A Leopard in the Mist

Book Three of
'The Kingdom of Durundal'
series

S.E. Turner

Acknowledgements:

Daisy Jane Turner: illustrator, for the magnificent book covers.

Jeremy Boughtwood for formatting and publishing, without whom the book would still be in its manuscript form.

My friends and family for their enthusiasm and encouragement.

My three daughters who continue to inspire me.

We are all connected.

Lyall groaned on the floor and shuddered as the General fell dead next to him. He looked up at Skyrah. She had broken the General's heart in two. He ripped the Seal from the perpetrator and clasped it to his heart. They had done it. They had killed the General. He had the Seal and he had Wolfsbane. He had his revenge. But at what cost?

He looked towards his brother and his own heart ripped in two. He let out a deep wail and clawed at the bloodied soil. Skyrah dropped down with him and they sobbed together in despair. They turned to look at Namir's body. He lay face up; a true hero and a true leader, a soul mate, a brother and the greatest friend to many. Skyrah pressed herself into Lyall's arms and wept again.

As the dust began to settle, the clans made their way towards them, united in numbers with a strength that defied their young years. They were all too weary and grief stricken for jubilation, but in their hearts they cheered. Lyall brushed Skyrah's blood stained hair from her splattered face and took a moment to look over her shoulder to his fallen twin.

But he saw a movement. He watched as his

brother struggled to motion a sign and he saw Namir raise his arm for help. His eyes widened, his lungs took in a slow rise of air and then he exhaled in a gust. 'He's alive Skyrah! Thank the gods, he's still alive!'

'It cannot be.' Her body trembled in response.

'It's true. Look. Unless my eyes are deceiving me. Tell me Skyrah, what did just I see?'

Her head turned and looked towards Namir. She felt as though she was drowning in tears, she couldn't breathe, she couldn't see through her weeping eyes and the putrid mist was overpowering. But when her eyes cleared she saw him. He looked quite still, laying there on the ground. He was pale. A corpse. She couldn't see any life at all. Lyall must have imagined it she thought. But then she saw it. He moved his head, he tried to raise his arm again. That's when she screamed. 'Help him! Help him!' She pulled away from Lyall and ran to Namir, calling his name all the way.

She fell at his side and kissed his hand. 'Thank the gods. Praise our totems. Hail the spirits. My love, he lives.'

He groaned in pain.

'Quickly! We have to get him back. My mother and Meric will know what to do.' She was still screaming out her orders to bring him back to life.

His comrades rallied round quickly and tried to lift him, but a gurgle of blood spilled from his mouth every time they moved him.

'Take Meteor!' Lyall shouted out to her. 'We can't move him, they will have to come here.'

'Lyall is right,' agreed Dainn, stemming the flow of blood from his own torn shoulder and being supported by Storm. 'We don't know what damage has been done.'

'We have stretchers ready, the women and children made them, I will bring one back.'

'Skyrah, you had better bring all of the helpers and all of the stretchers. A lot of our men are wounded.' Lyall looked over at Tore who was just about clinging on to life, then at Bagwa who was nursing a shattered leg. More and more casualties were exposed as the brume settled. Though as the moonlight rested on their bloodied armoury, Lyall could see that most of the bodies were the General's legions and whilst half of them were already dead, the other half would have perished by dawn.

'We need to burn these bodies,' called out Lace. 'They will remain the undead if they are not burned.'

Lyall nodded and breathed deeply, taking charge of the situation. 'Gather everyone you can and clear these grounds. But keep our men separate. They must be blessed before they are burned.'

'Of course Lyall, but I can assure you our losses are few.'

'That is welcome news,' he sighed.

'What about the General?' she cursed through tight lips.

He really wanted to bury that devil in the deepest pit he could find so that his soul would spend the rest of eternity rotting with all the other devils. But then he thought again, unless this monster was burned to a cinder, he might claw his way out. 'Burn that one first!'

She spurred her horse into a canter and recruited the strongest toughest men she could find for the harrowing job. Lyall deployed another group of men to round up the horses that were skidding on the blanket of blood.

'Ronu, Clebe,' he shouted out. 'These are fine war horses but they are maddened by the smell of slaughter, they must be taken to safety.'

'We're on it Lyall.'

Others were collecting the abandoned weapons and stacking them high. Some were finishing off the General's wounded before the night ghouls took them; they were doing the honourable thing they told eachother.

Darkness was descending and he could hear a rumble in the distance before the heavens opened. He lifted his face to the skies and let the cool water clear his face while his cries were muffled by the waves of thunder. He didn't even notice the hunched bodies of helpers working tirelessly against the driving rain, tending to the wounded and helping them to safety. He didn't notice Chay and Meric rush Namir away on a stretcher. He didn't see Skyrah beckon him over trying to get him off the field. The rain was heavy now, he couldn't see anything any more. He walked blindly through the battlefield, sodden grass squished and squelched beneath his feet.

Lace and her men had done a good job; the bodies had been cleared and stacked, the pyre was smouldering despite the flood. The smell of death still lingered even though the autumn rain had washed most of the blood and fear away.

A wind was swirling now, driving the clouds away, reddening his cheeks and stinging his eyes. The bright full moon peeped at him through the trailing gaps. He looked up to the skies and watched the moon and stars looking down on him. He found himself conversing with them, spilling his inner most thoughts, sharing his hopes and dreams and now the whispering wind was telling him what to do.

He could see the light. He saw his path vividly. And he knew, that come the spring, he would return to Castle Dru and take up his rightful place as Lyall, King of Durundal.

2

By the time he had got back into the camp it was a hive of people jostling from one place to another. The horses had been turned out and the stables now housed the wounded men; though Lace had been right, their wounded were few and their losses even fewer. The dead had been taken to the standing stones to receive a blessing from Zoraster whose haunting wails seemed louder in the catacomb of darkness. He went to the hut he shared with his brother and strained to hear what was going on inside, but with so much chaos and confusion around him, he momentarily hovered not knowing what to do first. Skyrah must have seen his shadow or heard his wavering breath because she was out in an instant.

'Where have you been?' her tone was anxious behind a tear stained face.

He looked at her blindly, not knowing what to do or say. She was covered in blood. Was it Namir's or the General's he wondered? He felt his face drain of colour and the vomit rise from the pit of his stomach. But it stopped midway and he was able to answer her question. 'I had to check the field Skyrah, I had to make sure that no one had been left out there in the dark.'

'I understand,' her face softened and she touched his arm. 'But your brother needs you.'

'I know, I am here now.'

He went in and saw him laying there.

Meric was cleaning the wound while Chay ground leaves and birchwood to be administered later. Laith had aged about a hundred years and was rocking in the corner. Lyall went to him first and fell down at his side.

'I'm so sorry father, I'm so sorry that I couldn't protect him.'

Laith put an arm around the boy and said nothing. He was trembling too much to speak.

Namir reached out to him and he moved closer to his brother.

'Hold him,' said the physician. 'I have to apply this now.'

Lyall didn't know what 'this' was, but whatever it was made Namir groan in pain.

'Hold him tighter,' urged the physician applying even more of the thick tar to his stomach.

The hand he held was weak and pale. He held it up to his lips and kissed it. The strong body looked so fragile and yet his chest was keeping him alive as it rose and fell with each shallow breath. Lyall whispered with angst written across his face. 'Will he live?'

Meric looked up at him for a second. 'If we all pray and the gods warrant it, then he will live.'

Skyrah wept again and took herself outside. Her mother followed to comfort her child. Lyall felt the tears rolling down his cheeks but he didn't make a sound. He sat there for hours, holding his twin's hand, feeling him flinch inside an otherwise lifeless body. Spasms and twitches weaved between the shallow breathing while his eyes rolled beneath transparent lids.

'What is going on inside you dear brother?' he whispered.

Namir heard nothing, he felt as if he was flying. He was joined by the two eagles he saw that day on the mountain. He felt like one of them, free and unleashed and spreading his ever expanding wings. They swooped and soared, all three of them together. What a magnificent feeling it was, to feel this empowered with so much freedom. He looked down on himself and saw everyone around him; caring for him and preparing potions that would save him. But still he swooped and soared not strong enough to become a whole man again.

The nights rolled into days while the days rolled into nights. By the end of autumn the orchards had been stripped, the food was cured and the bees were now docile. Skyrah never left Namir's side. She washed him, talked to him, held him, told him how much she loved him; then Lyall came in and they took it in turns to sleep. Meric checked the dressing. Chay brought them food. Zoraster took Laith back to his hut every evening; but by dawn he was back again, rocking in the corner, praying, chanting, weeping, looking more fragile by the day. Outside Namir's hut the wounded had responded to treatment and the final few were now venturing back to their own clans before the hard winter set in.

Clebe returned from the fields and handed the mounts to their riders. 'They are all fed and watered and will get you home safely.'

'Thank you my friend,' said Dainn.

'Namir is in our prayers,' Tore said as he climbed into the saddle. 'He is a fighter and very strong, he will make it.'

'Yes, I know he will,' said Clebe. 'He has the finest people taking care of him.'

'Send word when you can,' urged Dainn.

'Of course we will, you take it easy as well though Dainn, you have only just got well yourself, and a hard winter is but a few nights away.'

Wyn and Hass ran up to them. 'Here is something to keep you going.'

From a basket of food they handed them a muslin of cheesy bread and a flagon of ale.

'Thank you boys, this is perfect,' said Dainn. 'And thank everyone for the hospitality,' he praised. 'All of you, drop by to the Hill Fort and let us repay you when Namir is well enough.'

'Of course we will, it will be good to catch up without hostilities at the forefront of our thoughts.'

'Yes, I look forward to that day.' Dainn nodded to Storm, kicked his mare into a gallop and chased Tore and Siri back to their respective clans.

Lyall was in time to wave them off and caught sight of Bagwa limping with the aid of a stick. 'How are you today?' he called out.

'Not so bad, have seen better days. Am dreading the cold weather with this leg of mine.'

'Meric will have something for it,' Lyall assured him as his friend hobbled closer. 'How is Norg?' he continued. 'I saw him being treated for an eye injury.'

'Norg is coming round, now that he is accustomed to the fact that he can only see out of one eye.'

'Poor man,' Lyall mirrored Bagwa's despondent face.

'He sees it as a blessing now. At least he is still alive, one eye is better than no sight at all and he can still shoot with a bow and arrow.'

'Yes I agree Bagwa, we have to count our blessings.'

'I missed the burning of our dead as I was in the infirmary for so long, I wanted to honour them before they went to the afterlife.'

Lyall put an arm round him. 'We were lucky that it was so few men that we lost, it was only one from our clan, the General wasn't prepared for the support that we got.'

'The gods were with us that day. So who did we lose?'

'It was Jonha the blacksmith.'

'Oh no! Kal will be distraught, they were the best of friends.'

'I know they were, he is there every day checking on the bereaved family and doing what he can.'

'He leaves a young daughter and a wife that is gravely ill.' Bagwa shook his head.

'Yes, that would be Arneb,' said Lyall. 'She has grown into a fine young woman and has already taken over his job.'

Bagwa raised his eyes. 'And the mother?'

'I fear for her with the winter upon us, so we must help them as much as possible.'

'Yes of course,' said Bagwa. 'I will go and honour Jonha and pray for Arneb. My own daughters are lucky that they still have me and my dear lady wife, albeit a bit frayed round the edges now.'

'They are very lucky Bagwa. As are all the children and wives and mothers and fathers who have their loved ones around them.'

'Indeed.'

'But go and stand awhile amongst the stones. What's left of the pyre is just about visible, you can still give your praises and respects.'

'Yes, I will do that, thank you.'

Lyall was thoughtful as he watched his friend take shaky steps towards the home of the gods.

'Bagwa,' he called out.

'Yes.'

'Say a prayer for Namir as well while you are amongst the fallen. Summon his leopard totem, summon all the guides of the spirit world. He needs everything now to help him.'

'Of course I will.' Bagwa waved and trod his unsteady path to hold a vigil with his fallen comrades.

Lyall returned to his brother's side and silently prayed for him.

He must have dropped off with the rhythmic sounds of Namir's breathing and the warm stillness in the hut because he awoke with a start. He had lost all track of time but the sun was going down so it must have been a fair while. Zoraster would be here for Laith very soon. It was an arduous trek now for the two old men. In their youth they would have sprinted up the mound to their accommodation; but now, coming down was just as hard as going up, even with an extra arm as a guide and an old gnarled stick as support.

Lyall's prime concern was the impending freeze, it would be treacherous to attempt to put a foot outside. Laith didn't want to be moved though and was adamant he would see out his days in the place he called home.

'I don't like change.' He would say defiantly if anyone suggested he moved into a smaller more accessible dwelling off the slopes. 'I have lived here for nearly twenty years now and this is where I will see out my days.'

No one liked change, and nothing did change as the hours became days and the clouds swept past the rising sun and the moon took her place at night. And right here, right now, as another day was nearing its end, nothing had changed. Every day he watched Namir's flickering eyelids, the tremble from within his soul and the rise and fall of his chest. He looked over to Skyrah and looked back at Laith. Their grim faces hadn't changed either.

Namir was still flying his lazy circles with the eagles. But he was getting stronger now. He saw Skyrah weeping and feared how she would cope without him. He saw his father rocking backwards and forwards, he saw Lyall praying for him. They all needed him. He needed them. He wanted that life on the ground as a man, not circling the clouds as a bird. He felt the warmth returning to his body and his muscles started to fire up. He felt his eyes able to see more clearly and the wind stopped carrying him away. The two eagles flew in to him on seraph wings and pecked at his own which caused him to fall. He was trying to scream but nothing came out. He was panicking. He felt like a drowning man and struggled to breathe. His family were rushing up to meet him. He took a huge gulp of air before he landed. He opened his eyes.

'Water!'

Lyall scrambled for a cup of warm liquid and threw out his instructions. 'Skyrah go and get Meric and Chay, he's awake.'

'Is he all right Lyall? Please tell me that he's all right!' she grabbed his arm.

'He looks fine to me, but we need Meric right now.'

Laith was bent low as he staggered over and fell at Namir's side. 'My son, my son.' And he clasped his hand in his own.

Lyall held Namir's head up to the vessel and gently let him take the life giving nectar.

'What happened to me Lyall? How long have I been here?'

'You have been here for weeks escaping death dear brother. You have suffered a terrible injury.'

Namir winced as he tried to sit up. 'To my stomach I'd say.'

'Yes. We have all been praying for you. Meric and Chay have been looking after you with their expertise and potions. Skyrah and Laith have kept a vigil.'

Namir smiled at his father and squeezed his hand. Lyall had difficulty in deciding who was the frailer.

'And you have been taking care of everyone else I am guessing.'

'Yes, it seems that the tables have turned doesn't it, from when I was the injured lad laying here and you were the one looking after everyone.'

Namir had to stifle his amusement as the action pulled on his stomach.

'Careful Namir. Don't try anything until Meric has seen you.'

'What, I can't even laugh?'

'You can't even sniff brother.'

They shared a smile before Skyrah burst into the hut with Meric and Chay. Lyall squeezed his hand and moved out of the way to make room for them all.

Meric gently washed Namir's face with warm spring water and checked his eyes. He then looked inside his mouth before listening to his heart.

'Everything is as it should be Namir, I am now going to take the dressing off. Stay calm and just relax.'

Namir lay very still as everyone watched the physician slowly removing the first layer of ground leaves and mashed bark. He then started to painstakingly peel away the dried tar. With slow and careful movements the edges of the black scab were lifted away to expose fresh new skin peeping out from beneath like a vulnerable pink newborn. He finally got to the centre and lifted the last piece away to reveal a perfectly clean wound. Chay then placed the pulp of fermented maple leaves and pure white birchwood to aid the healing. Lyall remembered having the very same cooling mesh on his torn body.

By now it was dusk and Zoraster came to collect Laith. Lyall went to help his father from his coiled position and steadied him as he stood up.

'I can never repay you, all of you for saving my son's life,' Laith's voice was gravelly.

'The gods have been kind,' sighed Zoraster. 'Blessings and peace of mind to all.'

'I will see you in the morning father,' assured Namir. 'Rest well tonight.'

'I will my son.' He turned to hug Lyall. 'My brave boy, thank you.'

Lyall hugged him back and gave his arm to Zoraster. 'Take care of him for me.'

'I always have and always will,' came the humble reply.

Namir managed to smile loosely at the two old

men as they left the hut, but the muscles in his jaw ached. Skyrah tilted his head up slightly and held the cup to his lips. 'Here my love, sip this, it will make you strong again.' He tried as best he could but then sank back again.

'You are strong with the heart of a leopard,' applauded Meric.

'I am that, I know, and I thank you for saving me Meric. And I have so much to live for; especially alongside my courageous, strong, loyal brother.'

Lyall flashed a thin smile in his direction as Namir continued.

'My comrades, my father. Where I live, my animal totem that gave me strength. There is so much to be thankful for.'

Skyrah was cradling his hand.

'But this lady here, my beautiful Skyrah, she is my life and I owe her so much.'

Tears were rolling down her cheeks now.

'I love her, I have always loved her and I know I can not live without her. I should have asked her a long time ago, but now is as good a time as ever.'

She kissed his hand.

'Well?' asked Namir.

'I think that is a marriage proposal,' said her mother beside herself with joy.

'Really?' she said as tears ran down her cheeks.

'Yes really.' Namir wiped them away.

'Yes,' she beamed. 'Yes of course I will marry you.'

3

It was always dark now. The great stone flanks of the mountains hid the sun for most of the day, so activity was slow in these cruel winter months. The breath of the living steamed in the biting air as icy fingers of water trickled down the roof tops and swelled into small frozen pools that cracked and broke beneath awkward moving feet. Dwindling piles of logs were constantly covered in snow and even the dogs didn't venture out in these extreme blasts from the north.

The clan were eager to see the thaw again, to let the bright sun soak through their clothes and chase the chill from their bones, to release the soil for growing again, to hear the joyous gurgle from the river, but most of all; there was a wedding on the horizon.

The fire was always warm and inviting in Namir's home, and while he lay convalescing, Lyall filled a cup of tepid nettle tea and handed it to his brother.

'How are you feeling today Namir?'

'I feel much revived Lyall, I do believe the remedies that Meric and Chay constantly give me have much to do with my recovery.'

'Yes, I believe they do brother. Zoraster is very

frail now, so we are lucky to have such equally skilled people amongst us,' agreed Lyall. 'Meric has been treating poor Bagwa every day as well; his leg has been playing up most of the winter.' He finished pouring himself a brew and sat down next to Namir. 'His range of medicines are amazing. I took Bagwa to the hut he shares with Chay for some healing potions, and it is very impressive in there.'

'How so?'

'Well, for a start, he has built a three tier shelf, which circles the entire hut.'

Namir smiled.

'And then you have rows upon rows of stopped vials and bottles containing various coloured liquids, countless jars of dried herbs, boxes of pressed flowers, bowls of every type of leaf, as well as piles of stripped bark and rolls of parchment everywhere. It is truly amazing.'

'That must have taken some time to accumulate.'

'I think it has brother, both he and Chay work tirelessly to keep the stocks high.'

'I should like to see it when I am able.'

'If there's anything left. I think most of it's gone on you.'

Namir's laugh turned into a hearty cough and Lyall gently lifted him forward to rub his back.

'Is Skyrah happy staying with Arneb? I hope she knows that it wasn't my decision that she should go.'

'Of course she knows,' said Lyall, still rubbing Namir's back. 'Kal suggested that she go and live there as her father died in the battle and her mother just recently passed away. She is on her own now so it makes sense for her to have some company.'

'My thoughts are with Arneb,' said Namir sympathetically. 'How tragic to lose both parents within weeks of each other.'

'Whenever we celebrate our own good fortune, it seems it is always tinged with sadness from someone else's pain,' lamented Lyall.

Namir bobbed his head in agreement. 'I can see that both women need each other right now, but it seems strange that she will be confiding in another woman and not me.'

'You will have time enough for that; and mark my words, one day you will be glad of Arneb's friendship.' Lyall rolled his eyes as he conjured up the image. 'Since Tali married Norg they don't spend as much time together, so right now it's good for her to have a female confident and close friend. You know how the clan women are; chatting about everything, giggling about nothing and then there's the deciding what she should wear on the big day. That's a lot of talking that we don't know anything about.'

'Yes you are right,' Namir smiled. 'I sometimes wish that things didn't have to change. There's something so refreshing about the innocence of childhood and I wish that we could stay just as it was back then.'

Lyall supped into his mug and agreed by way of a low 'hmmm' from the back of his throat. He hadn't told anyone yet about his decision to leave in the spring. The clan were all too raw and most were still recovering from the battle; it needed to be the right time to share his news. These emotions stirred familiar feelings of the time Laith had revealed his true parentage amid claims that the time was never right to divulge such sensitive news. He was beginning to understand more than ever the need for such revelations to be timed just right. But sometimes the time can never be right he thought.

'I haven't seen father for a while,' said Namir after the pause. 'Is he all right?'

'He is fine brother. The ground is unsteady for him and the air is too cold, so he sits by the fire covered in layers of fur wraps. You can be rest assured he is well looked after by everyone.'

But Lyall didn't want to burden Namir with the truth. In fact the past two years had taken its toll on Laith. Finding out about the death of his brother and the woman he loved had drained him beyond recognition. Then losing his sons and youngest clan members to the Emperor for nine months; not knowing if they were alive or dead, had aged him further. And now, with every last drop of strength and courage, he had willed the life back into Namir; it was as if he had made a pact with the gods to take his life in exchange for the life of his son. And beside him throughout it all was Zoraster, his aide, his companion, his closest friend. And everyone knew, that come the awful day when one went, the other would follow soon after.

4

The low rise of the huts weighed down in snow made them look like a field of squat toadstools wearing fringed hats of icicles that nearly touched the ground. From above they would have blended in with the white landscape. From below they were as wide apart as they could be. Laith's dwelling sat high on the mound, Namir and Lyall's was just below that, and Skyrah and Arneb's quarters where nearer to the stream.

The Blacksmiths was a quaint affair, it only served a small community and mostly it was responsible for forging steel utensils for eating and cooking, iron spear heads and arrow heads for weapons, and more recently the blacksmith made iron shoes for the horses and repaired the armoury. Outside the hut was the evidence of the profession; a wood and charcoal pit, a pair of wooden bellows, a small anvil, iron tongs and a range of smaller tools to practise the craft. Inside, two women were settling down for the evening.

Arneb was preparing the evening meal when Skyrah walked in, she looked up to her friend and smiled. 'How is Namir today?'

'He is much better thank you Arneb.' She

shrugged out of her big winter coat and threw a smaller wrap around her shoulders and warmed herself by the fire. 'I took him for a little stroll around the camp earlier, he hasn't seen his comrades for many months now, so it was nice for him to get out and see them.'

'Yes the only way to get stronger is to keep moving, especially in this weather.' Arneb handed Skyrah a bowl of chicken stew with diced vegetables and a wedge of bread.

'Clebe and Ellise were entertaining Ronu and Enelle this afternoon, so we shared a brew and a plate of oatmeal cakes.'

'Oh they are lovely people. Clebe is always bringing one horse or another to be shod.'

Skyrah looked up from her stew, wiped the gravy from her chin with the back of her hand and raised a smile. 'Those two and their horses. It was the gods will that they were able to find sisters of the same age to marry.'

The two women laughed.

'Did you get to see Norg? I know he has been a bit low with his injury.'

'Yes we did. He is much better and so much more positive about everything. He says he is still good with a bow and arrow and that one eye is better than no eyes. Tali takes good care of him though and it was great to catch up with her.'

'Here, have another spoonful of stew.' Arneb held out the ladle.

Skyrah gulped down the last piece of chicken

and held out the empty plate.

'And dare I ask about Laith?'

Skyrah sponged the remains of the gravy with her bread and sat the plate down. 'It's grim, very grim. We could only spend a little while there. Laith is so weak. He has aged so much with everything that has gone on.' She sniffed away a runny nose. 'Zoraster is just as frail, but my mother and Meric go to see them every day and do what they can.'

'Maybe the warmer weather will bring better news.'

'I hope so, I really hope so. Namir really wants his father there at our wedding and we are praying to the gods, but he seems to get frailer by the day.' Her nose was still watering so the edge of her finger cleared it away. 'And Laith has already given Namir his sword as a wedding gift.'

'Really?' Arneb tilted her head.

'Yes, Leopardsbane has a special meaning for both of them. It was Laith's as a young man and Namir found it for him in the castle.'

'What about Lyall?'

'He has King Canagan's sword; Wolfsbane, and he polishes it every day while he chats to Namir.' The thought of that brought a smile to Skyrah's face. 'It's good that Namir and Lyall can spend these last few months together. Come the spring and after the wedding he will be on his own.' She threw Arneb a wry smile and raised an eyebrow. 'He is such a good man and will need a wife soon.'

But Arneb didn't rise to the suggestion. Her thoughts had turned to a time long ago when her parents had high hopes for her.

'You are so special Arneb,' began her mother. 'That's what your name means, special hare.'

'Does it really?' she asked.

'Yes, Laith told us that, and he knows everything.'

'And I know that you will make a fine wife and mother,' heralded her father Jonha.

'She will marry a prince, Jonha, not just any ordinary man for our little hare, she is much too grand for that.'

'Indeed wife, one day a fine young prince will come riding through our camp. His horse will need shoeing, his spear will need lancing and his armoury will need fixing.'

'And he will see our Arneb and fall in love with our little hare and carry her off to his castle where she will be queen.'

How they had laughed when her parents had pretended to be her servants and placed a makeshift crown on her head and a yard of muslin around her shoulders.

The smile faded from her face instantly because everything changed when the boys were kidnapped. The whole camp was in perpetual mourning with a dark bruised cloud hanging over them daily. Then her mother got ill. She and father did their best to look after her, indeed all those left behind played a part in her recovery. Zoraster chanted, Chay came daily with remedies and mother did seem to be getting better, especially when the boys returned safely and the whole camp was suddenly lifted. But then there was the battle. Her father shouldn't have gone, he didn't have it in him to fight. As most of the other men had signed up, he felt it was his duty. Both women tried to stop him, but neither of them could.

'It's my duty dear wife,' he had said. 'I cannot be the only man in this community to stand back and watch the others go to battle.'

'But Laith isn't fighting, Zoraster isn't fighting, Meric isn't fighting,' pleaded his wife.

'Yes father,' Arneb remembered saying. 'They are not fighting because they have important roles here, as you do. What you do is a vital part of the community.'

'You have forgotten that they are much older than me. I am still a young man. Now please, I have made up my mind. It is important for me to show allegiance. I do not want to discuss it further.'

And that was that. They didn't discuss it any more. It was the last conversation they had. Her poor mother never really recovered and passed away in her grief, and with it went all their hopes and dreams for the future. Everything of her past was put away into wooden boxes and stored safely under the bed.

Kal had asked her to come and live with them. 'Please Arneb, you cannot be on your own, come with us. Myself and Orla will take care of you.'

But she had declined, for no other reason than she wanted to continue her father's business. She had a new role now and with that came tough hardy clothes, a long leather apron and an assortment of tools. She had a place in the community. They all needed her. Every one of them came to the blacksmith.

Coming back to the present, Arneb choked back the tightness in her throat and changed it into a laugh.

'He wouldn't want me, I am a blacksmith. He wants someone of high standing to sit alongside him in the castle, to be his queen and host gatherings and feasts and everything that goes with royalty.'

'No, that isn't so, he isn't like that.'

Arneb now threw the wry smile and raised an eyebrow.

Skyrah's face was suddenly ashen. 'Do you think he will return to Castle Dru then?'

'Well I don't know for sure, but he may do.'

'It will break Namir's heart if he leaves.' But then she remembered something, she remembered a time long ago when the three of them were talking in the fields, when they were still children, before the General had changed everything.

'You will make a fine leader Namir,' said Lyall.

'I hope so, my father has guided me and chosen a strong totem. I know it is my destiny.'

'And you will make a fine king Lyall,' purred Skyrah. 'That is your destiny.'

'I hope so, I hope that one day I will reclaim my throne.'

'Of course you will and we will govern the lands between us,' cheered Namir.

'He has always wanted to return,' announced Skyrah.

'We don't know that for certain,' Arneb drew a sad face.

'No, you are right, it's in his blood. When Namir is leader here, Lyall will return I know he will.'

'Well it's not going to happen right now is it.' Arneb sat next to Skyrah and put a caring arm around her. 'Please don't worry yourself.'

'It's all going to change isn't it? Why can't everything just stay the same.'

But as Arneb cradled her distraught friend, things were changing in the hut on the hill.

5

Meric skidded outside Namir's hut and burst in unannounced.

'Namir, Lyall, you must come quickly!'

Lyall shot up off his low chair first. 'What is it? Please tell me it's not Laith.'

The physician's anguished face told him what he already knew.

'We are not too late are we?' Namir dreaded the answer even as he said the words.

Meric's look was sombre. 'No Namir, but I don't think he will last much longer. He is asking for you both.'

The brothers looked at each other. Lyall was already climbing into his fur coat and with shaking arms helped Namir into his. With fur boots already keeping them warm, Meric led the small procession. The long walk up the mound was the most difficult challenge they had ever faced. Even with everything they had been through, nothing had prepared them for this. Not a word was spoken, just the immense weight of emotions filled the ghostly night air as neither wanted to confront what would be waiting for them at the top. They didn't even feel the bitter cold biting into their weeping faces or the snow crunching beneath their feet. They climbed the unbearable path together with Meric's torch as their only source of light.

Chay was waiting at the entrance with her head low, even she was numb to the berating elements and couldn't look at the brothers as her face was too stained with tears; instead she drew back the thick aurochs hide and let them all in.

Lyall held back to allow Namir in first and stood for a while adjusting to the frail figure before him. Laith had deteriorated so quickly, he couldn't believe that it was only the day before he had seen him. Now he lay there, shrunken into the bed, his grey face sagged into the pillows and what little muscle he did have had melted off his bones overnight.

His eyes opened to the sound of Namir's voice. 'My son, my precious son,' his voice was fragile and without strength.

'I am here father, don't strain yourself please.'

'Where is Lyall?' he just about managed to say the words.

Lyall knelt by his side and took his hand. The hand that was once extended to offer him sanctuary, the hand that reached out to him for forgiveness on the mountain, the hand that held him close as he went into battle; and now here was the same hand being offered as a parting embrace.

'I am here father, please save your strength.'

'I have no strength left my boys,' the whisper was slow and laboured.

'Just rest, please don't talk,' Namir pleaded.

'I have to speak - I have little time left.' He stopped to take in air. 'I love you both so much - you have brought me so much happiness - I leave my legacy in you.' A tremulous smile touched his face.

Namir was sniffing back the tears as Laith steadied himself again.

'I have something for you Namir - here - in my right hand - take it - please.'

Namir prised his father's fingers apart to reveal an exquisite gold locket. Namir knew immediately what it was. He opened it to reveal a beautiful miniature painting of his mother.

'I can't take this father, it has to stay with you.' He looked at Lyall.

'Please - I have spoken with Lyall - he is happy - really - please.'

'Are you Lyall? Are you happy for me to have this?'

'Brother, I had been lucky enough to spend fourteen years with our mother, while you had only two. You cannot remember her beauty, how gentle and funny and caring she was. I have a picture of mother constantly in my head - and you will too if you have this locket.'

'Lyall, that is more than love, that is more than generous. I cannot find the words to say.'

'I love you brother. You have shown me how to be gallant, gracious and loved. Please take it as a token of my love for you.'

Namir put the locket round his neck and kissed it. 'Thank you.'

Laith coughed weakly from the back of his throat. 'Be happy with Skyrah - you were made for each other - the thought of you growing up together - has touched my heart - and Lyall - my first born son - there is a wife for you - closer than you think - I'm sorry we didn't have longer together - but - you had the most wonderful mother taking care of you.' A stab of pain stopped him and his fingers grabbed Lyall.

Lyall kissed the fleshless hand amid his watering eyes and running nose. He wanted to say a thousand words in response but nothing came out.

'Take care of each other boys - you are a leader now Namir - and you are a king now Lyall - rule wisely - rule together...' His face winced with pain again, his breathing was shallow. He croaked the last few words.

'I will always be with you.'

His eyes closed. The pained breathing was unbearable. It got slower and slower. Namir sank down into his father's skeletal frame. Lyall watched Namir's head rise and fall with each breath. Lyall couldn't move. He held on to the ancient hand until it went limp. Then he knew. With one last sigh the breathing stopped and Namir held him with all his might. He held his head back and let out an anguished wail.

Skyrah heard his cry.

She sat up and looked straight at Arneb. 'Did you hear that?'

'Yes, what is it?'

'It's Namir. I must go to him. He needs me.'

They both climbed into their furs and hurriedly made their way to the source of the cry. They were not alone. Everyone had heard it and were heading in droves to the leader's hut.

Before the community descended, Zoraster staggered over to his old friend and kissed both cheeks. Without a word he hugged Namir and then went up to embrace Lyall. He looked at Meric then at Chay and nodded, he then crouched low and took himself out of the tent.

'Should I go with him?' asked an anxious Lyall.

'No, leave him,' said Meric. 'He has already instructed us not to follow.'

'But why? he will freeze to death out there.'

Lyall went to put on his coat and get Zoraster back inside but Meric stopped him.

'He has made me promise him Lyall. This is his way, we cannot interfere.'

'Interfere with what?'

'He has spoken to the spirits. He wants to prepare the funeral pyre on his own.'

'What! Right now? Why can't it wait?'

'I don't know. We have to respect him Lyall, it's what he wants. We cannot interfere.'

Lyall called to his brother. 'Namir please.'

But he was blind to what was going on around him. Immersed in grief he sobbed into his father's thin frame. Skyrah came in and fell at Namir's side, it was only then that Namir let go of his father's body and held on to her tightly. Arneb stood at the entrance in disbelief.

'What happened Meric?' Skyrah wanted to know. 'Yesterday he was fine.'

'We cannot know what the gods decide Skyrah, we cannot plan or predict life and death.'

'But I had no time to say goodbye properly,' whispered Namir.

'But you have Namir, both you and Lyall have been here every day. He got to know his other son. He knows your love for him. He knows that you are fine men and that it was time for him to go.'

'I was not ready though,' he cried.

'But he was ready Namir and the gods were ready for him. He has no use of his old worn body anymore. He is with Canagan and Artemisia. He is flying with them now.'

Lyall didn't register the symbolism, but Namir did and suddenly felt more settled knowing that they were all together again. He could almost see them welcoming Laith with outstretched arms. Perhaps they had gone back to being children once more, just like Namir wanted to; the three of them playing and talking for endless hours about the future. He cradled that thought for a while and it made him smile. Was there really a place full of love, peace and harmony? or was it just found in one's own heart? How cruel the real world is he thought to himself and soon he too was longing to be transported back to the time where he was without worry or concern, just living on wild hopes and unexplainable dreams for an endless happy future.

'Come Namir,' said Meric, jolting him out of thought. 'I have to address the crowd now. Will you join me?'

Namir looked anxiously at Lyall.

'You go brother. You have a community who want to welcome you. I will be right behind you.' He threw a thin smile and gave Namir the strength that he needed.

Meric made his way outside and stood at the entrance. The air was cool, but not freezing anymore. Above, the clouds moved quickly to allow the bright full moon some access. People did not shiver now. A blanket of warmth and love cradled each and every one of them. The thaw was on its way. And with the thaw comes new beginnings.

When all was hushed, Meric began his accolade.

'Friends, comrades, brothers and sisters of the clan - tonight our great ruler died.'

A gasp went up from the crowd and tears flowed.

'He died in peace with his sons at his side. He is at rest now.' His voice was shallow.

The men were shocked, the women wept silently.

'I know that all of you have looked up to Laith and respected him throughout your life. He has been a great man, a great friend, a great father and a great leader. I know he will be missed.'

As the crowd looked up to him, Namir stepped

out of the hut with Skyrah at his side and Meric continued. 'Laith would not want tears now. He would want you to rejoice and celebrate his life. He would want you to go forward into the future with strength, dignity and fortitude. He has set the way, it is now Namir's destiny to rule. This is Laith's son, this is your new leader. Embrace him, pray to the gods for him. Namir will now rule the Clan of the Mountain Lion, and with Skyrah at his side they will offer you the same support and guidance and they will lead you into a peaceful new kingdom. For they, and their children, are the future.

Chay had kissed Laith's forehead and covered his body with the white shroud. On the morrow he would be raised on to the pyre being prepared by Zoraster and his body offered to the gods. She heard the cheers go up for Namir, their new leader and his wife to be, and watched as Lyall put an arm around the new hare in his life.

6

'Meric says the pyre will be lit at midday tomorrow,' said Lyall as they descended the hill together.

'And that we should prepare any words we want to say by then,' reminded Namir.

'I will collect some Rowan berries to lay on the pyre,' said Skyrah. 'To feed his soul in the afterlife.'

'I think I will have time to forge a spear that will protect him on his journey.'

'Thank you Arneb,' Lyall touched her arm and his eyes softened. 'That is so kind of you.'

She looked to the ground. The moment didn't go unnoticed between Namir and Skyrah.

'Laith chose my name when I was born; it's a very protective name so I want to repay the gesture.'

'What does your name mean?' asked Namir with interest.

'It means special hare,' she said with pride.

'That is so beautiful,' Skyrah sang out. 'And so meaningful that Laith chose it for you.'

'I know, I am blessed and I feel that I will always have a part of him with me forever.'

Namir smiled and looked at Lyall.

'All four of us have a part of him,' he said

gallantly. 'And that is the legacy he has left us.'

'I understand now what Meric meant about embracing his life and rejoicing for him in the afterlife,' said Lyall.

'We are sad, but he has touched all of us in some way,' said Skyrah.

Lyall then thought of Zoraster. 'I hope that Zoraster is back now, did anyone see him return?'

'I can't say I did,' said Namir. 'But there were so many people up there, he could easily have slipped in unnoticed.'

'He needed some time on his own Lyall,' Skyrah guessed. 'He has just lost his greatest friend.'

'That's what I am concerned about though.'

The next morning the whole community was awake early. Arneb had donned her apron and huge gloves and was making a start on the spear. Skyrah had gone to the Rowan tree to collect her star shaped berries and decided she would make a rune stave as well with the precious wood. Namir was preparing his eulogy and Lyall had gone to check on Zoraster.

The day had started off crisp and clear with a warm glow amid a crimson sky. There were a few heavy clouds appearing over the mountain he noticed but they were too far away to bother the clan on this day of mourning. A scattering of snow drops were beginning to poke their heads up through the softening soil. That always heralded a change in the seasons. Everyone welcomed these jolly souls because they indicated that warmer weather was on its way. He side stepped graciously and made his way to Laith's hut following the rise that he had climbed so often before. He remembered the first audience he had there as a young boy; cold, alone and terrified. He smiled when he thought of Skyrah holding his hand throughout it all. How he needed her on that day. That feeling of dread and anguish would never leave him and he shivered at the memory, and here he was now with that same feeling of dread, not knowing what to expect, not knowing what was in store for him. The same shiver went down his spine.

The moment fast forwarded to when Namir came out of the enormous hut and ushered him in to meet his father, and after the initial introduction he realised that Laith knew his parents. The echoes of a past life played out as a conscious thought.

'Did you know them?'

'Many moons ago I knew your parents Lyall, so many moons ago now.'

'Perhaps they knew you would look after me, that's why they sent me.'

'Yes, perhaps they did.'

A cool breeze brought him back to the moment and he ventured into the dwelling. He bent down low as he entered and found himself in a cold blackened space. It took his eyes a moment to adjust and then he focused. A shrouded image on the floor greeted him with two candles flickering contentedly which became more illuminated with the fresh air he brought in. They were full of life and cast a brightness in the gloom, just like the snowdrops he had witnessed all but a few minutes ago. He gasped and shivered again. There was nothing else in there, it had all been removed. Meric and Chay must have worked through the night. He knew that Zoraster would return to his old hut to see out his final days and this one would be burnt down as an offering to the gods and to help Laith on his journey in the afterlife. He bowed to the corpse; even in death the image appeared strong, proud and regal. He sat on the cold floor, crossed his legs and remained in that position, thinking, reminiscing and bringing every memory back to life. The candles danced for him while time stood still.

'Thank you Laith, my mentor, my guardian, my father. Thank you for finding me, thank you for giving me a brother, thank you for giving me my life - twice. I never really thanked you. I always thought we had plenty of time. I thought you just knew how I felt.' He shrugged. 'But I should have told you. I should have told you many times over. I had already lost one father, I should have known how I would feel and not take your life for granted - I thought you would live forever.'

He paused to reflect on life. 'Is that why we mourn so much in death, for the unsaid word in life? Is that why we can't let go; for misplaced promises and the lost hours that we try to grab when it's all too late?' He wore a sad thin smile and dropped his head again. Two fingers of his right hand placed a kiss on the cloth.

It was like a stone statue; cold, hard, lifeless.

Eventually he whispered his parting words. 'I hope you are with mother now - I hope Canagan is at peace.' He stood up to take his leave and looked back when he reached the doorway. 'We will be together again one day. All of us - together.' He turned for the final time and went to the only other place that Zoraster could be; the standing stones.

The views from there were breath-taking and the immense weathered boulders stood proud like old decorated guardsmen with their white patches of lichen and beards of tangled moss. He gazed off towards the rising sun and witnessed the rays tinge the surface of the mountain range. A shiver passed through his bones; the wind had picked up pace on the higher ground and as he entered the sacred circle he was transported to another zone again. This was the time he witnessed the name giving ceremony where Zoraster had administered the tattoo onto little Arran's arm. He relived the moment the blood drained from his face and how his hands flew over his ears to block out the cries. He could hear those same sounds again; deafening in the silence and Orla's wails begging the spirits to give her tiny boy the strength to overcome his pain. Everyone just stood there; watching, waiting, mesmerised. He remembered all too vividly how shocked he was and really believed that a baby was about to be sacrificed. He smiled at the memory, for now Arran was so proud of his eagle tattoo and showed it off to anyone who would take the time.

He snapped out of his trance and looked around. At first he didn't notice them. But then he saw Meric kneeling by the pyre, hunched over a frozen figure, and at once he knew. He flew to his side and stood there disbelieving what he was confronted with.

Meric looked up at him immersed in deep remorse. 'You were right to be concerned and I'm so sorry.'

Lyall breathed in deeply and ran anguished hands through his thick black hair. He paced about exhaling heavily. 'Has he been here all night?' he managed to say but already knew the answer.

'He must have, he didn't come back while Chay and I were with Laith. Then we left to go home and I assumed Zoraster had found somewhere else to spend the night.'

'It seems he did.'

'I had no idea that he would do this. He said that he wanted to prepare the pyre on his own. He told us he needed to be with the spirits.'

Lyall looked up to the skies and shook his head. Breathing in deeply and sighing in despair, he was at pains and distraught. 'Does Namir know?'

'No one knows, I am the first one here.' His voice was low and sad. 'The pyre has been built and been made for two people.'

Meric had his back to him and head tilted forward. Lyall put his hand on the physician's shoulder. 'You are not responsible for this Meric. Zoraster was of sound mind. He knew what he was doing.'

The physician clasped Lyall's hand in his own and dropped his head further. 'I am supposed to save lives though.'

'You saved Namir's life and you made Laith's last few days more comfortable than anyone else could have. Zoraster decided that without Laith he would be too unhappy, that his life down here had no purpose anymore. And in making that decision he is up there with his lifelong friend.' He looked to the skies once more to see if he could make sense of anything.

Everything was changing he thought to himself. He too felt that he didn't have a place in the community anymore. Namir was leader, he was going to marry Skyrah and they would have a family. What was here for him now - be the devoted uncle trailing after Namir and Skyrah with no real purpose? That's how Zoraster felt, especially with Meric as the newly appointed medicine man and healer.

But unlike Zoraster, Lyall was still a young man, he had a home to return to and a whole life ahead of him. Zoraster didn't have that privilege. He understood the old man's dilemma. Perhaps he knew only too well and could foresee what Zoraster wanted to do.

'We have to cremate them together,' said Meric, shifting his weight to a stand. 'That's what he wanted, that's what they both wanted.'

Lyall sighed heavily. 'I believe you are right dear friend. I believe you are right.'

7

The ashes had fallen like soft grey snow and covered the camp with a delicate dust, and when he awoke, the pale light of morning was slanting through the gap in the animal hide shutters. He sat upright and squinted through slitted eyes as he adjusted to the daylight. Namir had left a mug of nettle tea beside his bed. The touch of it told him that it hadn't been there long. Pursed lips sipped at the piping hot liquid, filtering it slowly into the cavern of his mouth.

'Ahhhh,' he sighed as the nectar revived him. 'My brother can indeed make a fine cup of nettle tea.' He continued till only the dregs remained before climbing out of bed. 'I know exactly where Namir will be,' he said to himself as he climbed into his breeches and swung a coat over his shirt. 'He'll be out there practising.' He smiled to himself as he laced up his boots and threw back the door covers of their hut. This walk was one he had done so often recently and every time he looked in awe at the snug dwellings that harboured gardens of nature's allotment.

'Morning Clebe,' he said as his friend stepped outside for a yawn and a stretch.

'Ah! good morning Lyall,' Clebe responded with a smile. 'Off to your lessons?'

'Yes I am; the things we do for our siblings eh!' His expression sparked a raucous laughter.

Ronu appeared from the back of the hut with an arm full of chopped logs. 'The days of hunting are well behind us now aren't they,' he chuckled.

'Nothing lasts for ever,' Lyall answered back. 'Got to change with the times.' He stopped for a moment. 'How are Silva and Hali doing in their new roles as hunting tutors?'

Ronu held on to his pile tightly as he approached. 'They are doing really well.'

'I hear that Wyn and Hass are turning out to be model huntsmen as well,' Lyall remarked.

'They certainly are, but I think they've had a lot of preliminary training.' The two men shared a knowing look. 'As you say Lyall, got to change with the times and I enjoy working in the fields now.'

Their conversation was halted as Enelle came to the door to see what Ronu was doing. She was heavily pregnant and was about to give birth any day. She waved from her position while the other arm supported her lower back.

'Not long now Enelle!' Lyall called out.

'Thank goodness,' she shouted back.

'You'll be there for the wedding I hope?'

'You try and stop me,' she called back and waddled back inside.

Two young children rushed up to him followed by the family dogs. He reached down to pick up the younger one and tousled the hair of the oldest.

'Now where are you off to I wonder?' he asked playfully.

'Mother wants some poppies for father.'

'Is he running out already?'

Lyall knew that Bagwa smoked the poppy seeds and his young daughters were sent on errands to collect more while his wife ground them down to make medicine for him.

'Meric says to get a supply while we can, poppies are the best plant to stop his pain.'

'You carry on the good work girls, I'll be seeing him shortly.' He set the youngster down and straightened out the hair of the older one.

The children ran off as Lyall looked on after them.

'Perhaps I should offer Bagwa the invitation to come back with me to the castle,' he thought to himself. 'I'm not sure how many more winters he can cope with out here.'

He carried on immersed in his thoughts until he saw Namir practising his moves on the mound where his father's hut used to be. He nodded his head to acknowledge Bagwa, who was softly drumming on a taut animal skin and puffing away on a clay pipe. Namir was moving perfectly in time to the beat and holding his arms out to an imaginary partner.

'You're late brother,' said Namir catching sight of him as he turned.

'Sorry, got caught chatting to Clebe and Ronu.' He looked over to his old friend. 'How are you today?'

'Not so bad now we have the better weather, and of course I can't live without this.' Bagwa took a deep puff of his pipe and blew out circles of smoke.

'I'm glad you have got some comfort, Meric is full of magic tips.'

Namir carried on dancing as Lyall watched his moves.

'Tell me again why we have to do this Namir?' His look was perplexed as he tried to make sense of the steps.

'Because it will surprise Skyrah, she will not be expecting me to do this.' Namir continued as he spoke.

'And why do I have to do it?' he queried.

Namir stopped in his tracks. 'To help me of course. You thought it was a good idea a week ago and said you would help me practise.'

'Yes I know, and I still do, I still will, but I am concerned that Skyrah might be a bit shocked that she will be called to do it on her wedding day because she learnt it from the General.'

'Lyall, I have seen her do the dance loads of times. When she thinks no one is watching she performs the steps. She is such a natural at it. If anything at all has come out of that dark time, it was to show us all just how clever and resourceful she really is.'

Bagwa stopped tapping and took the moment to inhale long and hard on his clay pipe.

'Yes, I know, I'm sorry,' lamented Lyall. 'I'm overthinking it. So what do you want me to do today?'

Namir let out a long sigh under a withering look. 'You stand next to me like this.'

Lyall had to adopt the lady's position, left foot forward, hand raised, and Namir took his place beside him.

'Are we ready now?' Bagwa asked from the corner of his mouth and exhaled from his pipe on the other side.

'Yes please.'

The drummer began to play. Namir nodded in time to the beat and stepped lightly to his left. Lyall, also nodding to the beat, stepped to his right and promptly collided with him.

'No, Lyall, the left foot goes back and to the side...' Namir was already exasperated. 'You should know this by now.'

'Oh yes - sorry - I remember.'

'Lyall, we have less than seven days, we must get this right.'

'I'm sorry Namir, I'm not concentrating, I'll be fine now.'

'Bagwa, can we start again?' Namir's tone lacked patience and it didn't go unnoticed.

Bagwa looked up, drew on his pipe and tutted at them both. They all started again. This time Lyall concentrated. He was led by Namir and together they managed the side-steps, the dips and the turns. The drumming kept them in tight formation and they mirrored each others steps perfectly. Round and round they went; flowing, rhythmically, weightless, effortless.

Lyall didn't dare look Namir in the eye for fear of losing his focus. But when it came to the lift, Namir collapsed in a fit of laughter when he felt Lyall's crotch pressed against his face and struggled to hold the stance. It took a while for both of them to get the focus back and regain the posture. By now the precision was broken and they couldn't do the lift without falling about in giggles; even Bagwa was distracted and choking on his pipe. So by the fifth time, Lyall stepped out of the way to give Namir more room as he pretended he was lifting Skyrah. But the image still made Lyall splutter, so he had to turn away each time.

'I do hope Skyrah remembers this part,' he eventually managed to say. 'So that when you put her down from the lift she will do her spin.'

'She will remember, I've seen her do it a thousand times, she just won't be expecting me to be able to dance with her though.'

Namir came to a standstill and looked pleased with his progress. The pained expression of exasperation had been replaced by his softer tones through laughter. 'That's enough for one day.'

'Norg is making some wooden pipes,' said Bagwa. 'They will make a wonderful sound with the drum.'

'That's great,' chimed Namir. 'Can he come and join us tomorrow morning. We must get this right?'

Bagwa nodded, Lyall threw a thin exasperated smile and Namir patted them sharply on the back.

8

The preparations for Namir and Skyrah's wedding day had been more complex and grandiose than any preparation for the recent battle they had fought. The wedding of a leader was something that didn't happen very often, indeed some clan folk would never witness a wedding such as this in their entire lifetime, so when it did happen, nothing was left to chance.

This was a festival to be celebrated and a mammoth feast would ensure the longevity of the clan under the gods and totem's protection. A monumental banquet would be served on the eve of the wedding consisting of sweetbreads, tarts and pies. The wedding breakfast would be a range of fresh eggs, bacon, sausages and wild mushrooms, while the wedding feast itself would offer whole hogs and whole salmons, roasted chicken, quail and duckling; a selection of vegetables, salads, nuts and dried fruits with steamed apples, baked wild pears and honeyed wine to complete the course.

All this took time to prepare and the women were busy throughout the day while the wedding platform and tiers were constructed. Groups of men had been deployed weeks ago informing the neighbouring clans of the forthcoming nuptials, for not only would this union secure the dynasty of the Clan of the Mountain Lion, it was also to be a celebration of Laith's rich and wonderful life. It would give thanks for the lives of all the men who had fought the battle and pay homage for those souls who didn't survive; but most of all, it was to secure the continued allegiance and loyalty of the neighbouring clans.

Skyrah had enlisted the assistance of her mother Chay, to oversee all the decisions, and her two best friend's Arneb and Tali to see to all the arrangements. So on the other side of the settlement in the girl's hut, she was discussing her speech with Arneb. 'I have to say something that is meaningful to us,' she began.

'Well that can't be too difficult,' said Arneb sensitively.' You two have a lifetime of experiences and wonderful moments, it's a case of which ones are the most important.'

'I know, but that's my dilemma, which ones?'

'Speak from your heart dear friend, that's what I will do on my wedding day, it has to come from your heart.'

'What would I do without you. I will truly miss our time together.'

'Me too - but I will be busy with this place.'

'This is fine work, I do not doubt it, but you need to find a husband.'

Arneb laughed. 'Let us get you married first before we think about me.'

'Yes - of course - come on, help me write this speech, then I will help you find your soulmate.'

When dawn broke on the day of the wedding, a golden sun rose up high and cast pink and blue shadows across the stirring village, the sacred stones shimmered white behind a veil of rays, and the echoes of a memorable evening were just rolling out of sight. Rows of tents had been erected in the neighbouring fields and each one seemed to rise and fall with the heavy breathing of a successful night of partying. Though slumber was confined to minutes now as the pungent smells of cooked breakfasts began to waft round the camp and waking bodies twitched under the mouth watering odours. But before the wedding breakfast could be served, everyone would have to bathe in fresh water from the stream and don fresh new clothes. This was a new dawn, this was a new day, this was the start of change and the beginning of a very exciting era.

Namir was rubbing the dust from his eyes and Lyall was laying out his wedding attire.

'What time is it brother?' asked Namir with heavy eyes. 'Have I overslept?'

'No, you haven't overslept, the smell of cooked bacon is the alarm call and we have plenty of time. I have drawn your bath for you and laid out your robes. The fire will keep you warm.'

Namir swung his legs from under his blankets and sat upright. He was still adjusting to the light. 'What time did you get up?' he asked sleepily.

'Up with the crows this morning, I was the first one in the stream and then it took a few pitchers to fill your bath.'

'Many revellers abandoned in the fields?'

'None at all, which surprised me.'

'It was a good day yesterday.' Namir stepped into the warm water.

'It was indeed, here let me help you.'

'Thank you.' Namir lowered himself into the bath.

'I'll always be there for you, you know that don't you?' started Lyall.

'Of course I do, and I'll always be there for you.' Namir rinsed his face in the fresh water and shook his head like a wet dog.

'I'm always just a stone's throw away, whenever you need me I will be right there, there is nothing I wouldn't do for you and I will be telling Skyrah the same.'

Namir pulled a finger out of a cleaned inner ear and looked at him. 'Lyall I'm getting married, I'm not undertaking some mammoth adventure with Skyrah,' he paused a while and grinned. 'Though some might think it that way.'

Lyall smiled at the allegory. 'I just want you to know that whatever you need, I'll be there for you both.' He then joked to change the tone. 'But I don't want you getting too used to this bathing malarky, this is a once in a lifetime job.'

Namir threw a sloppy wet sponge at him.

'Believe me I won't. Besides, I am sure Skyrah will do a better job than you anyway, you haven't even done anything.'

Lyall threw it back. 'Here, you ungrateful sod, finish off yourself. I'll go and get us a plate of eggs and bacon.'

They both laughed as Lyall disappeared out of the hut. But Namir had an unsettled feeling that something was amiss in his brother's thoughts, and that whatever it was, he really wasn't going to like it.

9

By noon the stage was set. The standing stones loomed around them, shimmering in the light of the sun. In the sky above, shining like the sculpture of a bronzed god, a golden eagle looked down and carried on its flightpath towards the mountains. Namir had donned his full length white robes complete with a grand garland of impressive animal tusks and looked every inch the proud groom and new clan leader. Beside him stood his brother, wearing similar white robes with a smaller garland. The stag's antlers had been ceremoniously placed on top of the heart of the same beast that they had killed together a lifetime ago; and now they awaited the arrival of the bridal party.

Bagwa and Norg sat at the entrance of the standing stones and ushered the guests in with hauntingly beautiful melodies on the pipes and drums.

The sun was at it highest point and Meric had taken his place at the Altar. Chay sat in the front row behind the brothers. Namir and Lyall faced the clergyman, and Leopardsbane was placed on a horizontal stone protecting the rings amid a blaze of light that bounced off the blade as the sun pivoted on its axis. The glare lit up Meric's eyes, and the congregation knew that the bridal party was ready. Skyrah moved silently down the passageway with Arneb and Tali in attendance. Each of her maids carried a clear obsidian stone; a piece of natural glass that bore a lighted wick with a glittering natural beauty that rendered them sacred and were only used in important ceremonies such as this. The bride wore a pure white silk dress that had been woven by Chay; her rich raven hair was loosely scooped up, secured with flower buds and elaborately carved grips. There were gasps of delight as she glided lightly past her audience, keeping her eyes focused as she approached the Altar. Namir and Lyall looked at each other and then hung their gaze on the beautiful Skyrah.

When everyone was in place, the heavenly music stopped and Meric invited the wedding ceremony to begin. 'Welcome everyone to this special occasion. It seems not that long ago we stood here saying our farewells to Laith and Zoraster, and now here we are witnessing the union of these two much loved and well respected people.'

Skyrah and Namir nodded in appreciation of the acknowledgement.

'But be sure in the knowledge that Laith and Zoraster are here with us today in spirit and all those who have left this world and who want to share this day with us, they are here amongst us now.'

The congregation bowed in memory of loved ones and welcomed the spirits in.

Meric continued: 'Today is special because we

are hailing a new dynasty, we look to the spirit guides and totems to take care of these two young people as they begin a new life as husband and wife, and we ask the spirits to help you support them and protect them in whatever guise that might be.'

Lyall sought his guide to give him added strength and to protect Namir during this transition.

'We begin with the two speeches of declaration; so Namir would you please start with yours.'

Namir choked back a hard swallow and touching her light with his own, declared his love for her. 'The gods looked down on me the day that Laith brought me here, because you were here waiting for me. I remember the days when we ground up plants for your mother as she tried to save your father. He probably knew that I would take care of you, protect and love you like no other; so he left this world with peace in his heart.'

Chay could be seen wiping away a tear.

'I will always love you and take care of you Skyrah; twice you have saved me from certain death and many times you have given me the reason to live. My heart has always been yours my love, and now my body belongs to you. On this day, I take you Skyrah as my wife, I will love you for an eternity and I will honour you with my life, I will walk with you and guide you, and as we tread our paths and overcome life's challenges, I will always protect you. I am your guiding light.' He bowed his head and took the time to reflect.

After an appropriate pause, Meric invited the bride: 'And Skyrah, if you could respond.'

She had practised this a thousand times, but in front of so many people it wasn't so easy, she had to steady her nerves. Meric closed his eyes and breathed deeply. She watched him and mirrored him and as she inhaled the magic, she took a moment to relax.

'My dearest Namir, I have always looked up to you and loved you. I have always felt that I was the other half of you; and now, on our wedding day, in front of our guests and the sacred stones, I feel complete. You make me feel safe in a hostile world, you make me feel loved in the family we call Clan. Today I honour you. Tonight I will lay beside you and in the morning I will wake up with you. I am proud to be your wife. I will bear you many children and every day I will tell you how much I love you and tell you how happy you make me. I too will love you for the rest of my life on earth and then beyond this mortal world. Namir, I will honour you with my life and my word and serve you as I walk every path alongside you. I am your guiding light.' She summoned her totems and gave thanks to them for this special day.

'Thank you Skyrah and Namir,' said Meric humbly. 'Those beautiful words will resonate with your people and have been declared in front of them. Now, it is time for your totems to become as one.' He took Leopardsbane from the altar and held it up high to the gods. 'With this sword and with your blessings, I seek to join these two people through their blood so that their totems will become as one. This will strengthen their bond, unite their bloodline and children born unto them will inherit the strength of both guides.'

The sword was wiped again on his robes and he took Namir's hand first. Turning it palm side up he made a quick incision along the pad of his left thumb. Then he took Skyrah's hand and made the same incision. 'Now, press your thumbs together and let the blood flow freely round your souls.'

Namir and Skyrah stood joined together, under the watchful gaze of the high priest and the congregation witnessing the marriage.

Meric put the sword back on the altar and spoke softly. 'Let nothing part these two souls. Let no one come between them. Let the enemy weaken in their presence. When danger is imminent the other will know. When sadness is abound, the other will feel. Their totems have become as one, their souls are now a single entity. This is the word of the gods.' He held up his arms to the sky and waited.

After a few minutes of silence, Meric spoke again. 'Please, who has the rings.'

'I do,' said Lyall, choking back the tears.

He carefully took the obsidian stones and placed them on the sword. He then retrieved the rings and gave them to Meric who continued with the service.

'These rings are a symbol of your love. There is no beginning or end, love is everlasting and bound in these solid circles for ever. Namir, will you please place this ring on Skyrah's finger.'

The captive audience held their breath as Namir held it to his heart and fulfilled his part of the ritual.

'And Skyrah, could you place this ring on Namir's finger.'

She kissed the symbol and placed it on his finger. Meric placed Skyrah's hands inside Namirs'.

'And now please declare the covenant of marriage.' He held their hands together as they proclaimed the vow as one.

'Today we pledge our love.
We swear by the kingdoms and all that surrounds us.
We swear by The Leopard and The Hare that protect us.
We swear by the gods and the spirits who look down on us.
We swear by all those who are present.
This is our word.'

Meric concluded the ritual: 'In the presence of the gods and spirits and animal totems, and with these people here present, I now pronounce you husband and wife. Go and enjoy the day with your friends, enjoy the occasion with your loved ones and enjoy your lives as a married couple.'

After Meric's final words, the newly weds turned to walk up the aisle to their new life together. Namir took Skyrah's hand in his own. 'Skyrah, before we can share our wedding banquet with our guests, I have been practising something that I would like us to do together for our friends.'

He nodded to Bagwa who started to beat rhythmically on the drum. Norg tuned in after a few minutes and Namir adopted his opening stance. Skyrah knew instantly what to do and affectionately followed his lead with a smile; she just wondered how Namir knew the dance. She held his hand lightly in her own and her body tingled with excitement. She poised her body on her toes and nodding in time to the drumbeat they both began to move. First of all it was very slow as they dipped and turned, face in, face out, step in and step out. Turn around once, dip again and turn. Face in and face out, step in and step out. The constant drum beat keeping them in time. The congregation began to clap in time to the rhythm, others clicked their fingers or tapped a foot.

Lyall grabbed Arneb and invited her to copy him. Norg gave his pipes to a comrade and led his wife Tali into the dance, another guest took the drum from Bagwa as he guided his wife around the floor. They all became part of the sequence. Even the children of the bridal procession copied them as they performed outside of the stage. The novices kept to the simpler choreography around the perimeter as Namir and Skyrah moved to the middle and stepped up the pace. The spring in their feet, the grace of their posture, the strength in their control was mesmerising as the dynamics of the routine suddenly burst into a vibrant frenzy of intricate moves and complicated steps.

The emotion of the dance was absorbing when Namir scooped Skyrah up and held her there, a curved back supported a long thrown back neck and as he raised her up higher she reached out with her fingertips. The drumming stopped. The wooden pipes stopped. The people were silent. The supporting cast froze. Not a sound could be heard as he gently put her back down on her toes and let her spin around him, their index fingers touching all the time as if he were controlling the action. Everyone's eyes were on Skyrah as she spiralled round and around. Then, with just a hair's breath separating them, the pipes whispered again and the drum beat like the ebb and flow of a wave. Skyrah slowed, took Namir's face in her hands and held his gaze as the music stopped. Their beating hearts and panting breath filled the void. The crowd went wild. A new tradition had been born.

Lyall and Arneb were still dancing as they moved away from the crowd.

'It feels so good to dance with a woman at last,' he said as he led her around for the umpteenth time. 'I have danced with Namir for so long now I feared I was turning in to a girl.'

Arneb laughed. 'There is no fear of that Lyall.'

'I was only joking of course, but really, this is such good fun.'

'You must have been practising for ages, you are a really good dancer,' she praised.

'Do you really think so? I think I have some good moves you know,' he laughed. 'Not as good as

Namir though, he is seriously good.'

'He has done so well, you would never have thought he faced death only a few months ago.'

'I know, I really thought we had lost him a few times back there.'

'Power of thought and prayer you know, that's what pulled him through.'

'Yes, I agree with you Arneb, but also the potions that Meric gave him, I think they went a long way to get him up and running.'

'How so?'

'They are very powerful herbs, I have to get them from Meric and prepare them daily for him. He was getting them three times a day. Now it is just the once, but Skyrah thinks he will need them for the rest of his life.'

'So Skyrah will have to do it for him now?'

'She will, but Skyrah is somewhat of an expert when it comes to powerful plants and saving lives.'

Arneb laughed. 'Yes, the hare is a good protector.' She looked at her own tattoo with pride.

'So will you continue to live in the blacksmiths cottage or will you double up with someone?' asked Lyall thoughtfully.

'I'll probably stay there, it will be lonely at times, but it's home. What about you?'

They had still been dancing, albeit slowly and just about managing a few side steps whilst holding hands. But Lyall stopped when faced with such a question.

'Shall we sit down a while,' he said. 'I'm getting a bit puffed out now.'

'Of course,' she dutifully agreed.

He took her hand and led her even further away out of ear shot. He found a patch of lush green grass, the blades silvered in the sunlight and the blooms of the buttercups and daisies moved about joyfully as if they had taken over the dance. Today the world was a joyous place, filled with the dawn of a beautiful spring day with its fresh new buds and rich azure skies. Neat little clouds puffed by quietly, only a light sprinkling from them would be required in the next few days. New stems rose from the ripened earth as honey bees threaded their way through the scatter of blooms strewn like jewels across the fields of the meadow below.

'Here this looks a nice place,' he held her hand while she lowered herself to the ground. When they were settled and he was sure that no one could hear them he spoke again. 'What I am about to tell you is just between us, you must promise me that you won't tell anyone.'

'I won't,' she assured him.

He took a deep breath and took her hands. 'Arneb, I will be leaving soon.'

Her face dropped and looked sad. 'Just when we are getting to know each other.'

'I know, it's not good timing, but I feel a bit lost now and I have to do something about it.'

'But why? You have so much to offer here and you are still Namir's brother.'

'Dear Arneb, I share your thoughts, I really do. It's not an easy decision believe me.'

'Then stay,' she found the words tumbling out of her mouth.

'I can't Arneb, really I can't.'

'Please.' She couldn't believe what she was saying, had she gone mad with love? She tried desperately to turn it around. 'I think Skyrah might already have an inkling.'

Lyall looked shocked and retracted his hands. 'How? Why? What did she say?'

She started to fidget with the dancing daisies fully aware that Lyall was willing the information out of her. 'She remembered something you said,' she fumbled. 'That when Namir was leader of the clan you would return to the castle to take up your position there.'

'That was ages ago I said that, I remember the conversation, and it's true. I felt that when Namir was leader here, I would take up my position in Durundal.' He sat forward and pulled his knees up.

Arneb found herself stammering. 'She said that you have always wanted to return, that it's in your blood to become king and restore Castle Dru to its former glory.'

'Does Namir know?'

'No, I'm sure he doesn't. Like you, Skyrah swore me to secrecy.'

'Goodness she has kept that quiet; she hasn't given anything away,' he paused, reflecting on the revelation. 'How has she kept that to herself and carried on as if nothing is amiss, preparing the wedding and keeping up her spirits?'

'The same way you have Lyall - you both love Namir and don't want to hurt him.'

A voice behind them snapped them out of their conversation.

'Come on you two, the guests are asking for the groom's man and maid of honour, we need you at the feasting table.'

'Just taking a five minute break brother,' shouted back Lyall. He grabbed Arneb's hand as she stood up and went to join the newly weds.

'What you two talking about then?' asked Namir, putting an arm round his brother. 'Anything I need to know about?'

'Nah, we were just chatting.'

Lyall winked at Arneb who retracted a coy gaze, but the look didn't go unnoticed by Skyrah. She knew, and right at this moment, Namir was the only one who didn't.

10

On the other side of the world, some ten thousand miles away, a lone man sat in a small tavern at a candlelit table surrounded by darkness and drunken strangers. Golden streaks of tangled limp hair reached his shoulders while a heavy woollen cloak hung almost to the ground covering a torn grey shirt and very worn breeches. A paralytic lout on the street had lost his shoes to him, plus a handful of loose change. Under the growth of a few days stubble a handsome face was etched, though some would argue it didn't exist at all. The saturated straw didn't bother him either as he supped on his ale and he barely noticed the pungent aroma of body odour and stale beer. Outside was a maze of twisting alleyways and hidden corners, best to keep away from those places, people would tell him; but he wasn't scared of those places, nothing scared him anymore.

'Gimme another flagon of ale!' he caught the passing serving girl by the arm.

'Are you sure sir? I think you have had enough for one night.'

'I'll be the judge of that you useless wench, just do as I ask.'

She pulled her arm free and slammed another tankard on his table. He tutted and buried his face in the goblet. When she reached the bartender she jutted out her chin in the vagrant's direction. The huge man instantly stopped towel drying the tavern mugs and made his way over to the table, but an outstretched arm blocked his path.

'No need for that Shorty, I will take care of him.'

'He can't keep coming in here Beauchamp, he's upsetting my girls, and good staff are hard to come by in these parts as well you know.'

'It's all right... I've got this... and give this to your girl... for her trouble.'

Beauchamp reached in his pocket, took out a sovereign and gave it to Shorty. The two men nodded by way of an agreement. Beauchamp pulled up a stool next to the lone man and the bartender went back behind the bar.

'Ah here you are Beauchamp,' started the young man. 'And where have you been hiding this evening?'

'I haven't been hiding at all,' answered Beauchamp.

'So what you been up to then?' the young man enquired.

'This and that,' came the short response.

'Boring stuff as usual then,' the vagrant disappeared into his beer.

'On the contrary, I think you will be very interested in what I have been up to.'

'Really, you really think so? I'm not much

interested in anything anyone has been up to these days.' The vagrant took a huge gulp of beer and wiped his dribbling mouth with the back of his hand.

'I think we need to get you sobered up first young man,' suggested Beauchamp.

'I think not, I am quite happy where I am thank you very much,' retorted the vagrant indignantly.

'If you are sure Cornelius, then take a look at this.'

From his sleeve, Gye de Beauchamp took out a scroll. Looking over both shoulders and lifting his chin high in front of him, he made sure that no one was looking as he unravelled it.

'What have you got here Beauchamp?'

'Read it for yourself.'

Gye de Beauchamp put an empty container on one corner and the now half empty one on another corner and held the bottom corners with his fingers.

'Go on, read it.'

Cornelius sighed and couldn't really be bothered. He took the flagon and knocked back three gulps. The parchment tried to spring back into its roll. Beauchamp put the flagon back.

'Cornelius, read it slowly and digest it.'

Cornelius rolled his eyes and sighed again. 'Then will you leave me alone?'

When he had Beauchamp's assurance, he began to read the document.

'This is a proclamation ordered by His Lordship

General Domitrius Corbulo. Governor of the province of Ataxata. Supreme Commander of the Colonies. Lord Protector of the Ataxatan Empire. Soldier of the Realm and Master of the Ataxatan Army.

Upon this day, the 10th of June, after faithfully serving our country for thirty years, the Emperor Gnaeus 111 of Ataxata was pronounced deceased.

Unless a legitimate claim to the throne can be found, the title will go to Lord Domitrius Corbulo. This has been bequeathed by The Emperor himself and can be duly seen in his Will if a legitimate contender can prove his or her claim.'

Cornelius scanned the proclamation over and over again. Flipping the document over for any hidden unread detail. He was now acutely interested.

'Where did you get this Beauchamp?'

'Down at the docks my dear friend. It fell out of a pile of books that some sea farer was bringing in.'

'What month is it now?' Cornelius needed to be sure of dates.

'It is the end of May,' confirmed Beauchamp.

'And when did my father become Emperor?'

'This year would be his thirty first anniversary, from the dates we have discussed in the past.'

'My father died eleven months ago then?' said Cornelius in a thin strained voice.

'That would be correct,' confirmed Beauchamp again.

'I remember Corbulo very well,' sneered

Cornelius behind clenched teeth. 'Sinister, horrible man, I believe it was him who got me exiled.'

Beauchamp agreed with a long sigh and a puckered chin. 'Unfortunately I believe you are correct in your assumptions in this case as well.'

'So he has been bequeathed the title - all worked out for him in the end then didn't it?' He seethed and disappeared into his flagon again.

'Not necessarily Cornelius.'

The young man tipped back the dregs, slammed the tankard on the table and cocked his head. 'Tell me what you know.'

'I perchance happened to ask the same sea farer about this proclamation and I made enquiries about the afore mentioned General.'

'And?' he gestured with an opened hand and raised eyebrows.

'It appears he is dead as well.'

Cornelius' brows met in the middle as his expression turned into a question. 'How?'

'The Emperor was killed in an uprising and the General was killed in a battle when he tried to avenge the uprising.'

Cornelius sat back in his chair. 'So I am free to return, I am not exiled anymore.' His tone was one of disbelief.

'You are a free man Cornelius.'

'Do we know who killed them both?'

'I can find out for you.'

'Good, because when I return, I need to know

70

who I am up against. I need to make sure they don't try and overthrow my Empire. I need to get an army and defend my title.'

'That is just what I was thinking Cornelius.'

'Excellent work Beauchamp. My father sent the boy away, but a man will return. I will take back what is rightfully mine and put to death to anyone who gets in my way.'

Gye de Beauchamp smiled knowingly.

Cornelius furrowed his brow in thought...'So how quickly can we get on a ship?'

11

Cornelius had been born twenty five years ago, the only son and heir to the Empress Eujena and Emperor Gnaeus. By the time he was five years old his mother had gone; it was said that she had given birth to a deformed daughter, not of this world and certainly not sired by the Emperor. What ever the truth was, Eujena had been banished from the court and Cornelius grew up without his mother or a sibling.

By the time he was twelve years old he was a tall strong boy with a taste for music, poetry and the arts. He loved singing and had a wonderful voice. So many times the palace was alive with the sounds of his warbling while the corridors and galleries rang out daily with his harmonious melodies. This disappointed the Emperor who had wanted a boy who enjoyed hunting, sword fighting and horsemanship; all the things he wanted to share with his only son. The Emperor had little time for 'women's stuff' as he called it. As the Emperor lost interest in Cornelius, people were brought in to try and change him. No one succeeded.

The Marquis De Beauchamp was one such man, and although he was skilled in hunting, sword fighting and horsemanship; he appreciated the gentle side of Master Cornelius and was more sympathetic and understanding, so he encouraged his softer side and formed a strong bond with the boy.

The Marquis was a few years older than Cornelius, though some said they looked about the same age. Cornelius had been given a privileged life, whilst the Marquis had covered his well. He was slight of shoulder, not overly tall but a medium build with a kind face and sparkling eyes. The Marquis kept his head shaved and wore a tattoo on his left arm; a Smilodon, the emblem of his tribe and a reminder of his forefathers from whence he had come; though no one ever knew from whence he had come. No one knew his roots or how he had learned his craft; only that he was skilled in many things.

After answering a notice to be an aide for Master Cornelius at the palace, he had been assessed by Domitrius Corbulo by way of a sword fight with his best swordsman, in addition to trapping a boar in the forest and skinning a rabbit in less than twenty seconds. He was given the position immediately. Cornelius liked him because he was always smiling, he had a soft kind voice and he always had an answer to everything Cornelius asked him.

'Where do dragons and witches come from?'

'On the other side of the world Master Cornelius, that's where they come from; they can't hurt you because they are so far away. Strange people live on the other side of the world, that's why no one goes there, only deviants and non human souls.'

'I won't be going there then.'

'Of course you won't, you are a kind and gentle boy and have no place with those kind.'

By the time Cornelius was fourteen years old, his father was obsessed with even more power and driven by avarice. He was fearful of his dynasty and how Cornelius would fare in matters of war. Would he even be able to father a son, or would he just breed more weaklings like himself?

'How come I am blessed with a fool for a son, how will he sit on the throne and rule when I have gone?'

'Maybe he should come with us when we search for the Seal of Kings, Your Excellency,' Domitrius Corbulo had suggested. 'That way he will have to face death and will definitely toughen him up...it's the only way to make him a man.'

'Excellent idea Corbulo,' the Emperor had agreed jubilantly.

But all that had happened was the General and the Captains put Cornelius in perilous situations and he always came off worse for wear. He got knocked down by more experienced men and he vomited when he saw death. He was put on the most difficult stallions that he couldn't control. Every day there was something more challenging that Master Cornelius couldn't handle. And every time, General Domitrius Corbulo and his captains sat laughing while he struggled.

The Marquis had observed all of this and went to the Emperor many times. 'My lord, if I may be so bold, I am concerned that Master Cornelius is being subjected to a form of bullying and expected to do things that he is not yet proficient in.'

'Beauchamp!' The Emperor had turned purple with rage. 'When I want your advice I will ask for it. When I want a lecture on how to bring up my son, I will ask for it. When I want to know the musical arrangement of a string quartet, I will ask for it. As I haven't asked for any of those things, will you leave me to do as I see fit!'

'But my lord, Master Cornelius offers other gifts that are far superior to killing and fighting.'

The Marquis was kicked out of court with the Emperor's wrath still ringing in his ears.

By the time the boy was eighteen years old, the Emperor had witnessed enough, and of course, Corbulo was there with the solution.

'He will never be fit to be an Emperor like yourself Gnaeus, he is weak with too much of his mother in him. He is a laughing stock and dishonours you.'

'So what am I to do with him Corbulo?'

'I have heard of places where boys such as him are sent away to become men.'

The Emperor was now interested and leaned in to allow Corbulo free passage.

'I can sort this out for you Gnaeus, I can send him to the other side of the world where he has to face his fears and become a man. It is not a nice place I can assure you; but then again, the world in which we live is not that nice.'

'Do it,' said the Emperor gleefully.

Cornelius was beside himself with grief and pleaded with his father to change his mind. 'Please father, please do not send me away, I will try harder, I promise. I will fight and I will ride a horse, I will hunt with the Marquis, just don't send me away to the other side of the world.'

The Marquis had also pleaded to no avail. 'Your Grace, you cannot send him away. Why do you want to change him, he has so much more to offer than fighting and killing and jousting on a horse. He is a kind and gentle boy who believes that dragons and witches live the other side of the world. You cannot do it to him, he is your son, he is your flesh and blood.'

'How dare you speak to me like this, who do you think you are? I had a wife once who begged me to let her stay here with another mutant of a child that was supposedly mine. And guess what I said to her?'

The Marquis suddenly lost the sparkle in his eyes when he looked at the madman in front of him.
'No, of course dragons and witches don't exist, there are far worse things to contend with,' he mumbled.

The Emperor continued: 'And you had better tell that pathetic excuse of a boy soon, because the arrangements are being made as we speak.'

'Please, Your Grace, he is your son and you do not know what it is like to be out there on your own with no one to look out for you.'

'Ha,' cried the Emperor with indignation. 'As I have already told you, I exiled my wife and her hideous excuse of a daughter to the great wilderness on their own, so I have no hesitation at all in doing the same to my son.' He paused to draw breath without a flicker of remorse. 'I am tiring of you and your ramblings. You forget your place in this palace. I should have you locked up in the deepest dungeon and throw away the key for speaking to me the way you do. But as you are so irritatingly concerned about my son's welfare, perhaps you should go with him; then I won't have to set eyes on either of you again.'

Beauchamp clenched his teeth. 'I will go with him... gladly. I will look out for him... happily. I will never leave his side... you can count on that.' He bowed his way out of the room.

The next day they were on a ship together; complete with a letter in the General's handwriting that this was a one way passage and that neither of them were allowed to return.

Cornelius began puking his guts up on the first day, he had never felt so wretched and cursed his father for inflicting this on him. The sea was rough and choppy with whitecaps everywhere; a flock of gulls and other monstrous sized birds escorted the vessel, eager for a discarded corpse he thought, or some other morsel of food. The huge ship rode the ocean as a hundred strong men pulled at the oars below; the oarsman beat a drum and the men sang out with each stroke.

Above them, the bulk of her body creaked and groaned with the weight of her cargo, and above that her sails cracked and snapped at each shift of the wind. Aside from the constant beating heart of the oars smashing against their port holes and smacking the bridge of the waves, the decks where alive with the rush of feet as crewmen ran to their tasks pushing past anything and everything that got in the way, which was usually him. So he decided to join them and earn a wage. For the first time in his life he was put to work. The journey would take the best part of three months, by which time he could assist hauling in the nets, scramble up a swaying cable ladder and manage to eat a meal without spewing it all up again.

Two times though, undesirables tried to take the clothes off his back and steal what was in his pockets. And two times the Marquis had finished them off and tossed them over the side. The fist time, Beauchamp saw two men trying to rob Cornelius on a late evening when the ship was quiet and the sea was calm. He raced up the ship's deck and yelled out to them. He ducked as one of the men turned and swung at him. Stepping back, he banged into the boom of the overhead mast as the big man came at him. He wobbled for a moment but had time to flick out his blade to deflect the blows that were raining down on him. The impact loosened his grip. He clenched his teeth and tightened his hold as the big man came at him again, each blow harder than the last.

Beauchamp had one eye on Cornelius who was still trying to fight off the scrawny thief while he had to fend off blow after blow. The big man had pulled out his own knife now and was swiping at his throat. He danced and parried while the attacker jabbed at him with lazy motions and narrowly missed his scalp with a well executed swipe. Beauchamp caught his chin deeply and while the bigger man put his hand up to stem the gush of blood, he reached up for the mast and swung himself round; he flew at Cornelius' attacker and dived at his sacrum with outstretched boots; the crack of his spine could be heard across the waves and the villain sunk to his knees. Beauchamp signalled with his hands and the paralysed man was hoisted over the side by Cornelius. Now, Beauchamp leapt from one cleat to another; with swift movements he catapulted himself onto the big man's back, pulled his head backwards and slit his throat. He too was sent over the side. He now always slept with a dirk in one hand and the other slumped over Cornelius. And that was just as well, for the second time another thief attacked them as they slept; but all he found was the end of Beauchamp's blade in his heart. He too was unceremoniously hoisted over the side.

'Next time we sail Cornelius, we are going to get a cabin.'

'What? Don't you like sleeping on the same deck as a hundred other men?' Cornelius smiled.

Beauchamp threw Cornelius a withered look and went back to sleep in his hammock.

Apart from the dreadful living conditions, the worst part of the journey was the dreadful storms.

'Bad weather coming!' warned a sailor.

'Best get below!' shouted another. 'Unless you want to feel the wrath of the sea, you either tie a tethered rope around your belly or you go down to your sleeping quarters.'

Beauchamp had gone below preferring the filth and the stench on the lower decks to risking his life to the waves. Cornelius though, decided to stay on the top deck and embrace the storm. The air was heavy and the clouds were thick, each one hardly daring to move until the winds opened them up with an unforgiving force. Crewmen were dashing about, battening down the hatches, reefing the sails; tying anything and everything down that had the potential to kill or maim. The sea grew rougher, the winds howled endlessly, pushing the ship down then whipping round to the stern and forcing her back up on her haunches again. Tonnes of gallons of sea and rain water deluged on her hull, soaking any crevasse or unattended door. Time and again the ship was thrashed about like a pawn in a tidal wave. The wind never waned and the sea never tired. Nothing was as strong and fierce as an angry storm.

But when it was kind, the sun came out and a gentle breeze helped glide the ship along as though she were a cradle taking care of a newborn babe. The vessel had been moving along at a good speed for days now; though their supplies were incredibly low, water barrels nearly empty and tempers short. Arguably, the oarsmen were the most tired, but all hearts were lifted when the lookout spotted cliffs and caves and the blisters of rocks made an appearance from the water.

When they docked, the port was crowded with sailors, smugglers and thieves alike. Thin and ragged peasants paved the streets, scrawny children dodged carts and legs. The people in the town always cheered the arrival of the ships, for the travellers bought in everything from rich fabrics to a range of exotic birds. There were fifty prisoners to be put to work on the farms and another fifty slaves to work for the gentry one hundred and fifty miles away. But most brought in money to spend in the town, and it was a thieves paradise when a ship docked.

The sprawling buildings covered the shore as far as Cornelius could see; tall brick storehouses, squat wooden outbuildings, crowded merchants stalls, loud taverns, bustling inns and places of ill repute. The fish wives could be heard for miles around shrieking and hollering while the squawking of caged hens pierced the air even more. A fan of quays lined the waterfront, and the harbour was bursting with ships, ferries, and fishing boats. On top of all this chaos, the day was uncomfortably hot and sticky and the two men waved off sweat and flies with the wrath of busy handkerchiefs.

The Marquis had been told of a bartender who owned several properties in the area; everyone called him Shorty, even though he was about seven feet tall and just as wide. They made their way through the jostling crowded streets; Cornelius had no money and could only offer the malnourished children a shrug and a smile, while Beauchamp resisted the women in the brothels with their pouting lips, beckoning fingers and inches of stockinged thigh on show. Shorty took his money and directed him to a weathered building that was wedged between a fish house and a manse house where the roofs of every building morphed into a crooked tunnel over the winding narrow street below. Their new home had a climb of two floors that took them to a single room. A bunk bed, a table and a desk greeted them. The toilet was outside, a pump and well with fresh water was further down the street and they had to pay Shorty one shilling once a week for the use of his bath.

12

The first time Cornelius had to use a knife was just days into their new venture. The two men had been navigating their way round the labyrinth of alleyways and taking note of the places to go and the areas to definitely avoid. Evading the countless buckets of dirty water thrown out of high windows was a particular necessity and they had to dance and pirouette along the narrow pavements, steps and doorways.

This particular fine sunny evening, two undesirables had hidden themselves in a darkened doorway; they obviously thought that the Marquis hadn't seen them as they tried to conceal themselves further, but Beauchamp had seen their shadows. Shadows always give things away. One should always be suspicious of a hidden figure he thought, they don't want people to see them, and in a place such as this, that's usually a dangerous thing. He felt the sheath clasped to his leather belt and kept an eye on Cornelius. The younger man was totally oblivious to the two scoundrels and seemed only concerned with the shop windows and what they were selling and looking upwards every now and then to avoid a soaking. The two vagrants were definitely following them though;

they had done this many times before, waiting to pull an unsuspecting victim into one of the hidden corners and attack them for their money or rob them of their clothes. Others worked for unscrupulous 'doctors' and those victims lost their lives.

Beauchamp was unsure of what to do at first; he didn't want to lose these two vermin and have them attack Cornelius when he was on his own, so he played them at their own game and deliberately meandered into a narrow passage down a secluded alley and pretended to be unaware. Almost at once, one of the men bounded up to him and grabbed him round the neck. Cornelius looked on horrified with no idea what to do. Beauchamp threw his knife to him so that he could defend himself while he grappled with the one that was hanging on his back and trying to gouge his eyes out. Beauchamp was having none of it though and with the ease of fighting off a small kitten, he pulled the vagrant over his shoulder in one movement and smashed the left side of his jaw with a heavy fist as he faced him. The opponent was dazed but not down.

'You bald bastard!' yelled out the street rat rubbing the pain.

'I've still got more,' yelled back Beauchamp.

'Oh yeah?' and the rat pulled out a knife. He smiled revealing crooked black teeth with two missing at the front. Then he pulled up his sleeves to display scars and other marks on his arms. This sign of menace meant little to Beauchamp, and he cracked a snigger. The vagrant tried to slash at his opponent, but

Beauchamp jerked back, just out of reach, and the silver blade cut only air. The attacker launched again but Beauchamp backed away, narrowly missing the rise of a moss covered stone. Beauchamp had to be smart about this now, he kept one eye on Cornelius, but his focus was on the one with the blade.

The other accomplice saw his chance and made over to Cornelius. The young man looked terrified and danced about with jutting movements and slashed the air with the knife. Beauchamp's adversary pressed forwards though, placing each foot carefully on uneven ground until Beauchamp was cornered, his back was nearly against the wall, but not quite. The attacker had the audacity to play another sinister smile on his thin pale lips. That angered Beauchamp. He smiled back, turned, launched himself up the wall, propelled himself from a sill and leapt behind the toothless grin. Without giving the smirk time to think, he rammed his face into the wall in front of him. The grin vanished as the lifeless body slid down the masonry and a thin line of blood trickled from a gaping mouth. Beauchamp took the knife from his opened hand and turned to face the other one. The second lout was now cornered and waved his arms wildly like a terrified bird, but Beauchamp was too quick and while the assailant was waving his arms in the air, the better man threw himself forwards and slashed the maniac across the neck; the razor edge of his blade left a bright red open wound that would show no mercy. He too slumped to the ground and would not bother anyone again.

'Two less vagrants to worry about,' he hollered to a totally shocked Cornelius, throwing the blade onto the dead man's coat and sliding his own back into its sheath. 'Look at them, they look like they've killed each other.' He pulled his own jacket neatly together and wiped his bald head. 'Now where were we? I think we've gone a little off course.'

'You have to show me how to do that,' said Cornelius in total amazement and went back to retrieve the knife that Beauchamp had abandoned. 'That's twice I have witnessed you taking on men bigger than yourself.'

'That's evidence you have taken Master Cornelius,' said Beauchamp ignoring the request.

'Maybe it is, but what if another undesirable takes it instead and tries to attack us again? I think it's better with me.'

Beauchamp nodded and grunted in agreement whilst watching Cornelius wipe the weapon clean on the deceased toothless vagrant and slip it into his belt.

'So will you teach me?' Cornelius asked again.

'Your father told me to look after you, and that is what I am doing.' Beauchamp quickened his pace to escape the scene, still ignoring the plea.

'But I couldn't help you, I was scared, I froze, I was no help to you at all,' said Cornelius trotting after him.

'But we're alive and those two are dead, that's all that matters isn't it?' Beauchamp turned into the street market with the young man close on his heels.

Cornelius tried another approach. 'Back in Ataxata, it wasn't really a life or death situation. Of course I had my father trying to turn me into a warmonger like himself or the murdering General, and all of his deranged captains, but my life was never really in danger was it?' He stressed the word 'really' to prove his point.

Beauchamp nodded and grunted in agreement and picked out an apple from a stall.

'Oi you!' shouted out the stall holder. 'That'll cost you 'alf a shillin'.'

He tossed her a full shilling. 'I'll be back tomorrow for the other one,' and winked at her.

The young woman put the shilling in her apron and tutted into the air.

'But here is a totally different place, my life is really in danger,' said Cornelius frowning at Beauchamp's audacity and putting a stress on the word 'really' again.

'Where do you suggest we learn then Master Cornelius? Because there ain't too many forests round here to hunt boar, we can't go about cutting people's throats on the streets and they don't run survival schools in a place like this..... so what do you suggest we do?'

Cornelius wasn't going to give up easily. 'We practise on each other.'

The Marquis stopped in his tracks, took three huge mouthfuls of apple and threw the remains on the ground much to the delight of a dozen squabbling sea gulls.

'Practise on each other eh?' he nodded and grunted, licked his lips a few times then wiped his mouth clean with the back of his hand.

'Well?' said Cornelius.

'Is that what you want, really, that kind of power? To be able to disarm me with a knife or a sword? Do you realise that power changes people. It attracts the worst and corrupts the best. You have seen it with your father. Is that the type of person you want to become?'

The words were a crushing blow for the young man. 'I won't become like that. I still like my music and my singing. I just want to defend myself in this gods forsaken place.'

'Good answer Master Cornelius. Come with me.'

Cornelius trotted behind him with a spring in his step as the Marquis led him down to the quay side.

'Down by the shore will be a good place to start, we can conceal ourselves in caves while we practise our craft.'

'That is such a good idea Beauchamp, such a good idea. I will listen and do exactly as you say.'

'Well I think you had better - otherwise you will find yourself in all sorts of trouble.'

Cornelius nodded earnestly and trailed after the master heading towards the coves.

The shore line was jagged with nooks and crannies, and a snarl of rocks tried to disengage them as they sought out the deepest cavern with sharp eyes and nimble feet.

Inside a deep hollow, the air was cold and damp with a strong smell of sea salt and littered with its debris. The same squabbling gulls had followed them from the town but soon disappeared when the two men settled on an appropriate cave. The mouth was a cavern in the rock barely wide enough for a man to get through, but Beauchamp had a nose for these things; they would be hidden from view and as it opened to the north, would not get too hot during the summer months. As Beauchamp had suspected, the small passage opened up into a huge cavity with an underground stream and a wealth of natural carvings born from the roof of the cave. Though when the sun filtered through, these carvings resembled mythical creatures that only appeared in the fragments of one's nightmares, and as the shadows played tricks on their eyes, the disfigured gargoyles took on human characteristics and appeared to move around them.

'These must be the witches and dragons you spoke about Beauchamp,' said Cornelius, studying everyone of them in detail. 'Perhaps they used to live here and have been turned to stone over time.'

'I think they must be,' agreed Beauchamp, just as mystified and glorified with the natural forms as the novice.

Cornelius was barely watching where he was going until Beauchamp pointed it out. 'Careful where you tread,' he advised. 'It doesn't seem to dry out in here very much.'

'We must be aware of the tide,' the boy's voice

echoed. 'We don't want to be marooned in here all night.'

'Oh yes, must rush back to the comfort of our splendid room.'

The two men laughed and began to arrange the area as best they could; moving the heaviest boulders out to the sides and levelling the debris on the ground.

The first lesson seemed straight forward.

'Take out your blade Cornelius, feel its weight, look at the shape of it, remember its dimensions. Look at your hand and see how it fits nicely into the palm.'

Cornelius did exactly as was instructed, examining every inch of the weapon and how it felt in his hand.

'Now I want you to extend that to your arm, I want you to hold the knife and just keep bending your arm from the elbow and out again,' he demonstrated the action. 'It's easy isn't it?'

'Yes, this is easy,' smiled Cornelius feeling quite pleased with himself.

'Wrong answer.'

'What?'

'If something is easy, you are doing it wrong, or you are not passionate about it.'

'It's easy for you.'

'Proficiency comes with experience. If you take the easy route and don't challenge yourself then you will never improve.'

'So what am I doing wrong then?'

'You're not holding it right, you're not standing

right; look at you, your posture is all over the place. Stand like me, upright, strong, in control, legs balanced, shoulders square, eyes forward.' Beauchamp stood behind him and forced his student's shoulders down, then split his legs wider apart and repositioned his feet. Turning his head face on, he ordered, 'Now do it again.'

Cornelius re-focused and moved his arm up and down but kept losing balance. 'I can't do it now, it's too hard,' he complained.

'Proficiency comes with experience remember. Focus on your muscles, feel them move around your bones, work with the tendons, they are the elastic hinges that guide you.'

Cornelius was using up so much energy now and tiring quickly.

'Move your legs, sway into the action, imagine you have no constraints, you are in charge of your own body. Keep moving your arms.' The tutor wasn't giving up on his pupil.

After several hours the boy shouted out. 'Look, look, I can do it, look at me, I can do it now,' and paraded round the cave for his weary instructor to see.

'Good work Master Cornelius,' championed Beauchamp. 'That's enough for today, we'll come back tomorrow.'

The next day in the cave, the tutor embarked on a new strategy. 'Feel your surroundings Cornelius, smell the air that makes you strong, listen to the breeze outside the cave, touch the walls that empower you, wait for the earth to guide you.'

Cornelius switched on his senses and intuition.

'Feel the magic of the earth, feel its power, for it is greater than anything you will ever know.' Beauchamp rang out his instructions.

The cave became a harmonious mix of vibrations and sounds in their dark compact world with only a few pores of sunlight seeping through the opening. This cave was alive with a beating heart.

'Now, with the cave as your guide, listen and feel and stretch your imagination, for if you don't engage with your surroundings, you can never be master of your craft. '

Cornelius didn't need to see what was around him, he could feel it. He could taste the salt from the most powerful element on earth and he let it slide down the back of his throat into the bowels of his stomach and held it there as a powerful ball of energy. He listened hard until he could hear a change in the direction of the wind. He breathed in deeply until he knew what the weather would be in the next hour. He felt the strength in his blade. His fingers curled and spread with added strength, he flexed his arm with power. He knew the importance of the senses now.

The next day they practised, and the day after that. Hour after hour, day after day, moving with the tides and the phases of the moon while the shadows in the cave changed with the sun. The cold was his nemesis, the rain even more so; for they challenged him and trained his hunger.

The following month he was leaping round the cave over the huge oval sea stones. Within six months he could dance around the cave in the dark. After nine months he could scale the cave walls and do a back flip in the air. After eighteen months he could disarm the Marquis and position the knife to slit his throat. After two years they had come out of the cave and were practising their sword fights on the precipices of overhanging rocks; stabbing, thrusting and circling the steel. Sharpened blades sang out a tune as they split the air into mischievous particles, dancing from edge to corner, springing from a shoulder of granite to a narrow sandy track, tumbling to the pebbled reef below and leaping back up again. Practised feet made expert climbers. Engaged senses created power.

After three years he could walk the streets without his bodyguard, day or night. Only a handful of times he was approached by attackers, but the swift removal of an eye or a quickly severed ear was all it took to get a reputation and before long no one was bothering him at all.

Beauchamp was a little sad that the young man who loved music and singing had gone, for there was something very vulnerable and sweet about that boy. The man before him could kill in an instant now and not think twice about it. But it made him smile the day when Cornelius had said: 'Now could you teach me to steal an apple from a street seller and get away with it.'

Perhaps some of the vulnerable young lad was still in there somewhere.

13

It was about the time when Master Cornelius had been exiled for two years, that a disturbance in Ataxata meant that the search for the Seal of Kings had to be put on hold. It was the end of the year when the State Marshals came to the palace seeking information regarding a washed up body.

'What do they want with us?' stormed the Emperor. 'Coming here looking for vagrants, the abomination of it!'

'I believe the authorities want to ask about the people who were employed here over the last five years.'

'What? Really? Corbulo this is just too much!'

'We have done nothing wrong Gnaeus, all we have to do is answer their questions.'

'All right, all right let them in, I will receive them in the mosaic conservatory. I prefer the view from there.'

'As you wish Gnaeus.'

The General went to instruct the guards while the Emperor took his position on the raised mosaic dais and looked around admiringly. An ornate crystal hall studded with precious jewels and dazzling fountains, it was indeed an exquisite piece of workmanship that ran along the south side of the palace. The floor was solid marble as were the monumental pillars and statues that were strategically placed around the perimeter of the building. Two spectacular water features of solid gold and lapis lazuli were positioned in two corners, adjacent to a range of ornate plants and exotic blooms of white, purple and yellow. At the end of the palisade was a magnificent bust of himself; sitting on a plinth of white alabaster with a granite column, the bust was the most incredible likeness and he considered it the most precious item that he owned.

His self gratifying was halted with the entrance of the General.

'Everything all right Corbulo?'

'Yes, the guards have been given the instructions, they will be here shortly.'

The General sat back and breathed in the sweet fragrance of rose, jasmine and honeysuckle. 'How wonderful this place is Gnaeus.' And he breathed deeply once again.

The two men sat up straight when the guards opened the doors allowing two visitors to enter. With the doors closed behind them, they removed their official hats and bowed to the Emperor. When invited, they strode the length of the mosaic hall. The peaceful image was tampered as hard soled boots clattered on the marble floor and green cloaks swayed against the swords at their sides.

'Gentlemen please, sit down, we are ready to

answer your questions.' The General pointed to two chairs that were positioned opposite them.

The visitors bowed again and sat down. A pause followed while the two officials took out their notepads and pencils. The taller one spoke first. 'Thank you, your lordships, and apologies for inconveniencing you in this way. It is most gracious of you to see us at such short notice.'

The Emperor nodded at the introduction and gestured to continue.

'My name is Dalton and this is my assistant Benfry, and we are here on a very grave matter.'

'Yes, we have heard; so how can we help you today?' responded the General with a thin wavering smile.

Dalton peeled back the pages of his notebook and stopped with a raised eyebrow. He read what was written to himself then conveyed the message out loud. 'Two years ago a body was found on the shores of Ataxata. It had been washed up several miles from here, a lone fisherman spotted the body and alerted the authorities.'

'Two years ago?' questioned the Emperor, raising his incredulous tone.

'Yes,' said Benfry. 'And it was already a two year old corpse by the time we found it. The man's throat had been slit, the body was white and bloated; quite hideous in fact, but the sea water had preserved it sufficiently and that made it easier for us to identify.'

The Emperor and the General sat aghast as to

why they were part of this investigation.

'Since then, we have been conducting our enquiries,' continued Benfrey.

'A very slow and difficult enquiry as you might appreciate,' added Dalton with a raised eyebrow.

'So how can we help with a four year old enquiry?' searched the General.

'Because we now know the identity of the deceased and we now know who probably killed him.'

'I'm sorry, you have lost me,' said the General and looked witheringly at the Emperor.

'The deceased is one Marquis de Beauchamp,' continued Dalton. 'An aristocrat who had recently come to the area to spend his fortune, or that is what we believe.'

The Emperor stroked his beard, his pained expression mirrored by the General.

'Is there something wrong my lord?' asked Dalton.

'It's just the name you mentioned,' he coughed to clear his voice. 'Because if it is Beauchamp, then it doesn't make sense,' the Emperor's voice was thick. 'Because he was in my employment then.'

'Yes, our line of enquiries gave us the same answer, but it seems that your Marquis and our Marquis are not the same people.'

A look of bewilderment followed the revelation. 'Please explain,' the General said massaging his chin.

'Of course, and please bear with us,' Dalton creased his eyebrows. 'We have managed to piece together certain facts; firstly, it seems that a young man was in the area at the same time as the Marquis; secondly, we understand that his name is Gye. And thirdly, our enquiries have led us to believe that he got into a fracas with the Marquis.'

'A fracas?' questioned the Emperor, receding into his double chin.

'They argued about a game of cards,' explained Benfry.

'The young man was doing very well apparently, until the Marquis accused him of cheating.'

'And was he?' asked the Emperor.

'By all accounts he wasn't, but the Marquis took all the money anyway and left shortly afterwards.'

'Carry on,' said Corbulo leaning forward.

'We believe that the young man followed the Marquis and they got into a fight as they argued about the winnings. A witness confirmed to us that the Marquis pulled out a knife on the youth. We are not sure of what followed next but the Marquis ended up with his throat cut at some point. Believing he was unseen, the youth threw the Marquis in the water and ran away. We have since found out in the last few months that the young man adopted the Marquis' identity.'

'Why would he do that?' posed the General.

'It has taken us four years to piece this all together, so please excuse us if it seems a bit patchy in places,' apologised Benfrey.

'Of course, but please carry on with what you

know,' encouraged the Emperor with his finger tips pressed together.

'It seems that the youth had come to Ataxata to make his way in the kingdom as well.'

'Really?' the Emperor looked bewildered.

'We believe that Gye, the youth who killed the real Marquis and then took his identity; answered a notice from this palace to work with the Master Cornelius.'

'Well, yes, he did, he did answer the notice and we gave him employment.' The Emperor nodded his head emphatically. 'He was with us for two years. It was two years wasn't it Corbulo?'

The General's face was a quandary of facial expressions.

'Corbulo,' began the Emperor again. 'Do you remember how long the Marquis, I mean Gye, was with us?'

Corbulo shrugged, 'yes...two years.' And returned to his tight facial expressions.

'So where is he now?' asked Dalton seeking clarification.

'Goodness knows,' began the Emperor.

'He's the other side of the world,' answered the General quietly, his eyes focused on a thread of jasmine.

The two men looked at him.

'I put him and Master Cornelius on a boat to the other side of the world,' the General's voice spoke out directly but his eyes were focused elsewhere.

'What for?' came the astonished reply.

'Because we had a disagreement, we fell out. I felt the Emperor's life was being compromised after a long series of arguments, so they have both been exiled.'

'Exiled?' The officials raised their voices together amid the Emperor's raised eyebrows.

'Do you have documents that prove that?' asked Dalton.

The General's face tightened with displeasure.

'I am sorry to ask, but I hope you understand why we need proof.'

'Of course we do,' interjected the Emperor and he found his face looking directly at Dalton's.' We don't want to be seen to be harbouring a criminal and covering it up. I mean, anyone could say anything just to protect someone.'

'Precisely' said Dalton, somewhat relieved at the tone of agreement as the air had suddenly turned quite sour.

'I will send you the paperwork this very day,' confirmed the General. 'One of my captains will deliver it to you personally.'

'Thank you, that would be very good of you.' Benfry wrote the details down in his notebook.

'I am sorry he is not here but I can assure you I put them on the ship myself,' continued the General finding his stern voice of authority once again. 'I doubt if they are still alive anyway. The stories I have heard about the other side of the world are quite horrific.'

'Yes of course,' agreed Benfry.' And no doubt a court would have put him on that same boat to befit his crime.'

'We know it was in self defence,' intercepted Dalton. 'Nevertheless, a death was inflicted, and he has been punished now, so we should be thanking you.'

'Just one more thing,' added Benfry. 'Did you by perchance see the young man with a pouch of diamonds at all? Some witnesses have said the two men were playing for diamonds.'

'No,' said the General. 'We paid him with sovereigns and shillings of the realm, we never saw any diamonds.' He puckered his chin as he nodded with the Emperor.

'All right, not to worry,' said Dalton. 'The diamonds are probably long gone by now, just like the young man.'

The General creased a thin smile from his puckered chin in response and the two men stood up to take their leave.

'Thank you for wrapping this mystery up for us,' said Benfrey. 'We can close the file now.'

'Glad we have been able to help,' said the Emperor. 'I really had no idea that we were harbouring a criminal.'

'Well things have a habit of catching up with felons,' said Dalton, tucking away his notepad and pencil. 'In my experience, perpetrators can't hide forever.' He cocked a smile and patted the contents of his pocket.

The two men bowed again and strode the length of the mosaic conservatory, their boots clattering on the marble floor as their green cloaks sashayed against the swords at their sides.

Behind them they left two deadly assassins planning their most monstrous atrocity to date - the capture of clan boys to fight to the death in a public display of betrayal - and wipe out the murderous conniving scum forever.

14

It began with Cornelius not returning home for just one or two nights, then it became three and four; then he rarely came back at all. Instead, he caught himself a fish or a crab or a lobster which he cooked to perfection over a low simmering fire; or he stole out under darkness and found a solitary loaf within arms reach of an open window, and if he was really lucky, there would be a freshly cooked pie right next to it.

This labyrinth of darkness soon became home. Something had awakened him and released him from the shackles of life. Now, his friends became the shadows and his allies were the wraiths. And soon, the serenity and peace that he found amongst the protective cavernous stone meant he was about to make a monumental decision.

'I think I'm going to move into the cave permanently,' he said after living with Beauchamp for four years. 'I prefer it in there, I like the quietness and being at one with nature.'

'Being at one with nature eh, that's a very profound statement Master Cornelius, are you sure you are not just tiring of my company?'

Cornelius laughed out loud, 'ha ha, not at all

dear friend, it's just that I am twenty two years old now and I feel that I can take care of myself, so I want to move out.'

'Is it a lady friend then, have you sought to court someone?'

'Beauchamp that is even more preposterous than saying I have tired of you. How on earth could I take a lady to live in a cave with me? Think about it, that is just not going to happen.'

'Well if you are not courting a lady friend, perhaps I could come with you then, there is plenty of room in the cave.'

'Well that kind of defeats the object doesn't it? we would be living together again and I want my own space.'

'Your own space! To do what may I ask?'

'To sing, to dance, to practise my craft in the dark, to walk outside in the rain under a moonlit night, to sit and watch the sun rise first thing in the morning. To weather the storms, to embrace the sun. To dual with the wind on the wing of a gale. All those things. That cave has changed me Beauchamp, it has made me strong with a sense of freedom; I am a different person now and I seek my independence.'

'Master Cornelius, I understand what you are saying, I really do. But I am worried that being on your own out there might affect you. Remember what I said about power and changing people? I am just concerned that's all.'

'Beauchamp I am not going to ban you from

seeing me ever again. Of course we will see each other; but just not as much as we do now.'

'Well, if that's what you want to do, then who am I to get in your way. Shall I draw up a timetable of when I can see you?'

'Now you are just being ridiculous and taking it way too personally.' Cornelius was getting exasperated now, he felt like he was letting a loved one down, or breaking up with a partner.

'Well, we have been inseparable for six years, it's going to take a bit of getting used to that's all.' Beauchamp sighed and pondered again.

But in all honesty, Beauchamp did feel like a let down loved one, he did feel like he was breaking up with a partner. He had been at Master Cornelius's side for six years now, and that was a long time. He had turned the boy into a man, he had made him strong and able to defend himself, even against a great master such as himself. Cornelius had fought the dragons and the witches in the cave so that he didn't fear those anymore. And now, the master felt redundant.

Beauchamp harrumphed. 'I'm not sure Cornelius, I don't feel right about this, there are so many undesirables out there, and I still feel responsible for you.'

'Look I will try it for a month, if I don't like it or I am getting beaten up,' he raised a solitary eyebrow at the idea. 'Then I will come back here to your hovel or you can come and live with me in my cave.'

Beauchamp pondered and Cornelius could see

the cogs going round in his head as he contemplated the notion.

'It doesn't seem right that you should live in a cave though.'

'Come on, how old were you when you left home?'

'Sixteen, but that was completely different.'

'How was it completely different?'

'Because I didn't really want to leave, I was forced to go.'

'You've never told me that.'

'Well, I'm telling you now, it was completely different and I was completely on my own.'

'But I'm not completely on my own am I? I still have you a stone's throw away from me.'

Beauchamp reluctantly let him go to his cave, and he stayed in the hovel. But Master Cornelius did change; he became a vagrant. After six months he was barely speaking to anyone, he even lost his appetite for bartering with the market sellers. He had lost all his charm and humour with the ladies. After a year he only came into the town to drink at the inn; the ale could sometimes make him magnanimous in spirit but more often than not he was particularly rude and unpleasant to everyone. After two years he barely saw his good friend Beauchamp and when he did he was a fragment of his former self.

Beauchamp remembered that night in June very well. There had been a festival out on the quay; it was always held in June, this year it was on the 10th day of the sixth month. Stall holders sold their wares, sea farers made a coin or two from exotic gifts they had brought in on a ship. There was singing and dancing, magicians and acrobats; it was a colourful and vibrant affair and the inns did a roaring trade. Cornelius used to love these occasions. But this was the second year he hadn't been. His second year in the cave.

'I don't know what I am going to do Shorty,' he said over a tankard of beer when everyone had gone home. He had been waiting for Cornelius, but he hadn't come in.' He's been in that cave for two years now and he barely sees me.'

'I sympathise with you Beauchamp, I really do.' Shorty spat on the glass and held it up to the light. He looked pleased with the final result and put it in a row with the others.

'I have tried my best to keep in contact, but he doesn't want to know me. And have you seen what he looks like now? He used to be so handsome and particular; now he just doesn't care.'

Shorty didn't have to respond to that one, he carried on with what he was doing, raised his eyebrows and settled his face into one his three chins.

'So you have seen him then and you know exactly what I am talking about.'

'He doesn't bother me Beauchamp, I mean goodness, we get all sorts in here.' Shorty held another spat on glass up to the light, put it down and leaned in to his tenant. 'But it's my staff, it's my girls, he can't go

107

round talking to them like he does; do you know what I mean Beauchamp?'

'I know, Shorty, I know exactly what you mean,' he sighed heavily. 'What I need is a miracle.'

He supped up, put what he owed on the counter and went back to his hovel alone.

15

Back in his room Beauchamp lit a candle and took it to a desk. He pulled out a sealed goblet and spilled the contents; fifty diamonds shone like dragons eyes in the pit of the night.

'These will get us back Master Cornelius, these are our tickets back home.'

'Where did you get those?'

'Never you mind where they came from; all you need to know is that they will get us on the next boat out of here.'

'When though Gye, when can we go?'

'I will go to the quay tomorrow morning first light; I will speak to the jetty master and find out when the next one sails to Ataxata.'

'I can hardly wait, I fear I have been here far too long.'

Beauchamp put his hands on his friend's shoulders and looked him in the eye. 'We have both been here too long my friend. Tomorrow I will go into the town and find a bathing house for you to wash and scrub up. Hopefully a barber can give you a wet shave, we can't have a newly appointed Emperor arriving in Ataxata looking like a street beggar. I will buy some new clothes for you; the ones you have on are practically falling off your back.'

Cornelius hugged his friend. 'What would I do without you? I know you have worried about me these past few years.'

'Few years!!' Beauchamp corrected. 'I have worried about you ever since you decided to move into that cave three years ago,' and he emphasised the three.

'Is it really three years?'

'Yes it is, three awful, worrying, lonely, three years. But all that is behind us now. You will stay here tonight and I will sort everything out in the morning. Now get yourself to bed and we shall resume our plans tomorrow.'

Beauchamp couldn't believe the change in his charge. He had miraculously morphed overnight. His prayers had been answered on that day in June last year. The Emperor had been killed and that one momentous event had given Cornelius his life back and his safe passage home. Thank the gods, thank who ever had served this justice; for who ever had killed the Emperor and the General would have his sincerest blessings. He owed them his life, not just Cornelius' life. This was indeed a miracle. His master was a broken man who had fallen into a severe state of depression, and this wonderful news had brought him out of it. He didn't have to beg him to stay, he didn't have to plead and point everything out to him. Master Cornelius was back.

In the morning Gye de Beauchamp descended

on the sleeping man. 'Master Cornelius, I have secured a place on a ship that leaves at noon in seven days time. I have also got you into one the bath houses for this morning. You will dine there and be fitted out with new robes.'

Cornelius sat up yawning. 'What! you have done all that this morning?'

'Diamonds talk and get things done,' he winked. 'And we have to get you back on track.' A raised eyebrow and thin smile from Beauchamp told Cornelius just how selfish he had been.

'I am sorry Gye, I really am. I am so sorry for everything and you have always been so good to me.'

'I care for you Master Cornelius and I am just relieved that this notice has brought you back to life.'

'I can hardly believe it Gye, I can hardly believe that we are going home. I can hardly believe we are leaving this dreadful place.' Cornelius looked around him, moved his frayed blanket aside and picked at the straw mattress he had just spent the night on.

'I know, at last we can look forward to a wonderful new life. Now get yourself down to the bath house and come back looking like a new man.'

Cornelius swung his legs out of the bed and threw on his rags. 'On my way my lord.'

'Take your time young man, I have paid good money for this.'

'Oh the joy of it, I fear my skin might wrinkle and peel off in the bubbles, it has been that long since I bathed. Truly, I am so looking forward to going home.'

He ran to the bath house with ludicrous alacrity and was particularly civil to the bathing maids. 'Now please tell me there is a hot bath waiting for me and that I can have something decent to eat; and please don't offer me anything cold bloodied or spineless, I don't think I can ever look at another aquatic in my life.'

The maids giggled and attended to him with fastidious detail.

'And be careful with that blade,' he joked. 'There is a very handsome face under all this dirt and facial hair.'

The bath was hot and soapy, the maids had scented it with aromatic oils and herbs and it felt so good to feel the warm liquid dissolve the dirt and grime on his weathered skin. The maid picked up his clothes and held them at arms length.

'You need to burn those please my beautiful lady, they have served me well, but not needed anymore... I am going home.' He sank into the steaming tub of water with a contented sigh, closed his eyes, and slid his entire head beneath the surface.

The last few days before the ship was launched, the Marquis and Cornelius spent every possible moment shaking hands and saying their farewells to the community that had been their home for seven years. Cornelius apologised for his unreasonable behaviour during the past three while Beauchamp was also apologising for his master's behaviour. That last night the two men strolled along the sloping cobblestoned street for the final time and walked towards the jetty that extended like long breaded fingers into the sea. Cornelius looked behind him and towards the cave.

'Please don't tell me that you want to spend our last night in the cave Cornelius,' Beauchamp looked aghast.

Cornelius laughed and shrugged his shoulders. 'No, dear friend, I am a changed man, 'he looked down at his smart apparel and pinched the collar's of his jacket. 'Do you really think I want to rough up these fine clothes?'

'I am relieved,' said Beauchamp. 'You had me worried for a moment.'

'Come my friend, let us go and have that farewell drink with Shorty.'

16

As usual a huge crowd congregated to bid their farewells on the quay. It was always full of excitement. Broad shouldered men filed aboard carrying crates of cured meats, dried fruit, bottles of wine, kegs of beer, caged birds, grain and fresh water. The voyage would take them nearly three months to complete and most of these supplies were for the duration; the rest were bound for the market in Ataxata.

Cornelius and Beauchamp made their way up the steep plank to the galley and looked down upon the cheering crowd from the high deck of their homeward bound ship. They looked like lords in their silk and satin robes with jewelled belts and flowing sleeves. The new clothes had cost a fair penny, alongside the jewelled rings that they displayed; even their scabbards were heavily enamelled and inlaid with burnished copper, shining silver and soft red gold. Cornelius had his blond hair cut into a better shape and his tanned skin set off those deep blue eyes. And now, without the crudity of facial hair, a strong and chiselled face emerged and his manner was deemed entirely charming and quietly powerful.

'I don't think we will be needing these this time,'

Beauchamp patted his sword. 'But it doesn't hurt to have a weapon or two on show.' He winked at Cornelius and showed him the hilt of his dirk concealed inside his sleeve.

Cornelius responded with a subtle nod towards his boot. 'Easy access in there.'

Gye put a loving arm around his friend's shoulder.

Cornelius reached round to Gye's hand, turned his head and kissed it. 'Always there for me my dear friend, what would I have done without you?'

'Probably die,' came the honest response.

With all sails set to catch the midday breeze and the ties set loose from the dockside stanchions, the ship pulled away from the wharf. From the stern, the passengers watched the cheering crowds and waved furiously back to them. None more so than Cornelius and Beauchamp and when the people were nothing more than dots on a hazy horizon the two men walked the decks, climbed down a ladder into the quarters and checked out their cabin below.

It was of a comfortable size and offered bunk beds for two people; a wash basin, a large leather captains chair and a rosewood chest of drawers with a crystal decanter and two silver goblets on the top. One panelled wall was lined with rows of books while the opposite wall housed a bundle of rolled up parchment. And the glorious sun filtered through the porthole to expose a rack, three tiers high, of the finest vintage wine.

'Goodness Beauchamp, you have surpassed yourself this time,' said Cornelius launching himself onto the top bunk, kicking his boots off and slipping his arms behind his head.

His friend perched on the edge of the lower bunk and removed his hat. 'Like I said, diamonds talk the loudest.'

'You never did tell me where you got them from.'

'Didn't I?' he replied, wiping the sweat mark on his bald head from where his hat had been.

Cornelius turned upside down and faced him. 'No you didn't.'

'I'll tell you one day,' he said, trying to avoid the question.

'Well we've got three months of nothing to do on this boat, so this might be as good a time as any.'

He swung himself down, sat by his friend and peered into his face again. 'Well?'

Beauchamp couldn't hide anymore. Cornelius was hungry for knowledge now. The diamonds had intrigued him and stirred his curiosity. All these years he had kept his past safe and secure. No one knew. Not a soul. And now he was about to divulge everything. He would get no peace until he did.

'I ran away Master Cornelius.'

'From whom?'

'I will be telling you things now that you might not like Master Cornelius.'

A dipped frown from Cornelius was enough for Beauchamp to continue.

'I was sixteen years old when they attacked us.'

'Who attacked you?'

'That does not matter for now, let us just say it was an army intent on death and destruction for their own elixir of power.'

Cornelius' brow stayed furrowed and his expression fixed.

'That was eleven years ago,' said Beauchamp.

'A year before you came to the palace?'

'Yes, a year to the day near enough.'

'So what happened?'

'At sixteen years old I was a scared young man, I was too frightened to fight. I hid away and watched as my family and friends got butchered.' Looking to the ground he sighed heavily. 'I can still hear their screams in my nightmares Cornelius, I can still see the stream running red with their blood. Our fields raging with burning fires, our homes ablaze with vicious tongues of yellow and blue. The smoke, the smell, the burning flesh.' He looked up to his friend with tears streaming. 'We were humble farmers Cornelius, we weren't prepared for anything like it.'

Cornelius looked ashen, but then he pieced together something else. 'I don't understand Beauchamp. If you come from a farming village with no soldiers to protect you. How come you are the Marquis de Beauchamp?'

'I will come to that later; that is much later.'

'All right, so back to the slaughter,' Cornelius grimaced.

The Marquis stood up, selected a bottle of vintage wine and poured himself a glass. Returning to his seat, he put the bottle by his side on the floor and continued his story. 'Even though my own mother and father got hacked to pieces in front of me, I could not do anything to save them. I was too afraid.' He knocked back a mouthful.

'What did you do?' Cornelius waved the offered goblet away.

'I waited till dark, until it was safe. The soldiers had taken some prisoners, but the rest were dead. Men, women, children were either taken as slaves or lay mutilated on the ground. The crows had already started pecking on the bodies of some, and I knew that before long the wolves would be down to finish the rest off.'

'Your mother and father?' Cornelius asked, fearful of the answer.

'I buried them, along with my younger brother and sister, I wept and prayed for their forgiveness. I prayed that they would give me strength to avenge their deaths.'

'So what happened next?'

'I walked and walked, I didn't know what direction I was going in, I just thought that south would be warmer with more food and that my chances of survival would be better.' He poured another glass of wine. Cornelius shook it away again. Beauchamp returned to his story.

'My legs ached after wandering for so many miles over hills and through dense forests, but the pain was nothing compared to the tortured soul of a coward.' He took another gulp of claret and savoured the taste as it swirled around his mouth, smacking his his lips and wearing a thin smile as it went down. Cornelius remained fixed.

'I carried on across the landscape with no particular destination in mind, just heading south with the sun guiding me. I lived on nuts and apples and managed to snare a rabbit or two along the way.' He paused at the memory. 'I remember that third night so well. It was dusk; the evening was still warm and the sun was just going down. I had sat by a tree to rest. I had built a fire to keep away the wolves, but I could scale a tree quick enough if the fire didn't deter them.'

He took another gulp of wine. Cornelius supported his chin on the palm of his hand. His face was wrinkled and his elbow formed a dent in his knee.

'Then I heard a twig snap, I grabbed a branch and lit it to keep away the monsters. I thought it was a witch or a dragon. But I told myself they lived on the other side of the world. They couldn't hurt me, there were far worse monsters out there.' He grimaced at the memory and sneaked a cheeky look at Cornelius. 'My heart was pounding now, I was exhausted, I felt useless because I had watched my family die. I just wanted to die myself.'

He paused and sighed. Cornelius saw a tear run down his face. Wiping it away he carried on.

'A stranger came out of the trees. He was so silent, all I heard was that one twig. He was an old man with a kind face, white hair, long beard, his clothes were worn not tattered. He needed a walking stick to aid him. He reached out his hand to me. I offered him some of my food. He sat down beside me and we talked. 'Are you lost boy?' he asked me. 'Sort of,' I said. 'Where are your family?' he asked. I couldn't even say the words Cornelius. I couldn't even tell an old man what I had done, what a coward I was and that I was responsible for my parents' death.'

'But you weren't responsible dear friend. It wasn't your fault.'

Beauchamp took another swig of wine. 'The old man stayed with me that night and in the morning I awoke to find he had prepared a wonderful breakfast of rabbit, eggs, mushrooms and fennel. He had a fresh flagon of water that I wolfed down.'

'Wow!'

'That's what I thought; then he said to me; 'You can't learn to fight on an empty stomach.'

'Really? He said that?'

'He did Cornelius, that's exactly what he said.'

'So what happened then?'

'Well, you remember how I taught you to fight in the cave?'

'Yes,' Cornelius was now sat upright.

'I was taught that way by him.'

'An old man taught you?'

'But this was no ordinary old man, he had skills

120

that surpassed those that I have now. His walking stick was an extension of his mind, and his mind was still young and active.'

Cornelius had so many questions now but didn't want to deviate from the story too much. 'How long were you in the forest?'

'Eight months, maybe a year. I had already learned to hunt and kill small mammals and rodents as a child in the village, so I could use a knife well. I could skin a rabbit in thirty seconds and help my father butcher a deer. It was courage and strength that I lacked, and of course sword fighting skills.'

'And he taught you all of that?' Cornelius' eyes were wide open with surprise.

'He did, just like I taught you; but he was undoubtedly a better teacher than me, so it didn't take him long.'

'Or maybe you were a better student?' Cornelius smiled.

Beauchamp shrugged and dismissed his praise. 'No, my tutor was the best.'

'So what happened?' Cornelius was still hungry for the story.

'One morning I awoke and he had gone. Nothing remained of him except the dent in the matted leaves where he had slept and the book that he always carried with him and referenced. I was distraught, I didn't even know his name, but he taught me everything I knew. I looked for him for hours, hoping he had just gone for a walk, or gone to see someone else for a few days. I stayed in the same place and waited, hoping he would come back. But he didn't. All I had of him were my memories and the book.

'So what did you do?'

'I didn't look at the book for days; I felt that it was his personal possession so I didn't have any right to it. But when I realised that he wasn't coming back and he had left the book for me as a parting gift; I opened it and read it from page to page with amazement.'

'What was inside?'

'Its pages were of the finest calf vellum and the intricate lettering was penned in iron gall ink, with detailed drawings and illuminated with such colours that could only have come from a far superior kingdom.' He breathed in deeply at the memory. 'Page after page of amazing information; mostly fighting skills, protective stances, defence moves, how to disarm someone; as well as nature's harvest that would help me along my way such as herbs, plants, wines, foods. But at the back was a whole section on the meaning of cards and how to play them.'

Cornelius was opened mouthed with astonishment. 'How to play cards?'

'Yup, how to play cards...' His voice lowered. 'In times of solitude cards are an insightful tool; a game to share with others or to be used as an almanac.'

'An almanac?' Cornelius found himself repeating the last words that Beauchamp said every time.

'Well, for example, the king and the queen of

kingdoms, the knave is evil and the ace is the god we worship. There are fifty two cards in a deck of cards, the same as the weeks in a year. Four suits which symbolise the seasons in a year that we farmers work by. Diamonds and hearts illustrate life, clubs and spades portray the after life. The two colours interpret the red blood of life and the black darkness in death. The ten numbered cards are a family. Do you see the the importance of them now Master Cornelius?'

'Yes I do,' Cornelius tightened his bottom lip, puckered his chin and nodded in agreement.

Gye looked satisfied that his student had understood and carried on with his tale.

'So I walked further south and the road took me to Ataxata.'

'And you answered the notice to be my aide?'

'Well not quite.'

Cornelius' silence urged him to continue.

'I had nothing, I had no money, I had no decent clothes. The rags I wore were the same ones I had been wearing for a year. So I took my chances and went into a tavern by the quay to challenge someone to a game of cards.'

'What were you going to barter with though?'

'My book.'

'What! But that was your prized possession now, how could you do that?'

'Because I knew I wouldn't lose.'

'It was still a risk not worth taking,' Cornelius looked shocked.

'At that point I didn't have too many options,' Gye poured another glass.

'All right, so what happened?' Cornelius waved his offering away again.

'At first I wasn't let in, I looked like a vagrant, my clothes were worse than a peasant. I stank, my hair was matted and stuck to my head. I must have looked so dreadful. The bartender had me by the scruff of the neck and was going to throw me out. But I spotted this man in the corner, he was on his own getting drunk. I could tell he was rich by the clothes he wore, what he was drinking, and his manner.' He finished off the bottle of wine and showed it to Cornelius. 'Get me another bottle could you good man, this is very thirsty work.'

'That was the real Marquis de Beauchamp then?'

Cornelius dutifully got up to get another bottle and filled the goblet to the brim.

'It was.'

'So what happened?'

'I said to the barman that I knew him, that I was an errand boy called Gye and I had been told to deliver him this book. The bartender looked at me and said, 'You know the Marquis de Beauchamp?' I said that I didn't know him personally just that I had business with him; so the bartender let me go in. I went up to the gentleman and with a bit of persuading patter, I challenged him. He laughed at first but he soon accepted my proposal when I told him that the book was full of spells and magic. Remember, the book was a very old specimen; with worn leather and ancient parchment; it certainly looked like a book of a warlock. Fortunately he was drunk enough to believe my story so he offered a pouch of diamonds as his stake; but of course he never really thought he would lose to me.'

'So I'm guessing you won as you have the diamonds and no book?'

'Not exactly... I won all the games... we played three times and it was the best of three... but he accused me of cheating, raised his dagger to me and I got thrown out.'

'So you had lost the book and the diamonds at this stage?'

'I had lost everything, so I had nothing now except the knowledge in my head. But I couldn't let him get away with it. I concealed myself in a doorway and hid myself away. It was very dark now, so no one saw me. But I had been taught by the master how to be like a cat, how to press yourself into alleyways and corners and wait for a victim to make an appearance. So I waited and waited until the thief came out.'

'Was anyone around? Did anyone see you?'

'I didn't see anyone and it was very late by now.'

'So what did you do?'

'When he came out I approached him and asked for my book back or the diamonds that I had won. I reminded him that I had won fair and square, but if he wouldn't honour that agreement like a gentleman then I wanted my book returned.' Beauchamp took a gulp of wine and wiped the dribble from his mouth with the back of his hand. 'He laughed out loud and pulled his knife out on me; he was clutching the book with one hand and the knife with another. We were by the quayside and getting nearer and nearer to the jetty. The Marquis was totally drunk and kept stabbing at me. I could easily have disarmed him and killed him, but I just wanted my winnings or my book returned. But he kept goading and laughing, taunting and teasing, jabbing and fooling around, getting nearer and nearer to the jetty's edge. I was trying to pull him back to safety but he was so drunk, he had no idea where he was. Eventually he slipped out of my grasp and he fell in. I dived in after him and we were grappling in the sea. He was trying to drown me now. The book had gone and I couldn't get to it. I reached out for it desperately... but I couldn't get a hold of it and I watched it disappear. The Marquis was pushing me down with one hand and trying to stab me with the other. But watching my gift disappear fuelled the rage in me, and now I found my strength. I wrenched the knife free from his grasp, slit his throat once and felt the life go out of him straight away. The book was long gone, but I had time to get the pouch out of his pocket plus a handful of notes and heaved myself to the surface. Once I got my breath back I ran off, found some dry clothes hanging on a clothes line and hid myself in a doorway for the night. Fearing I would be recognised I shaved my hair off with his knife. The next day I saw the notice to be your aide. I brought some new fine clothes in the town and called myself: The Marquis de Beauchamp.'

Gye finished off the rest of his wine in one go with a cracking 'aahhhhh,' and filled the goblet up again. Cornelius was still looking at him opened mouthed some two minutes later.

'So who are you then?' He managed to articulate some words round a heavy mouth. 'And what do we do if the authorities have found out about you and what you did?'

'Well it happened two years before we were exiled, so I expect the body was eaten, devoured, or certainly lost at sea. I am sure the body would have been found in that time if it was still in one piece; so I am not too concerned. But please remember that it was in self defence; it wasn't cold blooded murder. It really was either him or me. I was acting honourably when I challenged him to a game of cards; maybe I took advantage of him in his drunken state, that would be my only crime. And yes, the gods looked down on me that day.'

'Of course,' said Cornelius.

Gye took another large mouthful of the claret and swilled it round a dry exhausted mouth before swallowing and closing heavy eyes in satisfaction.

'But the authorities won't be looking for a woman will they?' A completely new thread was weaved into the story.

'What? Gye! you would change your identity? Surely you don't have to go to such extremes.'

'I don't need to.'

'Sorry, you've lost me. I am not following this at

all now,' Cornelius shook his head and furrowed his brow again.

'I am a woman Cornelius, I am not a man. I changed my identity to get the position in the palace.'

'What?' Cornelius stood bolt upright, got a goblet, poured himself a full glass of wine and knocked it back in one go. 'I don't believe you!'

'It's true! I can show you if you like; I have pert breasts, a womb that swells my stomach and a slit between my legs instead of a penis.'

'No, no, that won't be necessary,' and sitting opposite her on the stool he recoiled at the thought. 'You have felt like a brother to me all these years but now you feel like my sister.' He looked her up and down, totally bewildered at her revelation. 'How come I have never known, how come I have never seen, how come you have never told me?'

'There are ways and means. The last three years you have lived in a cave anyway. Before that I had my own room in the palace. It was tricky when we were in the hovel; but we paid to use Shorty's bathroom which we did separately. But to be honest, you weren't really looking, so I managed to conceal everything quite well. And I didn't want to tell you you dismissed me at once. Great women are often overlooked you know.'

Cornelius rolled his eyes in response. 'So what is your real name?'

'Gya, my name is Gya.'

'Did the wise man know that you were a woman?'

'Yes, he knew, but he knew everything didn't he? I was a scrawny frightened slip of a girl when he found me, but he turned me into the warrior that I am today.'

'It's unbelievable Gye, I mean Gya. How you managed to fool everyone. Me, my father, the General, everyone at the inn, including Shorty. I don't know how you have done it.'

'Where there's a will there's a way,' she smiled. 'As a woman I found my strength, but as a man I was able to prove it.'

'And now?' Cornelius asked.

'I don't need to prove anything anymore,' she began. 'I am not hiding from any monsters either.'

'So you will revert back to your true identity?'

'Yes I will Cornelius, I will let my hair grow out now and become a woman again. And I will go into the palace as your companion if that is all right with you?'

'As you wish dear friend, I do not mind at. You are the most courageous woman I know. Strong, fearless and I know the gods look down on you and protect you.'

'Thank you Master Cornelius.'

'And if I'm going to call you Gya from now on, then will you please drop the Master bit and just call me Cornelius?'

'Of course,' she expressed a look of satisfaction.

Cornelius smiled at his friend's bravery and then thought of her saviour: 'Talking of gods, I wonder who that old man was, where did he come from, where did he go?'

'I have often wondered the same thing myself Cornelius. Was he a hermit, was he a wise man, or was he my destiny? I do not know, but everything that I am today, I owe to him.'

'Well Gya, I raise a toast to the old wise man, I raise a toast to you, and I raise a toast to the deceased Emperor and his General, for their absence has allowed me safe passage back home.'

He poured himself another huge goblet of wine and finished it in two gulps. Gya was now laying prostate on the bunk, out for the count and snoring like a warrior. She had dropped off at the second toast. Cornelius draped a blanket over her and took himself up to the top deck.

17

Lyall had found himself in bed with Arneb on the morning after the wedding. He opened his eyes and thought he was still dreaming.

'Oh no!' he exclaimed. 'What on earth have I done now?' He ran his fingers through his hair in desperation and checked beneath the sheets to see if he still had his clothes on. He breathed a sigh of relief when he saw that his lower undergarments were still intact. Gazing around his room he saw the discarded clothes that had obviously been thrown off in a hurry. Arneb was still sound asleep. He watched as the sheets rose up and down in time with her breathing and could hear her purring softly. He smiled at her, resisting the temptation to stroke her cheek. He really wanted to kiss her now, but he knew that it wouldn't be fair. He would be leaving soon. It wouldn't be good for either of them. Instead, he got out of bed as quietly as he could, grabbed his clothes and hurried towards the stream.

He sat on a tumble of stones that had been abandoned there for centuries it seemed; white lichen and bearded moss made up the outer dermis now, much the same as the standing stones that he had become so accustomed to seeing on a daily basis. He looked at the small ripples, rolling by under the haze of a new dawn; skimming over vivid green reeds and washing the arrangement of pebbles below them. He let out a long sad sigh. He still hadn't told Namir about his intention to leave, and how many chances had he forsaken since that life changing day on the battlefield - which was months ago now. How could he possibly have left it so long?

He looked back at the cave, it still had the power to haunt him; but now he was able to embrace the cavern as it had opened up a whole new life for him and given him a new family - a family he was now poised to leave.

He heard footsteps behind him and turned to see Namir approaching.

'You are up early brother,' called out Namir.

'Yes,' he answered, quickly swallowing the lump in his throat. 'I have left Arneb sleeping.'

'Oh really,' Namir's tone was full of questions.

'Nothing happened,' said Lyall tutting under a raised chin.

'Hmm,' Namir's response was more incredulous. He sat down beside his brother and started skimming stones.

'It wouldn't be fair of me to start anything with her,' said Lyall.

'Why not? you are eighteen in a couple of months, it is time you took a wife.' replied Namir.

'No, I can't,' came the thin reply.

'But you like her don't you? And from what I

have seen over the past few weeks I would say that you two are becoming very close.'

'We are, we are very close, but I have my reasons.'

Namir stopped skimming stones and looked at his brother. 'Tell me your reasons.'

Lyall swallowed the pain in his throat. 'Because I am leaving soon.'

Namir looked at his brother, then at the water and felt his eyes sting. He couldn't speak.

'I'm sorry, but I need to return to the castle.'

'Why?' came the croaked response.

'Because it's my heritage, it is my home. I can be someone there,' Lyall strained.

'But this is your home, you can be someone here,' Namir begged to differ.

'How can I be ? You are the leader here, you are now married to Skyrah, I am just a nobody now.'

'You will never be nobody. We have always said we would be leaders together. All this time that is all I have ever wanted, to share all of this with you.' Namir jutted out his chin as he surveyed the surroundings.

Lyall turned to face him and took his hand. 'Namir, you are everything to me, my inspiration, my rock, the person who I admire most in all of this kingdom.' He took a big intake of breath to settle his nerves. 'But I can't live in your shadow forever.' His voice became hushed. 'You have made me strong. From the first day I came through that cave, all I have ever wanted is to be like you.'

'But you are like me,' Namir interrupted. 'We are the same, we come from the same blood, we have the same parents.'

'I know,' his tears spilled silently. 'But I want to do something for me now; I want to return to Castle Dru and restore it. I want to be a king now. I am ready for that.'

'And what about me? What about Skyrah? What about the clan?' Namir's grief was immeasurable right now.

'We have the cave that joins us, we will keep it open, we will make it safe. Every year we will make sure the structure is sound so that we are not kept apart.'

'You can't go, I won't let you go.'

'Please Namir, I beg you, please don't make this any more difficult than it already is for me.'

Namir sighed heavily, he wore the guise of pain on his face, his body was shrouded in grief.

'Please.'

Namir saw the angst of his brother, the difficulty he had born for these past few months must have been an incredible weight. Who was he to deny him what he really wanted. His face softened. 'I suppose we will still be neighbours.'

'We are more than neighbours brother,' Lyall kissed Namir's hand. 'I can never repay you for everything you have done for me. I have become a man and faced my fears because of you. But now I need to see if I can do it on my own.'

He covered Lyall's hand with his own. 'I

134

understand and you have my blessing, really you do. But we must make a pact to keep the cave open. It must never be closed.'

'That goes without saying. Our battle is over with the Emperor, and with the General. We can live in peace now. Without fear of retribution.'

Namir slipped his arm round his brother's shoulders. 'So when are you leaving?'

'Probably in a couple of weeks. I haven't got any possessions to speak of, but I want to make a start on the castle while the weather is good.'

'How will you finance it?'

'There is a casket of treasure in Canagan's apartments, I will use that.'

'And who will you get to help you?'

18

'Thank you everyone for agreeing to this meeting so soon and I know you must be wondering why I am heading this meeting while our leader stands at the back with his wife.' Lyall raised a thin smile and tried not to gaze too long at his brother for fear of crumbling at the last minute. He tried to assemble some words to lessen the pain, but they didn't formulate quickly enough to give it poetic justice. So he just came out with his intension.

'I am leaving.'

The room fell into a tense silence after the initial gasps of astonishment had abated.

'I know you will be shocked,' he continued with a strained voice. 'But I have talked to Namir and I have his blessing; but be rest assured it is with a heavy heart and a lot of soul searching that I have made this decision.'

'So where are you going?' asked Ronu hardly believing what he had just heard.

'Well that is why I am holding this meeting, to inform you of my intentions.'

The room was in unbearable stillness now. Even the breeze outside had come to a pivotable stop and the clouds overhead had become static in movement.

'I am returning to Castle Dru and I am offering the chance to come with me.'

'But it is a ruin!' exclaimed Clebe.

'You are right, it is; but there is treasure in the king's apartments. We can use that to restore the building.'

Hushed voices and excited murmurs trilled round the echoing room.

'I know it won't be easy, it will be a lot of hard work, but at the end of it we will have a fortress that offers safety and security for our people. All the rooms will have beds, carpets and furnishings. There will be kitchens and pantries and store cupboards full of food. I will offer rooms for the children to be taught lessons. I will offer bathrooms with running water; there will be torches that give light in the dark. It will be a growing community with the offer of work for everyone. A new skill for each of you. A bright new future for all.'

Namir stayed quietly at the back, fearful that he would lose most of his clan to that promise.

Silva spoke up. 'Will you keep the cave and the tunnel open so that we can come back and see our loved ones if we choose to go with you?'

'I have already given my word to Namir that is what we will do. And I can promise even better than that. Every year we will send a group of men to properly assess the tunnel for continued safety. But for now, I will put in brackets so torches can frame an otherwise treacherously dark chasm. The floor will be lined so it is not damp and flooded in places. A proper door will be mounted that is safe to use in an emergency. Never again will anyone have to go through there in the dark. Never again will the door seal itself rigid.'

'When do you leave?' Came a voice from the back.

'I will leave in two weeks, in that time I want to secure the tunnel straight away, so that the women and children will be protected with their possessions. The men will travel with their animals over the mountains.'

'Count me in,' said Silva over the murmurs.

'And me,' said Hali.

'I don't think my leg will stand another winter,' said Bagwa sadly. 'And I want my daughters to have more opportunities than me. You don't mind if I go do you Namir?'

Namir shook his head in response.

'I will go as well,' said Norg. 'I feel like half a man with only one eye, at least I can be useful in the castle. I am still a good carpenter.'

His wife Tali threw a concerned look at Skyrah, but Skyrah's expression gave her safe passage without fear of reprisal.

'Thank you everyone. Remember it will be hard work, but the rewards will be so much greater. Thank you for your time.'

He stepped down from his dais and went to embrace Namir and Skyrah, but Skyrah was already chatting with Arneb.

'Are you going with him dear friend?' she asked earnestly.

'I can't, I have a job to do here.'

'What?' the answer jolted Skyrah.

'I can't just leave,' said Arneb, noticing her friends shocked reaction. 'The blacksmiths was my father's pride and joy, I can't just abandon it.'

'But Arneb, this is your golden opportunity. You can't tell me that you don't have feelings for Lyall.'

'Of course I do, I love him, I really do, but I can't leave here.'

'I believe you are making a dreadful mistake,' said Skyrah with conviction. 'Think what your parents would want you to do.'

'But I don't know what they would want me to do. All I know is that my heart won't let me go... and besides...' her voice trailed off.

'Yes,' queried Skyrah, eager to sort this out.

'Lyall hasn't even asked me.'

'Does he need to?'

Arneb shrugged her shoulders and Skyrah knew what she had to do.

The fourteen days that followed saw much soul searching as members of the tribe discussed with family and friends what they should do. A lot of the older generation didn't want change and would definitely stay behind, it mattered not to them what was on offer, they were the ones who were used to the old way of life and would find it difficult adapting to a completely new environment. These were the people who had lived off the land for years and who had embraced nature at an unseen level. They had grown up in the knowledge that it was the animals, birds, plants and rocks that had lessons to teach and not the voice of a human being telling them the way of the kingdom. For this was all that was instrumental for them to survive; the things that had been passed down from their gods and from their forefathers, providing all the direction, protection, and healing that they needed. They didn't want new walls, new skills, new messages.

But for the younger ones it was completely different. This was a window of opportunity.

Arneb was busy making brackets for the tunnel so that lit torches could be lined, and the men started chopping down trees for the carpenters to start carving and planing them so a track could be laid. Someone had already gone through the tunnel to start on the door the other end. It was actually going to happen and Skyrah didn't have much time.

She approached Lyall one day as he stood resting from chopping up wood. He had talked to Namir and Skyrah for several hours every day about his passion and his fervent determination to restore Castle Dru, eventually they had to accept his decision, though it was never going to be an easy transition.

'I'm going to miss you Lyall, you know that don't you?'

'And I'm going to miss you too Skyrah, but it's not the end, you know we will always be in each other's lives, that is why we are fixing up the tunnel now.'

'I know, it's just such a drastic change that I can't get my head around. '

'I know,' he smiled compassionately as he agreed with her.

A pause followed as he remembered the very first day he saw her; how beautiful he found her; her strength, her intelligence and captivating wit. He still found her all those things, but now his heart belonged to another.

'So is Arneb going with you?' she asked coyly, playing with a strand of her hair.

'She hasn't said anything?' he answered, oblivious to Skyrah's subtle investigations.

'Have you asked her?' she said.

'Well no,' he stammered. 'Not exactly.'

'So what's stopping you?' she wanted to know.

He thought long and hard about his answer and then looked her straight in the eye. 'You know something Skyrah, the thing that is stopping me is because she is a woman.'

She frowned in response. 'And what does that mean?'

'I just don't understand women, I really don't.'

'Not many men do,' she looked away and sighed.

'We were getting on so well, and then I said I would be leaving in two weeks and she has ignored me ever since.'

'Maybe she wants you to ask her.'

'But that's just it, I don't think she would want to come.'

'And men think women are difficult,' she mumbled under her breath.

'What was that?' he didn't hear her exasperated reply.

'I think you should ask her,' she replied. 'I think you two are made for each other, and if you asked her I think she would say yes.'

'But she is loyal to her father's memory,' he started. 'We have spoken about it, and leaving the blacksmiths would be a hard thing for her to do.'

'But if you knew she wanted to go with you, would you be happy?'

'Of course I would, I had half hoped that I could ask her to marry me one day,' he paused as he remembered the time they had spent together. 'I feel so easy with her... she makes me laugh...we chat for hours ... I like to dance with her,' he smiled at the recollection.

'Anything else?' asked Skyrah tilting her head to one side.

Lyall laughed a breathless laugh. 'Her life is here Skyrah, she won't come with me.' He looked up to the skies. 'I had better carry on chopping these logs up, I think there are rainclouds coming.'

'Of course, I will see you later.' She smiled at him and went off to visit the next person on her list.

Toady was in his workroom welding some hinges for the barns.

142

'Toady, how would feel about taking over the blacksmith from Arneb?' she began.

The eve of the departure had seen laughter and tears at the same time; Namir and Lyall relived every minute since he arrived at the camp; reliving the fun times, the challenging times and the time in the arena where they faced the monsters. But they always came through it, they always survived and lived to tell the tale. Now, this was a new chapter in their lives and with much trepidation, Namir and Skyrah had to say farewell.

The morning came too soon. Lyall searched everywhere for Arneb but she wasn't to be found. He had now given up hope of ever seeing her again, certainly she was not going to say goodbye to him.

'Where is Arneb?' Skyrah faced Lyall as the rest of the clan stood around in their numbers saying goodbyes to loved ones.

'I don't know, I haven't seen her all day, I really wanted to bid her farewell.'

'Where is she then?'

Lyall shrugged. 'I don't know, but I have to go now, I have all these people waiting for me.'

'I will find her.'

'Skyrah, I have tried to find her but now I am out of time. Tell her....well...you will know what to say.'

His look lingered, his sigh was long. He smiled, then signalled to his band of pilgrims, kicked his horse into a trot and with a congregation of well wishers behind him, made his way out of the camp.

Skyrah ran to the blacksmiths, Arneb was not there. She went to the stream, she was not there either. She even went to Lyall's hut, but that was empty. Finally she went to the meadow and saw Arneb looking out over the horizon and picking at the daisies.

'Arneb, what on earth are you doing? Lyall is leaving right now.'

'There's no point, Skyrah, I have a duty at the blacksmiths, I can't go.'

'Nonsense! I have sorted it out with Toady, he is more than happy to take over from you,' her voice was becoming more urgent.

'I can't leave, you know I can't, I have gone through the scenarios until I am quite exhausted.'

Skyrah wasn't listening. Nothing her friend said was a good enough excuse. She shook her head at each line of defence and closed her ears to things that would never happen. She was bobbing about and stretching her head in Lyall's direction...until she heard those final words.

'...and besides, I don't have a horse.'

'You can take mine,' her voice was anxious and hurried. 'No more excuses. Meteor will take you.'

'It's too late,' persisted Arneb. 'It's all too late.'

'Nothing is too late, but if you watch the best thing that's ever happened to you walk out of your life then you will regret it for the rest of your days. Now get up, wipe that sad look off your face and race like the wind to catch up with him.'

The sky was as clear as it could be on this warm sunny day in this first week of June. Lyall could hardly believe that a year ago to the day, Skyrah had saved them all from certain death when she burst in to their dormitory having poisoned most of the palace. What a difference a year makes he thought to himself and glanced over as he heard the thunderous sound of hooves approaching.

Arneb fell in next to him on Meteor and they both looked at each other and grinned.

'I didn't think you were going to come,' his face looked relieved.

'I just had a few things to sort out and needed to have a little chat with Skyrah.'

'Women's talk?' he raised his eyebrows.

'Something like that,' she smiled.

He leaned over to kiss her on the lips, and with a congregation of people clapping and whistling behind them, they held that moment for as long as they could.

This was without doubt the longest way round, the women and children who were taking the carts through the tunnel would have the job done in a couple of hours. But this trail way, taking the horses and animals across the mountains and through the paths, would take much longer. There was a quicker route that one of the men had suggested doing, but that was even more treacherous with deep ravines to get lost in, and cracks big enough to swallow a whole horse, places where the sun was never seen, so that idea was abandoned.

The party rode north, away from the Clan of the Mountain Lion, following a beaten path across fields into the woods and streams. The ground from here to the mountain ridge was mainly grasslands, parched fields and rolling hills, high meadows and lowland marshes. Here, the sun beat down on them softly and the steady muffled sound of horses walking over the sandy tracks filled their ears. Lyall knew that this was the easiest part of the journey and they would camp at the edge of the forest before dark; he kicked his horse into a brisk trot until the trees opened up into the beginning of the mountain path. He stopped at this point and waited for his party to assemble.

'We will camp here tonight,' he said. 'We will rest, have food and get going again in the morning.'

The clan dismounted and relieved the horses of their cargo; the small herd were led to a stream to drink then tied loosely to tree branches and left to feed on bags of oats. The moon was rising behind one mountain and the sun sinking behind another as Zak struck up a fire. Men laid out their provisions and talked about their futures. Arneb settled Meteor and came over to sit with Lyall.

'It would have been a catastrophe if you hadn't come you know,' he said.

'And why is that?' she snuggled deeper into his arms.

'Because we both have so much to offer each other.'

Her heart fluttered and she felt the pit of her

stomach knot. 'This is what my parents wanted for me.'

'What did they want for you?' he asked.

'They wanted me to be happy and to follow my dreams.'

Lyall squeezed her hand and kissed the top of her head.

She smiled and continued. 'They told me that a fine young prince would be my saviour and whisk me away to his castle where he would love me and protect me for the rest of my life.'

A short laugh rose in the back of his throat. 'Well, maybe they knew your future dear Arneb.'

'I think they did, they knew my destiny from when I was born.' She sighed and looked up at the new moon. 'It's so beautiful and bright tonight Lyall... she's looking down on us and keeping us safe.'

She squeezed his hand tighter and closed her eyes. Lyall lay back with Arneb in his arms and looked up at the great magical sphere lighting up his homeward bound path. Smiling up at the huge orb of white light, he pulled a blanket over them both and bowed out to another successful day.

The cool of the night gave way to another bright morning and the sounds of dawn drifted through the camp as birds trilled out their awakening chorus and squirrels gorged themselves on a feast of nuts; the horses snorted and tossed their heads and soon the party was ready to go again.

For a long way they stayed to the trail,

following its twists and turns as it coiled around the side of the mountain. The ridge began to ascend slowly as they gained height and debris spat out from beneath the horses hooves as they carried their cargo homeward bound. Fortunately they were nimble on their feet and it made for better hacking while the path was covered in weathered stones and gravel. Whilst the conditions on the ground were favourable, the turns were treacherous and the narrow path would be fatal at any other time of the year. Above them a long fold of granite curved over them like a huge tidal wave, and under the ridge it zig zagged, going a quarter of a way round the circumference of the mountain before it started to descend again. The sun hung even higher above them now, perched on the crest of a wave of high ridges and immediately below was the Kingdom of Durundal.

It sprawled out before him like a long lost friend, the trees and hills welcoming him back with waving arms; he thought it to be the most beautiful place on earth, breath taking and magical at the same time. From out of nowhere an eagle soared, the sun caught the bronzed tip of its tail and turned it into a spectrum of light. He smiled at the image thinking it resembled his sword. He felt the weapon at his side, concealed safely within its scabbard. He followed the eagle's flight with squinted eyes and from this highest point he could see more of the mountain range and witnessed the unfathomable power of the Claw. He gasped in wonder as he saw unforgiving waterfalls plunging over tongues of stone into ravines that were so wide and brutal he could see whole trees still stranded at the side from the punishing winter months. Displaced boulders of rock had been pushed out with such a force it would be feasible to imagine that Giants lived in these peaks and why the range was given its name. But this was the eagle's home, and another giant of a beauty came into sight looking for rich pickings from the disturbance on the trail.

'Everyone all right?' he shouted back to his troops.

The single file caravan all confirmed that they were.

They had descended the north face of the mountain by the afternoon and stumbled across a disused archer tower. A section of the four hundred foot long spur wall had collapsed taking the gun ports with it. In its day the tower would have reached to one hundred and twenty five feet, now it was a fraction of that; and the long wall that once stood at thirty feet was now a ghostly ruin of a once proud monument, beaten and worn down by the work of a hundred murdering soldiers.

'What is this place Lyall?' called out Arneb.

'It's supposed to defend the castle.'

'Did the General do this?' her gaze followed the endless mass of fallen stones.

'He probably did, I can see that the gun ports have been smashed in as well.'

'What a despicable creature,' she grimaced.

'One of the very worst,' his voice was scathing.

'It will be back to its former glory one day,' she tried to lift a scraping of hope.

'That it will, I can assure you; but the castle has to be much better defended in the future. There will always be another General Domitrius Corbulo for us to contend with and we have to be better prepared.'

But that was only a fraction of what the General had done; for a much greater savaged dwelling greeted him as his party got closer. For the first time he could see that nothing remained of the castle grounds at all, it was a graveyard of ashes and bone buried deep within layers of dirt, soot and mud. Nothing of the beautiful apple orchard remained, it was trampled flat and bare; he looked for some saplings, but even they couldn't find any sustenance in this lifeless place. The rows of bee hives were flattened, none of the residents had even attempted to re home or build their nests close by. It was like walking into hell itself, and he had already seen several places that were comparable.

It took them the rest of the morning to make a slow circuit of the castle. Most of the stone walls remained, albeit fragments and charred beyond recognition, but the foundations were probably still strong and could be used again he decided. The wooden stable block was burned to a cinder; nothing remained of that except his memories. Lyall hoped that the horses had been able to escape, he didn't want to think about the terror and pain if they hadn't. Some of his most favourite ponies were kept in there; hopefully the stable boys and grooms had got to them in time and they would return one day. The new stables would be built from granite rock next time, he didn't want to put anything to chance again.

He had already seen the shredded core of the castle last year and was aghast then at how much death and destruction had been inflicted. He wondered then how parts of it had remained standing upright, albeit teetering on a splinter or a nail or a pole; but now, a year later, even the splinters, nails, and poles had given way. He had worried about the people coming through the cave and venturing into a room with no floor. He needn't have been concerned though, as all of them were there to greet him as he entered the courtyard.

It was only Bagwa they were waiting for. He had left the following day, because he knew he would be slow and didn't want to hold anyone up.

Bagwa popped his head from one of the exposed beams just as Lyall was thinking about him.

'Are you all right?' he shouted up.

'Yes I'm fine, we are all here, give us a minute and we will join you.'

'Hurry up guys, I think the whole thing is about to crumble.'

'It's been standing like this for four years,' Bagwa called back. 'I think it will hold for another four minutes.'

Lyall shook his head in desperation, he wasn't sure that Bagwa was right as he heard the castle creak and groan with the weight of new guests inching across its broken limbs. 'Just hold on for a few minutes longer please,' he begged the castle's beating heart.

Everyone felt his apprehension as the castle began to rock to and fro, they could hear muffled footsteps and ghostly voices telling each other where to go and where not to stand coming from within. Worried faces fixed on the fragile monument, guided the party safely out and a collective sigh of relief was heard across the estate when the family emerged safely.

'Got a fair bit of work to do then Lyall,' said Bagwa coming out into the light and stating the obvious.

'Come on hop-'o'-long,' and Tyna playfully pushed Bagwa out of the way.

Lyall had to laugh and greeted his old friend with a hug. 'You are not wrong there dear friend. Now, do you still think you are up to it?'

Bagwa ignored the raised eyebrow and thin smile from his wife and children.

'It's just a war wound you know, I can still build a wall,' Bagwa harrumphed and hugged his friend back.

'This will take a lot of effort and man hours to complete,' said Lyall. 'I hadn't fully appreciated how bad it really was.'

'Anything can be done if you put your mind to it,' said Bagwa, looking over at Tyna. 'You should know that more than anyone.'

'Yes, you are right, I can't be defeated before I've begun can I,' and his passion was rekindled once again.

Lyall called out to his people. 'Thank you for coming with me, thank you for supporting me.' He smiled to each of them as he looked around at his new recruits. 'I know this is probably worse than you were expecting, it's a lot worse than what I was expecting.' He looked sadly at the remains. 'But we will make this castle grand again, it will be safe and it will be a place that you can call home.'

'You are wrong Lyall,' called out Zak. 'We all knew it would be like this, of course we did, but we all know that anything that is worth having doesn't come easy, we all know that we will have to work night and day to get this castle to its former glory.'

A cheer and swivel of nodding heads went up from the crowd.

'Thank you Zak, thank you everyone,' called out Lyall in response. 'I will have to enlist a lot more men though to get this structure back up, maybe more women and children can help with the lighter work. I am sure our friends at the Marshland and Hill Fort and Giant's Claw can spare a few extra helpers. Are there any men who will get back on a horse in a couple of days to bring back support?'

A dozen hands went up and Lyall was knocked back with the response. 'Thank you, each and every one of you; I am truly honoured and overwhelmed and you will be duly rewarded.'

'The reward is the community we shall be building,' Tyna said humbly.

Another cheer went up and again Lyall had to

stifle his emotion. 'Thank you, I do appreciate your enthusiasm - but for now we need to build shelters. There is timber and wood littered around the grounds and I know a lot of you have brought provisions and blankets to share - so, we will make a base right here, and in the morning we start the real work.'

19

Across the still blue water came the soft swish of oars from the galleys. The great cog groaned with the effort and gentle breezes helped the ship on its way. Cornelius watched the sun bounce off the crystal waters beneath him and from the specks of nothing on a distant skyline. It reminded him of being in the cave, when he had come to appreciate the sharp salty smell of the air and the vastness of the horizon trimmed with a band of azure on a clear day, while the sea remained a rich shade of cyan. But now, on a ship with not much else but a crew of sweaty men, bilious passengers, and panicking animals, he had grown to love the freedom of the sea gulls in the air, their superb navigation skills, and their exceptional abilities when seeking out food.

He spoke to them often and sometimes wished he could fly alongside them, just for a day, even an hour, maybe a minute, just to feel that sense of power and unrivalled freedom. These masters could tell him in an instant of an impending storm; for they could see before the lad in the crows nest when a knot of dark clouds hovered in the distance, moving in like a giant shadow, following the ship at every turn, waiting to attack, and as the birds quickly flew low and changed direction, he would wave them off with admiration.

The animals below the decks also sensed a change; whether it was the smell of the wind, or the motion of the sea responding, they knew. But without their freedom, all they could do was panic; and as soon as the gulls had disappeared, you could hear the animals shrieking in fear.

The beautiful azure sky turned black and the crystal cyan sea morphed into an angered silver grey creature. As the wind howled off its back, the canvas snapped and cracked in response while the crew men reefed the sails. The hull bellowed undeterred and the crows nest stood firm as it was blasted with several tonnes of spray.

The squall picked up pace and the decks below were fuelled with screaming and stampeding, the galley boys were worked to their very core, cleaning up and settling the animals; it was frightful for everyone - except Master Cornelius. He gripped the rail at the bow of the ship and breathed in the voracious wind while the hammering rain beat down on him leaving him soaked and windswept; for he not only weathered the storm, he embraced it.

Day after day, the young man stood on the deck, drinking in the scenery of the vast horizons where an endless sky and a menagerie of birds flew alongside the ship, and he observed their behaviour to forecast the weather. On some occasions he was lucky enough to see a whale breaching or a school of dolphins jumping in time to the mechanical cog. The early morning was the best time to see them; it seemed they too were excited by the rising sun and after a long time brushing against the sea floor and hidden in the depths, would rise to the surface to take in the wondrous spectacle themselves. He had never seen that vision before, and because he thought he probably would never have the chance again, he stood at the bow most days watching for a glimpse of the great mammals of the ocean.

'Come up on the deck Gya,' he would say enthusiastically. 'It's going to be fine today so the turtles will be seen.' Or, 'best stay below, I sense a change in the weather.'

He preferred it up on the deck and would often sleep up there. Especially now he knew that Gya was a woman. For the first few nights he had found himself looking at her, trying to view unnoticed while she changed and washed her body. He found himself savouring the sight of her breasts and becoming increasingly aware of her sexuality, particularly the way she moved. Even her smell was different now and the tone of her voice. How come he hadn't noticed before. 'She is definitely more like a woman than a man, how could I have not noticed?'

Perhaps it's a case of believing what we are told he surmised. Tricks of disguise and camouflage. Nevertheless, it all got embarrassing for him, for now she was more like a sister to him.

'You don't mind if I sleep on the deck do you?' he asked poignantly one evening.

'Not at all Cornelius,' she had said kindly,

thankful for the peace and quiet and privacy without his lecherous eyes.

After a week, she had the place to herself.

Their cabin was very large, quite airy and handsomely furnished, which was forward thinking by Gya; as a three month journey on a ship was particularly arduous, and even more so in confined cabins. The journey outbound had been exceptionally difficult; sleeping in a narrow shipboard bunk or a swaying hammock alongside twenty other men, snoring, farting and belching had been one of the worst times of her life; so this time, Gya had made sure that their accommodation was much more comfortable and a lot more adequate.

She spent a lot of time in her cabin, reading the selection of books from the shelves and scanning the numerous maps about the surrounding continents. From her porthole she used a telescope to view the giant turtles, humpback whales and schools of dolphins swimming alongside them; while at night she followed the stars in a moonlit sky from the deck.

Occasionally she would accompany Cornelius up on the bow or the stern, but he was so engrossed with the elements around him that he was not very good company most of the time, so she took a few turns round the perimeter of the boat, went back down to her books and maps and enjoyed the evening sipping on the finest wines.

One evening, several weeks into the trip, she stumbled across an entry in a diary that fascinated her.

It spoke of an island, unknown to many, that had been kept hidden from the outside world for thousands of years. Ships would pass its sandy shores but few would ever stop there for the island offered nothing for them; little grew there, only tufts of yellow weeds and small clumps of trees. The inhabitants lived in scattered pods around the island; these were people who could talk with animals, who could summon storms and make men think they could fly. Sea farers kept well away from this place.

Most recently an old woman lives there with her three daughters, she is easily recognisable because of her long woollen robe. She walks barefooted. Her grey hair ends at her waist, her face is slightly wrinkled and yet her body is lithe and firm. Her three daughters are beautiful, tall, sculpted; the very epitome of a goddess. They have smooth olive skin, their hair is plaited with delicate orchids, they speak with the wind and are told things by the elements. They see cruelty spreading, they see cities burning and people running. They see the hatred in young mens hearts and know the killing will go on until the winds can change things. They hear a girl calling to them, a boy cries out for help, a mother weeps for her dead baby. They feel their anger, their weakness, their danger. The old woman talks to the storms and sends it with full force to eradicate the poison while the teeth of a gale tries desperately to swallow the evil, to clean the slate and pave the way for love and light. But all it does is delay things for a while; and the hatred and the burning and the running continues. The women don't like intrusion, they don't like visitors. Until the day the wind tells them of a change, bad things will happen to those who come to their island uninvited, apart from the giant that is.

Once a year, when the weather is warm and the conditions are right, a giant oval emerges from the ocean and its wet flippers soon become covered in pebbled sand. Slowly the hulking sea beast pulls herself up the beach's crest; she is not used to handling a four hundred pound frame on dry land; she is accustomed to the protection from the women though and she drags herself up on to the beach. Once in a safe place she begins to dig deeper and deeper into the sand. Soon a massive hole has emerged and this gentle sea creature begins to lay her eggs. When the duty is done, she covers the precious cargo and lumbers back towards the sea; into the quiet depths, into the safety of her vast home.

Gya closed the book and shut her eyes. She dreamed of such a place with such incredible powers. The wind and its offspring; gales, hurricanes, tornados. Were they really sent by some outside force to fight evil. Could they ever be that strong?

Into the second month of sailing a battering storm hurled them into unknown waters. A caravan of black clouds had piled up against each other and by dusk the crew could see lightning flickering to the west followed by the distant crash of thunder. As the sea grew rougher the angry waves rose up like serpents to smash their heads against the hull, splitting the crest with such force that the hundred oarsmen struggled to keep the ship on course. This storm was big. The winds began to howl, forcing the ship high on its stern and then sent it crashing down again, tossing every beating heart to the port and then to the starboard in quick succession. The galley boys tended to the shrieking animals while Cornelius stayed up on deck helping in the worst gale imaginable and the relentless driving rain. By the time the storm broke, morning was upon them, the weather had settled and the skies cleared. It was as though nothing had happened at all. The sea was calm and glistening again while small white clouds drifted nonchalantly by and the gulls had dutifully returned to escort the ship.

Those who had fought the sea all night were now standing or sitting in puddles of sea water; for that was all that remained of the storm and would dry up soon enough. But for now, the tall masts swayed and the weathered decks creaked as the battered ship made its way slowly to a remote bay that led to a wide stretch of land. The captain had decided to dock here to give the crew and passengers a few hours of shore leave and some well earned rest. The animals had to stay on board for fear of never getting them back on again, but the young boys stayed below; settling them, talking to them, feeding and cleaning up.

For the others, this idyllic tranquil beach led to a beautiful glade of palm trees, where pods of stones and driftwood greeted them. Although sparse with nothing more to do than when they were on the ship, it gave everyone time to rest and take in some much needed succulent fruit and fresh water from the nearby spring. The sand seemed to sway underfoot as the seafarers found their land legs again and the masses who descended on this remote, quiet island were soon treating it as their own. Cornelius was the first to spot a huge leatherback turtle to the right of him. An outstretched arm stopped him going over. The appendage belonged to an old woman who spoke in a strange language, but her manner and expression told Cornelius that she was not happy.

He pulled his arm away sharply and snarled at her even though he knew she couldn't understand him. 'The turtles are for everyone to enjoy not just you.' And he rushed over to get a closer look.

Gya looked at the old woman, her long grey hair reached to her waist, the long woollen robe skirted her ankles. She spun around looking at everything that was described exactly in the diary entry.

She noticed the woman's face becoming fervent with anger as more people went over to pester the turtle and witnessed the animal trying to get away from them bellowing in fear. Her roar was like a powerful stag during the rutting season, but it did little to thwart the masses. The old woman rushed over to get them away, spilling out words to pacify the frightened turtle; but her words and actions meant nothing to the unruly mob.

Gya ran and tried to appeal to Cornelius. 'Please Cornelius, I have read about this place and I know what will happen. This is unwise and you must stop.'

'What are you talking about now?' he laughed.

'This place, it is not good, please come away, we can't meddle with things here.'

'Have you been drinking again Gya, I thought you have been knocking back rather a lot of that vintage claret.'

'No, I haven't been drinking, I have read about this place in a book. This is not our home, remember we are guests here and have to respect that.'

'What?' he spat back. 'These mud huts and stolen sea shells make this place their land, I think not.'

'Cornelius please have you not learned anything from what I told you about my own experience and what I have recently read? No good can come of this.'

When that didn't work she went to the captain who was lounging in a worn grey hammock, his hands behind his head, his eyes closed.

'Please captain, call the men back, I have read about this place in your book. I know that bad things will happen.'

Lazy eyes and furrowed brows looked up at her.

'The book in my cabin,' she continued. 'The one with entries about destinations and different islands.'

'I haven't got a clue what you are on about.'

She sighed heavily. 'All right, so you don't know about the book, but you can see that we are upsetting the islanders and disturbing the turtle.'

But he wasn't interested in that either. 'Men will be men and boys will be boys, they've been at sea for months now and want to enjoy themselves. And it's only a dammed turtle.'

She still pleaded with him. 'That's what I am afraid of captain, they are out of control.'

The man was losing his temper now and spoke out abruptly. 'This is exactly why I don't bring women on my ship, they interfere and get in the way. You must have paid a fine price for this voyage young lady, otherwise you wouldn't even be here. Now leave me be and leave my men be.' He closed his eyes, folded his arms and went back to swinging in the hammock.

She hung her head in despair and noticed Cornelius sitting with his knees under his chin, perched high up on a rock. 'Run away why don't you,' she said under her breath. 'You start all this trouble when you could so easily have ended it and then just take yourself off and hide.'

It was only when a group of three younger women came out with trays of fresh oysters, crab, lobster and other shell fish that the men were lured away. The crowd eventually dispersed and the old woman tried to encourage the turtle back to her breeding ground; then she slipped quietly back into the safety of the water as the woman covered her eggs again with sand. But with the turtle gone, the men were now looking for other entertainment. While most of them fell asleep in the sun after the banquet, others tried to grope the younger women. Some were becoming quite violent and aggressive. The girls launched everything they could find, pleading and begging them to leave them alone. Gya was appalled at the outrageous behaviour, fearful that only one or two had the ability to destroy a peaceful environment. She looked at the three sisters and the old woman, the sisters were exactly how they had been described in the book; tall, beautiful, graceful. But how could that be? The conundrum went round and round in her mind as the mother tried to comfort her daughters.

Gya went up to them, knowing her words would not be understood, but hopeful that her tone would resonate. 'I'm so sorry, we shouldn't have come here.'

'No, you should not have come. Not while greed, lust and evil runs in the blood of men. And now, all but a few will perish from this curse.' The old woman looked around with malevolence and led her daughters away.

Gya was shocked. 'The woman speaks my tongue and her words sit like an omen.' She slid down against a tree and pondered. A discarded plate of lobster was at her side and she began to pick at it slowly. She couldn't eat very much, she was still recoiling in shame at being associated with such barbaric behaviour; instead she tried to unravel the prophecy.

By late afternoon, the captain ushered the crew and passengers back on to the boat. Cornelius was still perched high on his cliff taking in the view. He hadn't eaten anything at all. The ship moved out and left the bruised and battered island in its wake... but a scar remained and things would never be the same again.

20

The attack on Castle Dru by the General and his legions left Lyall no choice but to drastically secure the defensive measures of the grounds. The first task was to strategically place cannons around the perimeter and gun emplacements in the guard rooms. A drum tower was built with look out posts and a warning bell. Spy holes and archer wells were built into a crenelated wall and a secure parapet walk was raised within it; and since the entrance to the castle was likely to be the obvious target for an attacking force, it had to be fortified as heavily as possible. Lyall decided to put an iron portcullis in straight away for extra protection as well as a barrage of crossbow bolts. He put in a narrow roofed passage with arrow slits to either side in addition to the murder holes that would allow disarming debris and boiling hot liquid to be poured through. At the end of the passage was another set of iron doors with another set of murder holes and another set of arrow slits to maim or kill.

With an abundance of stone and timber in the surrounding forests, the main structure was the next section to undergo a radical change. Strong new fences had already gone up to replace those that had been burned. The collapsed roof of the main building had been cleared away and a new one raised hurriedly in its place. The huge doors into the Great Hall were even more impressive than the one before with detailed engravings of leopards, wolves and hares in panels, and blooms of aconitum, laburnum and hemlock embossed in the frames. Stained glass windows were even more elaborate with an image of every clan member's totem in each segment of glass and the chimneys and towers rose higher than ever before.

The refurbishment of the interior began as soon as the defence building was complete. No expense was spared with a resplendent and lavish style throughout. A magnificent new dining room was added to the state rooms whilst the Great Hall itself had been restored to an even grander magnitude than what Lyall could ever remember. Beaten silver mirrors backed every niche so the solid gold candelabras burned twice as bright and looked three times as impressive. The walls were panelled in richly carved wood, and solid oak boards replaced the once fragmented floors. A sumptuous carpet covered the planks, and woven into each corner was the wolf and hare totem of Lyall and Arneb, while running along the sides was the leopard totem of his brother. A magnificent fire surround stood staunch and proud, inlaid with exotic semi precious stones of jasper, agate and lapis lazuli. Either side of the fireplace stood two perfectly sculpted bronze heads carved in the image of a wolf and a hare, while portraits of the family hung on adjacent walls. An elaborately carved ceiling was made up of octagonal sunken panels, each one bore a central motif of an animal, while the exquisite Durundal crystal chandelier took pride of place in the centre. The minstrels gallery allowed an ensemble of the finest musicians to blow, pluck and thrum the most delicate of notes that would weave their way to the tender ears of any audience on any occasion. Outside, the estate was also given a makeover. Arneb had redesigned the gardens, including restocking the beehives and replacing the shrubbery with an extensive herb and apothecary garden. Lyall had created his very own aviary that housed a variety of birds as well as some very impressive peacocks.

The summer had been long and the harvests had been fruitful, and the people of Castle Dru had worked tirelessly to provide a rich and opulent lifestyle that would see them through the winter and beyond. By autumn, the store rooms were full to the brim. In the granaries were sacks of oats, corn, wheat and barley with kegs of milled flour and ground white salt. In the cellars hung the ripened looms of onions and garlic while bags of carrots, parsnips, potatoes and swedes were stacked high on top of each other. Another store room contained rounds of goats cheese while another housed iron hooks of rabbits, pheasant, woodcock, grouse and snipe; bound and hung to reach their peak. Racks of venison and pork were salted and layered in rafters. Crates of wild apples, wild pears, plums, damsons and cranberries were packed away in boxes.

Churns of mead were fermenting nicely and pitchers of shallots, cabbage and beetroot were pickling. Arneb's bees had worked hard all summer and their honey had been collected and poured into labelled jars. In the stable store rooms, bales of hay had been collected and buckets of oats were stored with lids carefully sealed. There was enough food for a small army for a whole year; and more than enough for a royal wedding.

21

The ship's crew went back to their duties, and the passengers watched from the decks as the ship surfed towards its final destination. The sea was incredibly calm with a smoothness that just rocked the boat gently. Though by the time the island had disappeared from view, Gya had already begun to feel unwell. She grabbed onto Cornelius.

'What's the matter with you?' he span round with a startled reaction.

'I'm not well Cornelius, could you help me down to the cabin?'

Her legs buckled as he took her weight.

'Everything all right there Master Cornelius?' asked the captain from the helm.

'Yes, just a bit of sea sickness that's all,' he replied.

'Take that bucket for her,' the captain pointed to a wooden pail by the galley doors.

Gya was now sweating profusely with a pallid tone to her skin. 'I have never felt like this Cornelius, what is wrong with me?'

'Too long at sea is my guess, come on let's get you into bed.'

She had vomited into the bucket twice before she was had reached the cabin, and fell onto the bed completely dressed. Cornelius took off her jerkin and boots and covered her with a blanket.

'Get some rest, I need to empty this bucket. I will be back soon.'

But she couldn't respond. She twisted in her bed for hours, holding on to her stomach, slipping in and out of sleep. She found a commode under the bed and vomited into that. Cornelius returned and sat with her and kept the fever down with sponges of cool water. She was still angry with him for not taking control on the island when he had the chance. Too many times she had witnessed destruction through lack of empathy and morality, but she was too weak to do or say anything to him now, she couldn't even think past the pain.

In and out of consciousness, her dreams were full of grey walls, stone stairs and hands reaching out to her. Was this her family she thought, or was she becoming delirious? She didn't know. All she knew for certain was the incredibly severe abdominal pain that caused her to vomit every hour and by the second day she thought she was going to die. She sent Cornelius to get help.

'She's got food poisoning,' said the ship's Bosun. 'We've already lost the captain and half the crew.'

'What?' shrieked Cornelius.

'Half the ship has died.'

'How on earth...?' Cornelius was more than shocked.

'Did you eat anything on the island Master Cornelius?' the Boson continued.

'No I didn't.'

'Neither did the galley boys or myself and only a few others are free from the sickness.'

'What are you saying?' asked Cornelius warily.

'I'm saying that it was something consumed on the island that made everyone ill.'

'Surely not.'

The Bosun nodded his head and raised his brows.

'Did you eat anything on the island Gya? It's important that you tell us,' Cornelius was at her side.

Her thumb and forefinger indicated a small amount and she mouthed the words fish.

'Just as I thought,' surmised the Bosun. 'I'm rarely wrong in these matters.'

'Did they know it was off do you think?' asked a disbelieving Cornelius.

The Bosun shrugged, 'I don't know. But we are the fortunate ones.'

'Will she be all right?'

'Well put it this way, she's lucky that we are docking today. Without treatment she would probably die like all the others.'

'It's that bad?'

'Yes it is Cornelius, it's very serious. Once she is back safely, you must get a doctor to see her at once.'

'I will do, and thank you for your help.'

The Bosun left and Cornelius went back up on the deck

to see where exactly they were. He knew he was approaching home when he saw the silvery hue of sunlight hugging the palace towers in the distance. He craned to see the bustling city and hear the market sellers crying in their fever pitched voices. He was to be disappointed. As the sea kissed the shore, the palace got swallowed up behind a jostle of buildings and the city of Ataxata looked very different now. His heart was pounding with fearful anticipation.

Down below him, Gya just about managed to put on her clothes; she struggled into her brown breeches, breathlessly donned a green tunic, while her tanned leather jerkin had so many studs and buckles it was ridiculous. With shaking hands and fumbling fingers she managed to pull them in extra tightly; she had lost so much weight on the journey home she wasn't aware how thin she had become. Sitting upright on the side of the bed waiting for the ship to anchor took its toll as well and she broke into a sweat as the room started to spin.

'I am going to die,' she thought to herself. 'I have brought Cornelius back home safely, but now my life is at an end.' She lay back on the bed and waited for Cornelius to come and get her.

She awoke to the sound of him coming into the room, the deck was moving under her and she thought they were still sailing. 'For a moment I thought we were back in Ataxata,' she murmured to him.

'We are Gya, we are home.'

'Why are we still sailing then?'

'We are not sailing, we have docked. Come on, let's get you off this ship.'

Gya clung on to Cornelius as they shuffled down the ramp. She had never felt so frail in all her life.

The port was now full of the remaining crewmen, sea merchants and animals. Those that had survived the journey were now facing another peril, for all were to learn that Ataxata was not the thriving place it once was, and now, most of these people were lost souls with absolutely nowhere to go.

Their driver was waiting for them beside his trap. Gya had got word to the port several months beforehand that they would be requiring transport to the palace. Excellent forward thinking she thought to herself again as she clambered meekly into the back of the carriage. The driver covered her with a blanket and helped Cornelius onto the seat at the front. As the rickety trap trundled along the cobbled street, Cornelius looked back at his friend being thrown about like a sack of potatoes, and then to the driver who was yelling foul mouthed expletives to anyone and anything that got in his way. The trap continued fighting its way through the dockside throngs but the horse was getting more skittish with a growing frenzy of people, vehicles and beasts; while the driver was becoming even more irritated and his language fouler by the minute.

'Top speed man,' Cornelius said, eager to escape. 'Find me a doctor when we get home and you will be rewarded handsomely for your trouble.'

The trap master tipped his hat and made haste to the palace. But it was a shocking journey.

Inside the city walls they rode past crumbling guildhalls with empty markets and stagnant dirty bathhouses. Fountains that once gurgled and sang in the centres of wide squares were now tortured with dryness, and places where old men sat at stone tables moving chess pieces and supping ale together were now derelict and void of human existence. All the statues were disfigured, ornate lanterns remained unlit and occasionally a gentle breeze would roll in a tumble of debris. They passed torn and tattered street advertisements flapping in the wind hanging like grey tangled beards; the painted frescos of boys fighting had been scratched away and left to rot. Whole porticos that had been ablaze with life size murals of young adult males had been ripped apart and all that was left was the skeletal frame of ghosts long gone. Sculptures, figurines, lamps, glasses, engravings; prints and paintings were all abandoned in neglected gutters and left for winter to dispose of at her will.

'What's happened here driver?' asked Cornelius in astonishment and disbelief.

'It's since the malady a year ago sir.'

'What malady are you talking about man?'

'Dreadful business the malady, t'was that what killed your father, Master Cornelius.'

'What do you mean?'

'The gods didn't like it did they? 'im killin' all 'em boys; all 'at death, all 'at fightin'. T'was what the

175

gods did as punishment. You mark my words.'

Cornelius was still vying the surroundings as upturned wagons and abandoned carts littered the road. Weeds had grown over the vehicles and looters had taken what they could.

'That's how I got this Master Cornelius, t'was abandoned, t'was left to rot, jus' like the rest of 'is place.' He shook the reins and the horse trotted faster.

They continued to make their way out of the gloom and moved into the staggeringly rich and opulent area. This was more like it Cornelius thought, this is still the same, of course it is, the coachman didn't know what he was talking about; for building after building was bigger and more impressive than the previous one, and Cornelius smiled to see the rich and beautiful colours once again. He beamed when he saw every house they passed was tinged in pink and clad in more gold then the preceding one. He remembered this; this was the sight he had carried in his mind for all these years. But his face soon dropped, for this time there were no peeping fingers of the summer's creeping jasmine or the remains of honeysuckle vines entwined round magnificent heralding fountains. This time, triffids had been left to strangle the life out of the delicate stems; shackled and tormented, the ivy had bled them dry. Dead leaves and discarded petals had withered away to a brown mush that congealed the weathered pavements; for this time there was no errand boy to clear it away.

And where were the women who wore fine dresses that skimmed the gleaming pavements as they walked, and the portly over indulged men swishing their long ponytails? Where had they all gone? He looked at the coachman who shrugged his shoulders and yelled out another obscenity to the horse to get through the carnage that bit quicker.

Their journey continued, eventually turning in to the wide entrance of a walled palace. The colossal marble statue had been removed, a crumbling stump was all that was left. Cornelius craned his neck to see if he could work out which bit it was. He couldn't.

As they turned into the palace grounds, a more familiar sight greeted them. Freshly painted walls could be seen, a clear driveway free from moss and lichens unravelled before them like a luxurious carpet. The windows shone and glistened from a washed exterior, and the sweet aroma of cinnamon and nutmeg wafted through the bricks, while the pungent smell of jasmine, honeysuckle and climbing roses was like nectar to the soul.

The trap came to a stop by the stables and Macus was the first one on the scene.

'Where's everyone else?' asked Cornelius in disarray.

'It is just me and a light skeleton staff been keeping the place running my lord.'

'So the disease affected everyone in the palace?'

'Yes my lord, killed nearly everyone. A few guards and cooks survived, but not many.'

A groan from the trap temporarily halted their discussion.

'Master Cornelius is everything all right?'

'My friend is unwell Macus, please give me a hand.'

Gya's short cropped hair flopped over her eyes and her head dropped as the two men supported her. Weak legs were unsteady and her fever had broken now.

'We have to get her inside quickly,' said a troubled Cornelius.

'I shall go an' get the doctor,' and the driver cracked a whip onto the resting horse.

'Please make haste, this is life and death now,' Cornelius shouted after him.

'What happened Master Cornelius?' asked Macus in total shock.

'She has food poisoning.'

'I will help you get her up the stairs and then I will get a fresh jug of water for you.'

Gya was in and out of consciousness as she was led up the grand carved staircase and along the corridor. She caught sight of the vast guest rooms with their magnificent marble bathrooms and painted ceilings with jewel encrusted chandeliers. She could see out of the huge fenestra window that faced the east wing looking out to a lake that was surrounded by ornate buildings, vineyards, pastures and woods. The beautiful rose window faced the west wing and looked out to the stable block that housed the horses, wagons and cages.

'I think she should be put in this room, since it is the most recently decorated one,' said Macus urgently. 'Will you be all right while I get some refreshments for you?'

'Yes we will, thank you Macus.'

Gya looked ahead at the magnificent arched window, framed with pale blue curtains that matched the colour of the deep pile carpet. To her left was a huge bed complete with a canopy on posts and blue and yellow damask silk covers. Opposite the bed was a dressing table and large ornate gilt edged mirror. A beautifully carved mahogany chair slid nicely under the vanity unit. Along the same wall stood a chaise longue covered in identical dusty blue and yellow material. Beside the door was a wardrobe on one side and a chest of drawers on the other. Cornelius pulled off her boots and she scrunched her toes into the warm wool that peeped through and separated each appendage as her feet devoured it. She smiled with the touch. He then helped her out of her leather jerkin and tunic but left her shirt and undergarments.

'I need a bath,' she croaked.

'Not just yet, the doctor will see you first.'

'But I stink Cornelius.'

'A couple more hours won't matter. Once the doctor has been I will find a maid to give you a bed bath.'

'All right,' she groaned and crawled under the sheets.

'Macus will be here soon with some

refreshments for you.'

'Stay with me Cornelius, just for a while.'

'Just for a while then.' He removed his jacket and sat on the chaise longue adjacent to the bed.

Macus knocked on the door and brought in a tray of hot tea, a jug of water and some fresh ham rolls.

'Water for Gya, but I will have the tea,' instructed Cornelius.

Macus poured a cup of tea for the master and a glass of water for Gya. She sat up against the plump pillows and sipped slowly on the pure crystal nectar.

'Please Macus, sit with us while we wait for the doctor to arrive and tell me what has been happening in my absence.'

'Goodness Master Cornelius where do I start?'

'How about the beginning.'

Macus pulled the vanity chair out, gripped his cap in his hands, and slowly began his story.

'Well the General used to go off periodically as you no doubt remember Master Cornelius. But now we know why.'

'And why is that?' asked Cornelius devouring a soft ham roll.

'To look for the Seal of Kings my lord.'

'Remind me what that is?' Cornelius chased an escaped crumb round the side of his mouth.

'The Seal of Kings my lord, a very important piece of the realm according to the General's literature.'

'Yes I remember its importance now,' Cornelius looked at Gya.

'So how did you come across this vital information?' he continued.

'The guards have seen maps and documents in the General's apartment, alongside lists of names of castles, villages and tribes to target.'

Cornelius harrumphed. 'So you have been rummaging about the General's personal belongings?'

'No it wasn't like that my lord, we needed to find if there was a next of kin to report his death to, that's all.'

Cornelius harrumphed again. 'I understand, and are the maps and details still there.'

'Yes they are my lord.'

'Good, I will look at them presently, but please carry on with your story.' He crossed his legs, one over the other and pressed his back into the padded support of the chaise longue.

Macus poured himself a glass of water, knocked it back in one go, wiped his mouth with the back of his hand and carried on. 'So, three years after you left, it seems the General found the Seal. The documents ended with an attack on Castle Dru in Durundal, with all occupants pronounced dead.'

'I can imagine,' said Cornelius, his voice waned. He saw that Gya had her eyes closed now but he knew she was listening.

'But I forget myself, apologies my lord. I can remember the marshals coming to the palace two years after you left.'

'And what did they want?'

'They were looking for the Marquis de Beauchamp, it seems he was a murderer and a fugitive.'

'Really, whom did he kill?' Cornelius tried his best to look as shocked and surprised as he could.

'He murdered the real Marquis de Beauchamp, stole everything from him, literally everything, including his name, and sought refuge in the palace.' Macus tried to play down his excitement.

'Well it doesn't surprise me,' said Cornelius looking at the pallid pallor of Gya.

Macus looked shocked at his answer. 'Please my lord, if I may be so bold, where is the Marquis' imposter now?'

'He got into all sorts of gambling problems and fights with sailors. We parted company long ago. To be honest, I don't know where he is Macus. I really don't have any idea. I had to rescue my friend here from his clutches a few years ago.'

Macus looked at Gya; she tried to smile at him. 'I would never have guessed it, he seemed such a nice young man.' He smiled back at her.

'People are never really quite what they seem are they?' Cornelius sipped on his tea and shot a look at Gya out of the corner of his eye.

'I suppose not,' and Macus looked to the ground.

'So, what happened after that?'

'Well it seems that the General and the Emperor thought that the imposter had come to kill them both. They had been told by the marshals that he was a tribal boy. So when the marshals left, they put together a plan; not just any plan believe me, this was a truly vile plan.'

Two faces looked at him opened mouthed.

He took a couple of deep breaths before continuing. 'So the following year, after they got the Seal, they rounded up a selection of clan boys as a punishment, brought them back here, and made them fight to the death. Out there, in front of the dignitaries and the rich folk of Ataxata. You can see the arena and the dormitory from here.' He jutted his head towards the spectacle.

Gya choked on her water. 'What?'

'I know, it was bad, really bad. We have been through some really despicable times here. One time the General got a peasant girl as his play thing, but she escaped from her room. As a punishment and a warning the General got in a huge cage, bigger than anything I have seen before; put her whole family, plus her guards and her maid inside and set light to it. We were made to watch so no one would ever cross him again.' He looked to the window as if he could still hear the screams, still smell the burning flesh, still see the black coiled smoke. 'It was dreadful, my poor mother has never fully recovered.'

Cornelius winced and Gya looked even more sickened.

'The following year they rounded up about twenty clan boys to fight to the death, but this time it was different.'

'How was it different?' enquired Cornelius,

pensively captivated now.

'Because they retaliated.'

'How?' his morbid curiosity wanted to know.

'The General acquired a new girl. Her name was Skyrah, we heard him screaming her name when he realised she had gone. But this clan girl was clever, she was so very clever. She was put in this room actually. I hope you don't mind being put here ma'am, but after she escaped, the General trashed it, so we put it back how it was.' He looked around. 'I think we've done a good job.'

'Of course I don't mind Macus,' said Gya quickly. 'But tell me how she did it.'

'Oh yes,' Macus was preening with his knowledge now. 'She poisoned them, all of them. On the third day of the games she managed to get out of the room and pass round her lethal concoctions to the unsuspecting guests; it was amazing really.'

'How on earth did she do that?' asked Gya.

'She got her maid to bring her deadly plants over the course of several months. Of course the maid didn't know they were poisonous, she had been told they were for artistic purposes. But Skyrah didn't want to paint them, she ground them down to a pulp and fermented them to a liquid. She then killed the maid and took her clothes to get the deadly liquid round to everyone.'

Cornelius frowned distrustfully. 'How do you know all of this?'

'The court physician, Meric, he conducted the search to find out how it had happened. He was the one who informed us through his enquiries.'

'So how many did she kill?' asked Gya.

'She killed the Teacher, the Emperor, most of the guards, most of the gentry. You must have seen the empty streets; that was her doing. She wiped out most of Ataxata. People were scared. They thought it was a malady. So they all left.'

'And the captive boys?' asked Cornelius.

'They took the horses to get away, all those from the stables anyway.'

'So they escaped too?'

'Yes, she saved them, she saved them all; all but two that had perished in the games. I was in the stable when she came in. She wanted the horses to get away. She was very beautiful and I believed her when she said it was a curse. But we soon found out the truth.'

'So what happened to the General?' asked Cornelius.

'He was so angry, beside himself with venom. I felt the wrath of his fist for letting them escape. But I believed her story,' he paused briefly at the recollection. 'Anyway,' he continued. 'The General decided to get an army to punish them and get the clan girl back.'

'So how come he is dead?'

'Because the clans got a bigger army than him; from far and wide, all across the subject kingdoms, all the clans he had attacked in the past, came together on the day. It was a total victory for them.'

'How do you know this?'

'Because a few of the soldiers were allowed safe

185

passage. They returned from the battle and told us everything. The carnage, the death, how they were totally outnumbered and overpowered. That Namir is their leader and Skyrah is his betrothed. They saw everything.'

But Cornelius was a troubled man now. 'So if they can get a bigger army than the General, then they might come back and finish me off. I am the Emperor's son. I am the enemy. They will come and get me.'

'No, said Macus, visibly taken aback. 'Why would they? What they did was in retaliation, in self defence, they wouldn't come back and attack you for no reason.'

'How can you be sure Macus, how can you be really sure?'

'Well I can't be sure Master Cornelius, but I would stake my life that they wouldn't.'

Cornelius pondered. Gya could see his mind working.

'Listen to Macus Cornelius, listen to him,' she pleaded. 'You are not their enemy. Vengeance has been done. It is finished.'

Cornelius looked at her, then at Macus and frowned fervently; but his answer was interrupted by an announcement at the door. Macus scurried away and Cornelius invited the doctor in.

The doctor prescribed a list of herbal remedies and treatments, all of which the driver with his pony and trap had been sent off to take delivery of immediately.

'She has the worst case of food poisoning I have ever seen,' said the doctor grimly. 'She is severely malnourished and dangerously dehydrated. On top of all that she is gravely underweight.' He held her wrist between his fingers to take her pulse. He then reached in his bag and took out a bottle of liquid; a measure was poured into a spoon and given to the patient. 'She must also take this three times a day.' He put the spoon on her bedside cabinet and took a pencil from his pocket. He wrote the date on the bottle and muttered to himself, 'twenty-fourth of September.' The pencil was put back in his pocket and the bottle replaced on the table.

'Will she be all right?' asked Cornelius.

'She will be now, now that she is back here. But her recovery will be long. She will have to remain in bed until she is strong again. I do not want her getting up or being concerned about anything. Her food portions will be small with regular amounts of water, only water mind you. Nothing else but pure water.' The portly gentleman began to put his instruments away and folded his spectacles into a brown lacquered eyeglass case.

'I can arrange all of that,' said Cornelius gratefully.

'It's imperative that she gets plenty of rest, I do not want her being moved at all. She has lost a lot of fluids and a lot of body weight. This must be replaced before she even attempts to get up.' He moved towards the door.

'Of course.'

'The prescribed dose will be on the bottles and they will provide her with all the minerals and vitamins she needs to help get her strong again.'

'Her maid will see to it.'

'Good,' the doctor smiled. 'If that's all my lord, I will bid you good day.'

'Good day to you sir and thank you.'

Cornelius turned round to Gya, but she was now sound asleep in her soft cocoon and layers of silk. He crept out of her room quietly and ventured back to the room he knew best; his own living quarters. He looked around the vacant space, it would be refurnished again soon much more to his liking. He sat in the comfortable arm chair and perused the days activities, and what a day it had been; what a few months they had been. So much had happened. So many life changing events and experiences that were now piling up behind each other, that with his increased tiredness it was becoming a blur. He went to the bed and lay down. He had forgotten what being comfortable was. For too long he had settled for hard surfaces with the raw elements brushing against his skin. Maybe he should embrace this moment and act more like an Emperor now.

It had been a very long day, he should be asleep by now, but too much was on his mind. The conversation that he had exchanged with Macus was consuming him and keeping him awake. So instead of giving in to the hours of the night, he lit a brass oil lamp, closed the door to his private apartment and moved about the palace towards the General's quarters. The moon was full, shining silver through the arches and windows; only a few lamps or candles were lit at this late hour. Cornelius moved silently with his long shadow for company, his silk slippers brushed the marble floor. The guard captain, always alert now for treachery and secret invaders, simply smiled at Cornelius and left him alone with his business. He opened the General's door and saw the maps and documents filed away exactly how Macus had described. He rifled through the scrolls in their neat little compartments and one by one he took them out and studied them. The oil lamp was burning low and the room was in shadow, apart from a slice of moonlight that slanted through the window. Outside an owl shrieked, Cornelius looked up for a moment but soon returned to his reading. He pressed the temples of his brow between a thumb and forefinger as the words on the parchment blurred into a range of undecipherable encrypted codes.

He had been in the General's quarters for hours now. He should have been asleep a long time ago. He leaned back in his chair and yawned. He looked at the ceiling then all around him, always searching for clues and hidden messages. He opened a small drawer on the side of the desk and in the dark he felt about. His hand rested on an item; small, neat and square, he retrieved the article and held it to the light. 'A pack of cards,' he sniggered softly and looked through them one by one; they were exactly as Gya had described. He liked the touch of them, the size was most satisfying and being accessible and compact he could see how they could while away the time and be of benefit to someone in isolation. But now the pictures and numbers were tiring him; so he patted them neatly together and slid them carefully inside his coat pocket. The only thing keeping him awake now was the thought of one last scroll, hidden right at the back of the three tiered bookcase that he had been rummaging through all night; but first he needed some empowering fresh air. He went to the window, opened it wide and breathed in the refreshing nocturnal breeze. The moonlight turned his skin the colour of ash and the contrasting shadows made knife edge angles of his enviable high cheekbones and triangular nose. The owl swept past him and dived into the eaves of the forest out yonder. Cornelius closed the window and pulled the last scroll from its hibernation. Taking it back to the desk he rolled it out under the light of his diminishing lamp. One corner of his mouth began to rise as he realised he had stumbled across a treasure trove. General Domitrius Corbulo had labelled all the castles and all the clans that had been attacked seeking the Seal of Kings. In addition to that, he had documented all the clans that had been targeted for the killing games. Cornelius rifled through the bureau and the drawers and found further lists of tribes and clans that had been interrogated about the Seal's whereabouts; some went back almost twenty five years, plus the names of those taken prisoner and held in the dungeons all those years ago. He scanned them over and over again. Then he discovered the lists of clan

190

boys who had taken part in the recent killing games. Most had been crossed out, some had been ticked, others had been highlighted.

Fully awake while the palace slept, he stared down at all the information in front of him. Meticulously detailed in its organisation were the compass points, the coordinates, latitude and longitude, crosses, ticks and stars. The best routes, the safe resting areas, the rivers, the glens, the passes; it was all there. He had spent half the night sifting through reams of paperwork, delving into dusty vaults, pondering over charts and then pouring over it all again for the umpteenth time, and by morning he had found what he was looking for. The Clan of the Mountain Lion had two dates. One was twenty years ago where a young man had been imprisoned while he helped the Emperor with his enquiries regarding the Seal and the other was a list of boys names from last year's games.

But even more interesting, was the name of the clan boy who had not only escaped amid a wrath of death and destruction, but who had led the revolt against the Ataxatan Army and won.

With jubilation and satisfaction, he looked up from the desk, sat back in the chair and displayed a gratifying smile. 'I've found you haven't I.'

22

A September wedding was considered most lucky in these parts and this was the twenty-fourth day in the month of September. With a successful harvest and the field being turned for another crop, a wedding in this month would surely secure riches and prosperity for years to come.

On this spectacular day of royal pageantry; peacocks fanned their impressive tails whilst meandering around the manicured lawns, snow white doves cooed from their very own ivory towers, patiently waiting for their turn to signal continued peace and prosperity, and gossiping guests swivelled round in amazement at the glorious sights.

Though the centrepiece and epitome was undoubtedly the most magnificent hammered bronze wishing fountain where an elaborate structure turned and twisted upwards and transformed into a wolf looking up to the skies howling into the moonlight with a hare at his side and a leopard ready to pounce; a cascade of shimmering water attracted an abundance of flying creatures and a raven sat at the very top keeping a keen eye on the proceedings.

Lyall entered the building by way of the huge double doors and strode into the Great Hall - a room decorated with rich tapestries and paintings of Lyall's ancestral family. Sensual jasmine and fragrant honeysuckle weaved itself round the carved oak pillars whilst gold venetian vases were ablaze with the rich vibrant colours of a late summer's day. A thousand mahogany chairs, bearing red cushioned pads and golden fringes, seated the honoured guests and dignitaries.

Looking regal in a weaved tunic of golds and reds, complemented with a decorative sash made from the most luxurious purple satin and held together with the King's Seal, while a green belt went round his waist with Wolfsbane's scabbard tied securely onto it. And to complete the ensemble, were the softest leather slippers crafted by the newly appointed cordwainer. He was preceded by his page, Arran, who carried the magnificent Wolfsbane, and was flanked by his groom's man, Namir. He walked slowly to the front of the Great Hall acknowledging as many guests as he could with a nod of the head or a shake of the hand.

At the front, the sword was placed ceremoniously on the altar and Arran stepped back to sit beside his parents. Lyall took his place on a raised dais where he sat with Namir.

With the sound of a drum beating softly and a hushed flute chanting melancholy in the background, he waited for his bride. He spent a few moments taking in the ambience and sat quietly immersed in private conversation with his brother. And then the atmosphere changed and all chatter was interrupted by a gasp from the congregation, and those at the front knew there was nothing more elegant in the room.

A beautiful woman entered, looking radiant in a dress of ivory silk, scattered with semi precious gemstones that hung so perfectly on her body it accentuated the round of her curves. On her head she wore a close fitting skull cap from which hung a simple square veil made of the lightest gossamer, so fine that it was almost invisible. Around her shoulders hung the priceless Queen's own Blue Diamond pendant that Lyall had given to her as a wedding gift, and spectrums of brilliance bounced from its many facets. The guests threw fresh petals at her feet as she glided down the aisle, her soft velvet slippers brushing the luxurious pile of the woven carpet that was now lined with a layer of perfumed flowers. The music stopped as she reached Lyall and he faced her with a look of pride.

A hushed audience eagerly anticipated Meric's words. 'Honoured guests and fellow countrymen, I am so very privileged and honoured to bring our very own King Lyall and our future queen, Arneb, together in marriage, and I am especially pleased to be able to conduct this service with so many of their friends and family here as witnesses.'

The congregation muttered and nodded in approval while others dabbed a tissue to stifle escaping tears.

'A wedding such as this can only bring prosperity and riches to our land and we thank the gods that Lyall and Arneb were destined to meet each other and we pray that they will live a long and happy life together with many children to come.'

The bride and groom acknowledged Meric as he continued. 'Marriage means so many things to different people; so I ask Lyall to speak first and tell us why he has chosen Arneb to become his wife.'

Lyall took Arneb's hand and held it gently. 'Once in a while, right in the middle of an ordinary life, the gods give us the person of their dreams, the love of their life, the person who they hold most dear. For me, that person is Arneb. When I am with you Arneb I feel alive. Every breath I take is so that I spend that moment with you. Your life is my life now. I serve to make you happy and I will never give you cause to shed a tear over me; for you are the key to my world.' He kissed her hands and then her face.

'And Arneb,' Meric looked at her. 'Please will you respond with your words of love for our king.'

She had rehearsed this speech a thousand times now and dutifully obliged. 'Lyall, when I sleep I dream of you, when I awake I reach out for you, and I know that the day will be full of loving you. Laith found me as a newborn and gave me my name; then his son found me as a woman and gave me his love. Both will stay with me forever.' She too kissed his hands and planted her seal of a kiss on his cheek.

'Thank you, you have pledged your love to each other; now you will become one with our customary ritual. Arran, could you bring me the sword.'

The young boy stepped forward and lifted Wolfsbane from its resting place and gave it to Meric. The blade was wiped with the ceremony ribbons as Lyall and Arneb knelt before the sword. At the same time they pressed their thumb on an opposite blade and waited for the blood to run. Then they pressed their thumbs together and watched as their bodies became as one.

Meric lifted the sword and proclaimed: 'Today we have witnessed the joining of two people. They have declared their love in front of chosen guests and loved ones. The spirits have looked down on them and have blessed them.'

He gave the sword back to Arran to wipe clean, and then held out his hands to conduct the next part of the ceremony. 'Who has the rings that will bind these two people in marriage?'

'I do,' said Namir. And he placed them on the blade of Wolfsbane that Arran held so proudly.

Arneb's was the brightest, purist most exquisite aquamarine set in the middle of a faceted collet with flawless rubies and amethysts embedded around it. Lyall's ring was the striking Lapis Lazuli stone of a king and set as the centrepiece flanked by rows of perfectly cut diamonds.

'I am so happy,' she whispered as Lyall slipped the jewel on her finger.

'We are blessed,' said Lyall as his was secured.

'With these rings and in the presence of these witnesses I now pronounce you husband and wife.'

The guests cried and cheered, the acrobats tumbled in, the minstrels strummed their lyres, the jesters juggled their bats.

Lyall held Arneb's face in the palms of his hands and kissed her lovingly. As he did so, the first few notes of the reed pipes began to shiver across the room. At the fourth quatrain, the dancers began to move. Not taking their eyes off each other for an instant, they kept their posture graceful and their stance defined. They moved with subtle gestures as they circled around each other; seductive, passionate, empowering; they had the congregation not daring to breathe. Arneb picked up a ribbon of blue silk and made circles around him with the streamer; entwining him and prowling round him as the silk touched his face. He reached out for her, so she stopped, let the ribbon fall to the ground and stroked his cheek. He took her hand and pulled her into him, she felt his strong arms around her as she fell back, confident that he would not let her fall, and felt his beating heart as she rose again, her breast pressed to his chest. She spread her arms wide and he lifted her, and as she dropped to the ground, feeling almost weightless, the drumbeat started. Without conscious thought they both slipped into the arise, parted, hands raised, meeting for the merest fingertip touch, parted again and then he lifted her high into the air before letting her slide down against his body till her feet touched the floor. They held the embrace until the music stopped and then wrapped their arms around each other as a final embrace.

In the next room a string of servants were waiting, and as the applause died down, the king led his queen to the head table and everyone followed. When all were seated, servers lifted the silver domes and exposed plates full of exquisitely presented food; pulled pork and shredded beef, roasted duck with brandy sauce, glazed guinea-fowl in turkey dripping, red cabbage with pine nuts, potatoes drenched in honey, carrots dipped in wine. And for desserts was a range of pastries, cakes, fruits and sweets. The congregation celebrated until the early hours with speeches, renditions, accolades, and songs; and when it was time to sleep, those who didn't have a bed, just slept where they lay.

As Namir and Skyrah slept in the grandest guest room in the castle, she had a dream that was so intense it woke her at an unearthly hour. She sat up in bed and found that she was sobbing. She was unable to stop herself. She tried to smother the sobs with the hem of the blanket, but this produced a snuffling noise that was even worse, so she got out of bed to pour herself a glass of water from the jug beside their bed. Once up she found she couldn't stand properly and she had to sit down again rather suddenly on the bed. That woke Namir. He saw the streaks of tears on her cheeks and became alarmed.

'What's the matter.'

'It's nothing, really it's nothing.'

'Is the baby all right?' he tenderly felt her

swollen belly.

'The baby is fine,' she swallowed her tears.

'Then what is it?' he persevered.

'I had such a vivid dream that's all.'

'You will have vivid dreams, you are with child.'

'But this was so real Namir, so very real.'

'Tell me about it then,' he urged, sitting upright again.

'I dreamt that men came, they were soldiers from Ataxata and they wanted to speak to you.'

'About what?' he asked.

'They said that the Emperor wanted some information and you were the only one who could help him.'

'But the Emperor is dead Skyrah, you know that.'

'I know he is, but this was so real.'

'Alright, so what happened next in your dream?'

'They said it would only be for a couple of days and that you would come to no harm, that you would be well looked after.'

'And then?'

'But you didn't return, after several days you still hadn't returned. Then, in my dream, as if no time had passed at all, I was running through the tunnel, in the dark; it went on for miles. It was awful, I was so frightened. My legs wouldn't carry me, I was getting nowhere. I was trying to get to Lyall to help me.' She dissolved into tears again.

'Skyrah, nothing will happen to me. You have

described what happened to my father all those years ago.' He wiped her tears away. 'This is just a vivid dream, it won't happen.' He brushed her face. 'Skyrah look at me.' She turned to face him as he continued. 'The Emperor is dead. We killed him. No, you killed him remember. I will not be imprisoned in a dungeon in Ataxata for two years like my father, and I will be here to see my child being born.'

She sniffed back a runny nose. 'You promise.'

'I promise.' And he held her close in his protective arms and watched her fall asleep.

23

It was now two weeks since the wedding celebrations. Clebe was sitting on his stool in the goat pen, his hands drawing hot milk from the udder of the patient nanny and watched the dawn spread over a misty land. The milk hissed into the wooden pail in rhythmic spurts, the sounds growing deeper as the pail filled. The goat munched on hay strewn on the ground as a hazy October sun struggled to rise above the rim of the far hills. The forest tinged and sparkled for a few moments until a cloud consumed the glow in one go, swallowing the golden scene for the rest of the morning.

As he finished the milking his herd and had poured the milk into large metal urns, he was aware of the sound of horses hooves rumbling into the camp. Looking up, he saw two soldiers approaching through the mist. As they got nearer, he recognised the uniform. 'Ataxatan soldiers, now what on earth do they want?'

Knowing that the camp was greatly depleted, he went out to see what was going on. Ronu and Namir were already there, while a stream of other men began to gather round them as well.

'Are you lost?' shouted out Namir.

The horses were reined to a halt and snorted

loudly while one of the soldiers spoke.

'I am looking for Namir.'

'Who is looking for Namir?' asked Ronu.

'I am General Van Peirs, and this is Captain Alverez, and we come in peace on behalf of the Emperor of Ataxata.'

'The Emperor is dead,' Alun's voice bristled. 'And most of Ataxata.'

Cheers from the camp supported Alun's reaction.

The General waited for the cheers to die down. 'Yes, you are correct, but I speak for his son, Cornelius, the exiled and now returned Emperor of Ataxata.'

'His son?' frowned Namir, stepping forward.

'Yes, he has returned and wants to personally thank Namir. It is because of Namir that the Emperor Cornelius has been able to return from exile and His Highness wants to show his appreciation.'

Namir smiled an embarrassed but unconcerned smile. 'Well, I am Namir, but I don't need to travel to see His Highness thank you. I just want to live alongside him in peace now.'

'He thought you might say that, but he wants an audience with you, as one leader to another. To ensure peace and harmony amongst our people. To form an alliance, so that these atrocities will never happen again.'

'Tell him you have my word but I can't leave my camp at this time.'

'And why is that?' persisted Captain Alverez, his

horse restless under the weight. 'Do you fear reprisals when you have gone, do you fear attack from other enemies?'

'I do not want to leave my people and my wife is with child. Right now is the wrong time.'

Namir turned, but the Alverez stopped him. 'On the contrary, it's the perfect time. To protect your loved ones, the safety of your child and your community.' His words followed his gaze as it navigated the camp.

Namir's face sought clarification, so Alverez continued to explain. 'The Emperor invites you to sign a treaty. This treaty will protect your people. We will ensure their safety. Together we will become allies and form an allegiance against further uprisings.'

'We have seen evidence of the former Emperor's crimes against your people and we want to ensure it never happens again,' General Van Piers added. 'With your mark on the treaty, alongside that of the new Emperor, we can implement peace as soon as the document is signed.'

Namir looked at his clan for answers, most of them shrugged not knowing what he should do.

'Why isn't Lyall here when I need him?' he muttered.

Unable to hear more than a few murmurs and unplaced tones, Skyrah came out of their hut and looked at everyone. The horses took a few steps back and seemed to bow to her as long arched necks dipped to the ground. Pulling up their heads, the soldiers kicked them in the side with hard boots; the destriers moved forward and shaking their manes stood to attention again. Van Piers and Alverez tilted their heads in respect. They knew exactly who she was.

'What's going on here?' she asked with suspicion.

'I have been asked to sign a peace treaty.' Namir started to explain.

She looked levelly at him without a word then cast her suspicious gaze towards the soldiers.

'Why?'

'To ensure peace amongst our people so that we can live alongside each other in harmony.'

'I still don't understand. Why do we need a peace treaty, our word is sufficient. Or is it not, gentlemen?' She threw her question over to the soldiers.

Fearing her gaze contained a poisonous glare, they looked to the ground and did not answer.

Her distrust was fuelled, so she pulled Namir out of ear shot and spoke with her voice held low. 'Do you remember my dream?'

'I do, but this has nothing to do with a dream you had.'

'I don't trust them and I don't understand how you can.'

'Well I haven't said yes yet.'

'But you haven't sent them on their way either have you?'

'Skyrah, this offer could mean peace across all the kingdoms, we wouldn't have to live in fear and be distrustful of our neighbours.'

'I don't believe I am hearing this, why would you believe them after everything that has happened to our people over the last three decades and more?'

'It is time for peace Skyrah. I am tired of fighting. I am tired of battles. I am tired of looking over my shoulder. I want my sons to grow up with freedom and prosperity. Not fear and constraints.'

She sighed a heavy sigh. Had he not learned anything of human nature, that sometimes it was not always in everyones best interests to form alliances with the enemy; to act as if nothing had happened before, to believe that people could change. 'You are a good man Namir, you want the best for your people, I know that. But I urge you one last time not to trust these men of Ataxata. Let them return to their Emperor with your word as a sign of peace. But do not go with them.'

'Skyrah, I must go and sign the document. I must put my mark on it for the future of our clans. It is the only way forward in these uncertain times.'

She was doubtful of this ruse, but she couldn't keep arguing with him, and certainly not in front of everyone; he was the leader and she had to support him. 'It is your choice Namir. But let me come with you.'

He looked at her swollen belly. 'You know that is not possible.'

She had to agree with him this time; he was still taking his remedies and she was with child, but she was not going to give in. 'I agree that I will not be able to serve you best, but I urge you to take a travel

205

companion, it will be two against one out there and then you face a long journey back alone; even the Ataxatan soldiers travel in groups.'

He looked over at the General and the Captain in their smart uniforms and sheathed swords. 'All right. I will agree to that.'

She faced the soldiers as a tall, strong, defiant woman. 'Namir will travel with a companion at his side. I trust you have no objection. Until this treaty is signed, you can never be too vigilant.'

They looked at each other, then the Captain replied. 'Of course, who will you be nominating?'

She addressed the clan with her eyes. She didn't have to say anything. A mass of hands went up.

'Alun, please will you accompany Namir, it's for the journey back you understand. He is still taking medication for his injuries and needs an aide.'

Alun stood tall. 'I understand Skyrah and it will be an honour to ride alongside him as his protector.'

She nodded to the soldiers with an air of majesty and they dipped their heads in response. She then disappeared into the hut, closed the door from prying eyes and released her overflowing tears.

Namir faced the officers. 'It is settled then, I will return with you as the Emperor has requested, with Alun as my aide. Though I suggest you rest here for a few hours. Please take your horses to our stables and join us for breakfast. We will make haste straight after.'

After a good nourishing meal, the soldiers were left to saddle up their destriers in the stables. While inside the leader's hut, Skyrah had prepared a months supply of herbal remedies.

'You must take your medication Namir, I have made enough to last you several weeks.'

'I don't intend to be several weeks my dearest, I want to be in and out as quickly as you want me to be.'

'I know, but just the weather changes or your horse gets lame; I would rather that you have too much than not enough.'

'What would I do without you Skyrah?'

'I never want you to find that out. Hold me Namir. I want to remember this embrace until your safe return.'

As they held each other tightly, the morning mist began to turn into a fog so dense that it chilled the very air. Skyrah lifted her head and breathed in the vapour. The horses in the stables clattered about restlessly. The goats in the pens rammed into the wooden enclosure. The clan became concerned.

'This is no common fog,' said Clebe warily.

'I agree with you,' said Ronu. 'I have a bad feeling about this.'

'There are restless spirits in the air right now to be sure,' Clebe's voice trembled.

'There was a time he would listen to us, but not now.' Ronu looked out to the invading mist. 'If Skyrah can't change his mind then nothing can.'

Skyrah saw the fog as a warning and it unnerved her. It had consumed everything now, even the totems were being suffocated. Why couldn't he see it. Was the fog making him blind as well. Was there some sorcery at work that was clouding his judgement?

'I do not like this Namir,' she said fearfully. Even though the gloom was outside, it seemed to muffle the sound of her voice making it small and hushed. 'The gods are warning you.'

He hugged her tightly. 'My love, there is nothing to be afraid of. Why would the new Emperor want to hurt me? Besides, I have my totem protecting me. I have your blood running through my veins. I am well protected and will be back in a few days. I promise.'

She leaned in to him and prayed, and she knew from that moment that she would be praying every minute of every day until he was safely in her arms again.

24

The path was hazy though the October day was free from rain. The journey shouldn't take them long at this time of year, but the fog was particularly dense and unnerving. The officers allowed the horses their rein to lead them back.

'This is a bad idea Namir,' Alun's voice was thin.

'Not you as well,' Namir waned. 'I've had this with Skyrah ever since the soldiers arrived.'

'But this fog isn't natural, can't you feel it?'

'Alun, you are supposed to be protecting me here, not the other way round. Look, the fog isn't going to hurt us.'

'This is bad, I can feel despair and death Namir.'

'Then turn around Alun, I will be fine.'

But the air was sharp and cold and brimming with terror, and Alun was fearful whichever direction he chose. He didn't want the fog to snatch him with fingers of death and devour him with its hungry tongue when he was on his own. Better that he stay with the group. But he didn't like it...not one bit.

They pursued the barren road, heading south towards Ataxata. The fog clung to them, damp and cold; they passed misshapen objects spiralling out of the swirl and ending somewhere in the air above. Beyond that, half seen, were other shapes that looked like headless bodies and trees wielding swords and axes. The elements were distorting everything now.

By eventide the fog was still with them.

'I suggest we stop here,' said Van Piers, unperturbed by the perilous gloom.

Their resting place was a short distance from the road by a copse of stunted trees, alongside it ran a narrow river, swollen by recent rains. The banks were shallow enough for them to water their horses, the trees were dense enough to give the travellers shelter. But still the long grey fingers of mist were spreading ever further.

'Are you sure this is safe?' asked Namir warily, his own senses beginning to shiver.

'I'm not sure it is,' Alun was deeply traumatised and ill at ease. All he could see around them was a swampy ground festooned with slimy white ghost-skin, and endless quarries of mires, quicksands and glistening swards. 'This is no ordinary fog dear friend; you mark my words.'

The soldiers vied each other surreptitiously. 'Here, take this.' Van Piers offered Namir a goblet of wine from a flagon. 'It will help you sleep.'

Namir begrudgingly took the offering.

'And you Alun, you will dream of orchards and vineyards ripening in the sun, and women so beautiful they will be like the golden goddesses of the moon herself.'

Namir and Alun drank the wine, but didn't notice that the soldiers took theirs from a different flagon; they failed to see the exchanged wicked smile and knowing look. Namir didn't notice either how quickly he had fallen asleep and succumbed to a sequence of torment that followed the initial slumber. With dreams that were chaotic and disturbed; he saw something huge rising from the river, clad in a black tar that was dripping from its face, body and outstretched fingers. Giant frogs sat on the river banks; squat, grey, menacing creatures with huge fat throats protecting a castle; high on a mound it was; rotten and overgrown, its spires snapped off like broken spears, its walls covered in old mans beard. A roofless tower appeared through the fog and then disappeared again. The hideous fingers of tar weaved through the hall doors, curled along the galleried landings, round the turrets, through archways and over the buttresses like a sinister vine devouring the entire body.

Amid the dense black he heard a high pitched scream and felt the earth thud with a dreadful force; the noise was followed by the gnarled fingers of death reaching up from the water, taking a drowning man down to the depths.

He tried to wake up but he couldn't, he wanted to run away but was grounded, he felt water splash him so he turned away. He sensed a commotion; a fight, a struggle, but still he couldn't move. His senses were heightened but he was locked in a sleep so powerful it rendered him paralysed. In the end he had to give in to the night and let his totem bring him out of the dream naturally.

When he awoke the following morning he felt groggy. Sitting up he rubbed his eyes and soothed an aching head. He reached for his medication that Skyrah had given and knocked back two of the ground down shapes.

'Do you want water with that?' Van Piers handed him a flagon.

Namir looked at him cautiously.

'It's all right, it's only water,' said the General reassuringly. 'I think you had a nightmare, you were thrashing around a lot last night.'

Namir didn't say a word, his eyes conveyed his thoughts.

Alverez was cooking rabbit and field mushrooms close by. The fog had cleared and Namir could see the land around him was red and gold with the colours of autumn. Beautiful trees spread their branches so they nearly touched the ground, whilst around them was a range of disused stone dwellings and further along the stream sat an assortment of abandoned boulders.

But he didn't see Alun. He stood up to look around. He couldn't see Alun's horse either. 'Where is my companion?' his eyes searched wildly.

'He went back first light,' said Alverez calmly, putting the rabbit and mushrooms on to three metal plates.

'Yes,' said the General. 'The fog really spooked him you know.'

'What! I don't believe you.'

'Well he's not here and his horse is gone,' barked the Captain.

'Did he say anything?'

Van Piers ripped a piece of meat off the thigh. 'He just said he wasn't man enough for the job, he asked us to tell you he was sorry.'

The Captain handed Namir a plate of food, but he was too taken aback to eat anything.

'I just can't believe he would do that.'

'So you think the fog monster took him?' Van Peirs laughed out loud as escaped fat ran down his chin. He wiped at it with the back of his hand, took a swig from the flagon and shook his head in amusement. The Captain laughed with him and sat down to gorge on his breakfast.

Namir threw them a withered look, put his plate down and went to stand by the stream. He was confused. His friend would not leave him. Yes he feared the fog, but he wouldn't desert him like this. 'I need to find him,' he said at last. 'He can't be far away. There has to be a good reason.'

'There is a good reason, he was scared witless,' mocked Alverez, disappearing into the bushes to relieve himself.

'We don't have time to look for him, we have to go,' Van Piers' tone was more harsh.

'I can't just leave him,' Namir persisted. 'He

might be hurt.'

'He is probably home by now,' snarled Van Piers. 'And we don't have time to go back there and check that he is safe. Now if you are not going to eat the food we gave you, leave it for the wolves. We are going now.'

'I can't leave my friend.'

'And we can't let you go back now,' Van Piers rested his hand on the hilt of his sword.

Namir was now truly vexed. 'What is going on here?'

Alverez brought the three horses round. 'Nothing is wrong, we have told you the reason for our visit and what has happened to your friend. Now please, we are just following orders.' He handed Namir the reins of his horse. 'Look, we haven't got far to go. You will be given a nice room with good food when we get there. You will sign the treaty with the Emperor and then you will be on your way.'

Namir reluctantly mounted his horse, but by midday the three men hardly spoke at all. Namir was tired of asking them the same questions and getting the same muted response.

'What happened to my friend? What does the Emperor really want with me?'

'We have told you, your friend went back. We are just following orders.'

'I do hope he doesn't keep me long,' Namir muttered. 'I don't have good memories about that place.'

That comment was always ignored.

Namir thought about how he would be on his way back in a couple of days. How he needed to get back to his home that breathed the pulse of the earth and laughed with the rising sun. Unlike this gods forsaken place where everything was either dead or dying.

As the destriers plodded south along the river, the cottages became more derelict and overgrown, the trees became more spindly and diseased while cobblestones gave way to grey moss and raging lion's tooth. Farms were ghostly, outbuildings were tumbled down and where many a homestead once overlooked the plentiful river, now stood broken gates with trampled fences and weeds in barren soil.

By the time they entered the town of Ataxata, it was very different to the one that greeted him last time. It was nearly dusk for one thing and the streets were empty. The was no market, no crowds, no hollow eyed children swarming underfoot and begging. No fish wives screeching or pot bellied butchers slaughtering. Not a soul abounded. No fountains spurted. Something wretched had caused so many people to vacate much of the city and Namir had a strange feeling he knew exactly what that was. The formation of pink clad houses stood in rows like platoons of defeated soldiers and the once flowering vines had been strangled dry by a carnivorous creeping ivy, while clawed triffids had populated every cracked wall and pavement fissure for as far as the eye could see.

By now the eventide sun was disappearing

behind the horizon and it's fading rays slanted down the slopes and washed the city with a pale golden light. Three stable boys were returning their horses to the fields after a day of riding, grooming and feeding. The road could be seen from the pastures and from there they could see the convoy approaching.

'We have company Macus,' said Keris despairingly. 'They have brought the clan boy back here.'

Macus looked ashen. 'What are they going to do to him this time?'

'Why has he even come back? I wouldn't have done that,' said Aart shaking his head.

'They must have promised him something important to get him back here,' suggested Keris. 'That's the only possible explanation.'

'Or threatened him,' said Aart with raised eyebrows.

The three of them watched the party until it had disappeared from view.

'I had better get down there,' said Macus when the scene was clear. 'Finish off here will you?'

The two other lads nodded to him and watched him descend the hill.

The sky above the lines of rooftops and chimneys was blue and silver in the fading light and it had now begun to rain again. In comparison, the palace had been looked after while the city had been left to starve. As they turned in to the wide entrance of the walled palace

216

Namir could see bright lamps burning as window after window spread a golden glow to illuminate their path. Their horses walked along the wide driveway flanked by the rows of manicured laburnum trees and aconitum bushes. Then they veered right and channelled around to the back of the palace. The pavilion was still huge; painted white with oval windows clad in pillars of gold sitting on a well-kept terrace and immaculate lawns. As they took the final curve round the building he saw the huge arena cut into the hillside, he shivered and turned away at the ghostly apparition. He felt sick instantly and brushed the memory from his mind.

The three men dismounted and gave the horses to Macus who had sped down from the fields at break neck speed. Namir was sure he recognised the boy and studied his face intently. Macus dropped his gaze quickly and led the horses away. The soldiers nodded to someone behind him and went into the palace. Two guards came forward and escorted Namir to his accommodation.

But instead of going into the main building for a proper meal and a comfortable room as had been promised, the guards took him further along to a tower tucked away on a high mound. It was empty and derelict, tall and crumbling with twisted bracken and treacherous stingers growing all around it. Perhaps it was some kind of look out post from a time gone by, but now, this really was his worst nightmare.

'What are you doing?' He appealed with wild eyes and stopped in his tracks.

The guards pushed him with rough movements. He tried to get away, but he was grabbed under the arms and escorted towards the towering stone edifice. The entrance was by way of a wooden doorway that had been recently cleared of debris. Behind it was three floors of stone steps, each floor stopped at a spy hole. The walls were cold, the tower was dark and at the very top was a vacant room. The guard released the bolts and pushed him in; a small prison in a disused turret, with a stool, a narrow pallet and a bucket in the corner.

'What am I doing here?' Namir cried out in total shock. 'I am here to sign a peace treaty.'

'We are following orders and the Emperor will see you in the morning.'

'I need to see the Emperor now, there is a mistake, I am not a prisoner, I am an ally come to help secure peace between the kingdoms as requested.'

The guard smirked at his outburst. 'You can vent your complaints in the morning.'

'I need to see him now!' Namir ran towards the door to get out but was pushed back with a heavy fist and he fell against the wall clutching his stomach. 'Damn you!' he shouted out, but his stomach knotted again and he grimaced. He reached for his bag of medicines and curled up on the palette.

The two guards had gone, and with a clanging of locks and bolts left him on his own.

The night was very long. He caught snatched moments of sleep and found himself shivering in a cold damp ball for much of the duration. Strange nocturnal sounds could be heard amid shuffling noises from way beneath him. He couldn't even be bothered to get up and seek out the disturbance.

'Was this how Lyall felt in the tunnel?' he said to himself. 'Alone, cold and terrified? Being forced out of the comfort and safety of your own home to find yourself in strange surroundings and not knowing what is going to happen next.' He saw the moon peeping through the bars of his primitive window. 'At least I've got the moon as a guide Lyall, but I fear that my captors will not be so welcoming as yours.'

25

Morning brought visibility and allowed him to view part of the outside world, so he pressed his face against the bars and looked out. In the distance he could see the dormitories where he had been locked up a year ago.

'How on earth have I got back here. What challenges does my totem have for me now. Have I not proved myself enough. Or is it to show me how strong and intuitive Skyrah is. That it is I who needs her and not she who needs me?' He berated himself constantly. 'I should have listened to her. I should have listened to the all knowing and powerful hare.'

He looked out of the opening and faced a carefully laid out central garden full of shrubs and herbaceous borders. There were bird statues everywhere. Narrow paved paths curved around flowerbeds, and miniature ornamental trees danced with the weight of dangling bird cages. Beyond the paved walkways and disappearing lawns, stood the arena; towering over the domain where they lived and trained for eight months. He shuddered at the memory.

'And she is not here to help me this time.'

He went back to his palette, sat with his head in his hands and wondered how on earth he was going to get out of there.

That same morning he heard a movement and a bracing noise. The bolts fought against each other as the door was opened. He waited with anticipation to see who it was. Black velvet slippers made a hushed sound on the stone floor as a tall man entered. Loose golden curls framed a regal face with handsome lines, chiseled jaw and deep blue eyes. He wore emerald green breeches with white stockings, a silk shirt was ruffled at the neck and the ensemble was finished off with a crushed red velvet jacket. But the man's demeanour was dangerous and his smouldering aura engulfed him.

'Good morning Namir, I hope you slept well,' his grin was wicked.

'Well actually I didn't,' Namir replied indignantly. 'And I was not expecting to sleep in a prison in return for being so compliant with you.'

The tall man laughed. 'I'm sorry, I know, but if I had told you that you would be sleeping in a disused tower, you may not have been so willing.'

'So what am I really doing here?' his voice was low and thick. 'I somehow doubt I am here to sign a peace treaty.'

Cornelius laughed. 'Well it is partly true.'

'Partly true?' Namir was tiring of these games.

His captor began to detail his true objective.

'Well, as you may know, I am the deceased Emperor's son. My name is Cornelius. I was in exile when you were last here. My father was a very wicked man as well you know,' he grinned at the recollection.

'But I have had a nice little chat with Macus the stable boy, and I have also spent many hours referring to documents left by the General - so I have built up a picture as to what has been happening here.' He played with the ruffle at his neck whilst focusing on Namir.

'And?' Namir's reply was curt and short.

'Well, I need to know that your army is not going to try to overthrow me.'

'What? Are you serious? Is that what this is all about?'

'You have seen the town and the villages, you have seen the death and destruction, the absence of people. My home is devoid of life. No one wants to live here anymore. And you know as well as I do how it has come to such a dismal state.'

Namir thought for a moment; a year ago not one of them would have even dreamt that an entire city would be virtually wiped out by a young girl who's only aid was her superior knowledge of plants. No wonder the Emperor was concerned. He answered the Emperor as best he could.

'Well, if you have spoken to Macus then you will know what happened. That we escaped from the killing games because of my extremely resourceful wife, and an army was gathered because we were informed of the General's planned attack.'

Cornelius rubbed his chin and pondered, he sat himself down on the stool and looked Namir in the eye.

'I'm just not sure that I believe you Namir. I mean the General was a very powerful man with a powerful regiment. I am at a loss to understand how a bunch of clan boys can overthrow his army.' He paused, furrowed his brow and tilted his head to one side. 'Do you see my dilemma?'

Namir sighed and pressed his back against the wall. 'Well I am sorry if you cannot see how a bunch of clan boys disengaged the Ataxatan force; but I can assure you we did. But it wasn't just boys; we had help from men and women, even children joined the mission and the elderly came together. The clans united because our cause was so great. But we suffered casualties as well, in fact I nearly died and am still taking medication. So if it's all the same to you, I really need to get back home now.'

Cornelius furrowed his brow even deeper, he was not going to be compliant. 'But I am not satisfied with your answers young man. So I can't let you go. You might have your very impressive army round the corner waiting to attack me, you might have your potions and poisons ready to unleash on my surviving staff. No, no, you are not going anywhere until I am sure. And until I am, you will stay here.'

'I don't have an army! I don't have any poison!'

'And yet a year ago, that's exactly how you overthrew the Ataxatan Empire. You've just said it. And now you tell me that you don't have those things.'

'That was in self defence, our people came together for protection. I don't have an army at my disposal, you must understand that. We are not like you. Just because you wear fancy clothes and live in a fancy palace, you think you can have whatever you want, and do as you please. We are peaceful people and want only peace, that's what I thought I was coming here for, to sign a peace treaty.'

Cornelius flashed his wicked grin. 'That was such a clever ploy on my part don't you think.' He inspected his finger nails and picked out a bit of dust. ' My officers told me how your wife saw through my cunning plan. Perhaps you should have listened to her; she seems to be the one who I need to be afraid of here.'

Namir sensed the danger. 'Don't you even think about it you monster.'

The Emperor leaned in to him. 'Be careful what you say to me young man, be very careful. You don't know what I am capable of.'

'You can't do this to me, you cannot keep me a prisoner!'

The Emperor sneered back at him. 'Just you watch me.' He stood up from his seat, put the stool neatly back in its place and without turning back, vacated the room.

Namir couldn't believe what had just happened. He went to his small opening and stared out blankly. 'Why didn't I listen to you Skyrah,' he called out as if she could hear him. 'Cornelius is right, you are the one with knowledge and foresight here. I should have listened to you.' His rims filled with tears and he felt them spill down his face. When he had exhausted himself with hopeless thoughts of escape, he returned to the palette, lay back on the straw and closed his eyes.

Two days later the Emperor came in again. 'Good morning Namir, I hope you slept well in your, err, comfortable surroundings.' He looked distastefully around and flared his nostrils when he caught a waft of the damp cell. 'I have brought you some breakfast.' He handed over a plate of fresh fruit and rolls with a warm mug of milk. 'I have brought these for you in the hope that it will tempt you to be more honest with me.'

'I have been honest with you,' Namir hungrily gulped the milk.

'Well can you tell me about the Seal of Kings then?'

'I don't know anything about the Seal of Kings,' he licked the remaining drops from the side of the mug.

'Are you sure?' Cornelius' eyes narrowed.

'I am from the Clan of the Mountain Lion, I know nothing of kings and Seals,' he stifled a belch.

Cornelius looked repulsed. 'I have been looking at documents left by the former Emperor and the General and it says about Castle Dru in Durundal being targeted because it held the Seal of Kings.'

'I'm sorry, I know nothing about that.' Namir had his mouth stuffed full of juicy ripe figs now.

Cornelius was not going to give up. 'But the Seal is missing.'

Namir selected the next fruit. 'Well maybe the General wore it in the battle and he was buried whilst wearing it.'

'Hmm, maybe, but I think you know more than you are letting on. I will leave you for a few more days and see if you change your mind.' Cornelius went to take his leave.

Namir shot up out of his seated position, the fruit and rolls tumbled to the floor in an instance. The empty mug span out of control across the room. 'No please, please, you can't. I am not well, I am getting worse, my medication is running out. Please you have to believe me when I say I am being honest with you. You have to let me go, I will die otherwise.'

'Do you have an army?'

'No!'

'Can you get hold of an army?'

'No.'

'Where is the Seal of Kings?'

'I don't know.'

'I think you are lying to me about at least two of those questions,' seethed the Emperor. 'My guard will come with rice and water. Every day he will ask you if you are ready to talk. If you are ready and you satisfy my questions then you can go. If not, well, I guess you will die in here.'

'No, you can't,' Namir grabbed him by the shoulders. 'I am a human being, you cannot treat me like this. I do not have an army to raise against you.'

Cornelius pushed him back onto his palette with one hand. 'You are vermin, you are scum, and don't you ever touch me again.' He wiped the imaginary infected part from a golden shoulder pad with the flick of a hand and stormed out locking the doors noisily.

'Barbarian!' Namir bawled out at him.

There was no answer.

True to his word the guard came in every day with rice and water and asked if he wanted to talk. Each day Namir said he had nothing more to say. So he was left on his own. He slept a lot and woke frequently. He thought about his father and remembered the recollection of his living hell.

'The General wasn't there then, he would have undoubtedly killed me. Instead, the Emperor imprisoned me for two years in the deepest dungeon in the Palace of Ataxata. I spoke to no one; I had no contact with anyone except the guards who threw a daily ration of bread and water into my cramped cell.'

'How did you survive that?'

'A belief in the protection of my totem, a hunger to live, the thought of Artemisia, my unborn child. All of those things. But every day the guard asked me if I wanted to talk to the Emperor, and every day I said I had nothing to say.'

And here he was, experiencing exactly the same torture as his father, except he was in a tower and not a dungeon.

The long hours passed in silence while he watched the slim fingers of dusk and dawn peek at him as shadows between the cadaverous rails. Eventide and day seemed the same now; long, lonely, empty, devoid of any contact with anything. Sometimes he wished a rat or a mouse would find its way up to him, just for company, something to talk to; but even species such as these kept in the gullies and the gutters below.

Every night he looked through the slats over to the dormitory; a huge lifeless tombstone. He wept each time he saw it. But somehow the quiet garden and the shapes of the trees and flowerbeds edged in silver from the moon brought him peace. For he knew that Skyrah could see the same moon. But while she enjoyed her freedom, his walls were closing in that tiny bit more each day.

26

It was now some two weeks since Namir had been taken to sign the treaty, and a group of children had been fishing by the stream early that morning when they noticed a floating log. But this log wore a dark cloak that was tangled in the roots of a fallen tree so it couldn't continue on its journey downstream. It bobbed up and down in the water as the current tried to free it, but the roots of the tree wouldn't release its grip.

Believing it to be a monster, the children had rushed to get help. To begin with, their mothers thought they were messing about and they got severely chastised for inventing such a story, but then it became obvious that they weren't making it up, that they were deadly serious about what they had seen.

The parents and the children followed Clebe and Ronu to the water's edge and watched them as they waded out to the monster. The men knew what it was straight away and told the parents to take the children home. Because what they saw was not a log covered in a cloak; it was a man with his head caved in so severe that half his skull was missing. They turned the bloodless, swollen corpse over, one eye had been devoured and a thin white snake slithered out of the empty eye socket and disappeared into the reeds. The two men jumped, looked at each other and carried on with their task. Brushing away the algae, they removed the mud and instantly recoiled in horror.

'It's Alun,' cried out Clebe, swallowing the rise of vomit from the back of his throat.

Ronu had already spewed up at the side of the bank. They looked at each other in disbelief.

'How did he end up like this? Do you think the soldiers did this to him?' Clebe was in total shock.

'What other explanation is there?' groaned Ronu, wiping his mouth clean with hands wet from the river.

'But why? - they were going to sign a peace treaty. But this suggests evidence of foul play.' Clebe was still trying to make sense of the heinous crime.

'Well if Alun is dead, what about...' Ronu couldn't even say his name.

'It doesn't bear thinking about,' Clebe looked at his friend. 'Come, we have to get him out, then we will take him to the standing stones so his soul can be received by the spirits. '

'We should clean him up a bit first,' said Ronu mournfully. 'We can't take him through the camp like this.'

They disentangled the cloak that was caught up in the branches and dragged him back onto dry land. Ronu took off his shirt and began to carefully wipe away the mud and grime from the corpse. 'No man should die like this,' he said fretting. 'I only hope his spirit guides were with him in his final moments.'

'Amen to that,' hailed Clebe.

In the distance a group of people were making their way to the site; Meric, Skyrah and Alun's widow Idia, had been alerted by the children and the mothers... and they were nearly upon them.

'Make haste Clebe, we can't let anyone see the body like this.'

'Poor Idia and poor Skyrah, she will be wracked with worry for Namir now.'

They cleaned him up as best they could in the little time they had. Meric held back Idia until the two men confirmed it was safe to approach. With most of his body covered, Idia fell at his side and wept uncontrollably. Skyrah stood tall, with the weight of a mountain on her shoulders and took in deep breaths.

Meric put an arm round her. 'Praise be to his totem who brought him to us, he must have given his life to save Namir.'

'So what has happened to Namir?' Skyrah bravely asked, controlling her breathing and caressing her unborn child.

'He would be washed up as well if he had met the same end,' Ronu offered consolation. 'He has to be safe.'

'How do you know that Ronu? How can you be sure?'

'Dearest Skyrah,' said Clebe, his eyes wet with tears. 'If I thought for one minute that Namir was in the water as well, I would be wading through these reeds until I found him. But the wash of the river doesn't differentiate, everything follows the same path. Namir would be visible to us, really he would.' He choked back the sobs and willed the strength back into Skyrah's heart.

'But Alun was caught in the branches, how do we know that Namir wasn't carried further downstream?'

His response was difficult to convey, probably because he didn't know for sure himself. 'We have to believe, we can't think like that.'

She looked at Idia, a widow with young children. She would need their support now. 'We need to get Alun's body to the stones,' she said earnestly. 'Meric, we need to perform the death ritual straight away. His soul needs to be released. Idia needs peace.'

'We shall have the ceremony tonight Skyrah,' said Meric. 'Under the stars and the moon. The spirits will be around us then.'

She nodded in agreement and walked away from the mourners. Back in her hut she sat on her bed and gripped the bed sheets. Her baby kicked inside the safety of its womb, oblivious of the turmoil its mother was in. She stroked her swollen belly and wept.

As Clebe and Ronu carried the body of Alun through the camp, many heads craned to see the deathly remains of one of their dearest friends. Clebe had draped his coat over the face, it would be too shocking for the people of the clan to witness. The motion swelled and the crowds began to hum softly as he was taken past. The children, the old folk, Alun's dearest friends, all followed mournfully in a procession, one by one, through the camp, eventually halting at the subdued standing stones. Clebe and Ronu laid out the body on the ceremonial slab and the crowd dispersed to bring in a huge collection of wood for the pyre later that evening. It was all done quietly, and whilst they expressed their sadness for this loss, their thoughts were also with Skyrah; who right at this moment didn't know whether her husband was alive or dead. She stayed in her hut most of the day; resting, sleeping, humming, singing her song to her baby and hoped the words reached Namir, wherever he was.

'The wild wind blows through valleys my love,
The wild wind blows through the trees,
The wild wind blows o'er the rivers my love,
But will n'er get closer to thee.
The wild rain storms through the valleys my love,
The wild rain storms through the trees,
The wild rain storms o'er the rivers my love,
But none will get closer to thee.'

The clan moved about silently that day. Some couldn't do much at all, others busied themselves as they found that was the only way of coping. Idia stayed with her husband; these last few moments were precious to her and she spoke with his totem, giving thanks that he had been brought back to her, albeit in death, for the unknown would have been a far worse fate.

By eventide, Meric had arrived with Skyrah and her mother, all looked ashen. Skyrah stood in front of Ronu and Clebe and their wives. Meric, the great medicine man and healer, giver of life and proclaimer of death; embraced Alun's widow with affection. He stood at the raised pyre.

'This is a most unexpected turn of events,' he began. 'We don't expect to lose one of our own in such circumstances, and we can only pray that his totem and spirit guide was with him when he passed away; to give him comfort and peace when his life was so brutally ended.'

The congregation could hear Idia sobbing in the deathly quiet.

'Our people will pray for Alun's widow and his children and hope they will get strength from his memory in the coming days.'

The people around the grieving widow held her and comforted her and took the children to one side.

'We stand here now waiting for the moon and stars to take our dear friend, we know they have shone down on him for many nights, but he needs to look up to them and view the new cycle of his journey and see where he will be taken. The spirits have given him back his sight for this one last crossing and we know that he is safe and will soon be with his ancestors.'

He began to sprinkle sacred essences over the

body and chant as he did so.

'Take these offerings from our life into the spirit world dear friend, and may you find glory in the after life.'

He prepared the pyre by pouring drops of fuel onto the wood and invited Idia to light it. A fanfare of deep toned horns rang out, the clan hummed and a soft drum beat echoed round the stones. As the fire took hold, the mourners threw back their heads and began the eerie and mournful howling of their custom; the notes rising up through the octaves and sent with power and love into the chasms of the ancestral home above them. Now the flames roared up to even greater heights, spewing its power and illuminating the autumn settlement with even more golds and reds and burning amber, the people howled longer and wailed louder with ever increasing tones that matched the intensity and noise of the inferno.

Skyrah's thoughts turned to Namir as the incredible heat source slowly unmade the body of the man who had been sent to protect her husband. She tried not to dwell on it, but thoughts could not stop her from thinking that Namir too, must be washed up on the side of a bank somewhere. Even though she tried to tell herself otherwise and believe what Ronu and Clebe had told her; she found it difficult to convince herself in such dreadful circumstances. Why should Alun have died and not Namir she thought to herself, what possible reason could there be? Her mind was spinning as her imagination wrote out a story that she tried so desperately to change. She started to well up and the fumes brought tears to her eyes. But the flumes of pouring smoke created a vision for her, and through a haze of tears and ashes and twists and turns of flames, she saw Namir behind bars. He was as grey as the clouds above and as thin as the corpse that had just been sent on its way. The sadness in his eyes matched the sorrow of a whole clan.

Suddenly a bitter wind scathed through the ranks of people, causing them to draw their coats tighter about themselves. The wind changed the direction of the smoke, she followed it with her eyes. She looked harder and deeper. She felt her unborn child kick the side of her belly, she felt the strength of the unseen forces - this was a sign - Namir wasn't dead, he was alive - and there was only one person in the kingdoms who could help her. The wind blew strong with its incredible power in a northerly direction and settled itself round the Kingdom of Durundal, the home of the new king. The home of Lyall, Namir's brother.

27

Skyrah wasted no time once the congregation of mourners had dispersed. 'Meric, Mother; I have to go to Lyall.' Her voice was frantic, her tone shaky.

'Why?' asked her mother, taking her daughter's trembling hands.

'Because Lyall is the only one who can help us now; he has better negotiating skills, his weapons are finer, his armour is more protective, the youngest, strongest men are there with him at the castle.'

Chay, looked round the camp; indeed it was primarily the older generation that had stayed behind with the clan. Ronu and Clebe were amongst the younger adults and they were married with young children now.

'We don't know for sure that Namir is in any danger though Skyrah,' Chay pleaded.

'Mother, he has been gone for two weeks now. A peace treaty was offered and now Alun has been discovered washed up with his head caved in and you are telling me that Namir is safe!'

Chay turned her head away with the horror of it.

'I think Skyrah needs Lyall's help my love,' said Meric. 'We all need Lyall's help now.'

'Do you think Namir is in danger then my dear?' Chay's worried expression sought clarification.

'It doesn't bode well does it? Skyrah is right; if a peace treaty was at stake here, why was Alun found battered to death in the water? It doesn't make any sense does it?'

'Well, if Skyrah is going to the castle through the tunnel, then I am going with her,' proclaimed Chay.' She is with child, my grandchild, and I need to go with her.'

'And I will come also, I can't let two women go through there alone,' advised Meric. 'We will leave Ronu and Clebe in charge of the camp.'

'It is agreed then, we will pack our provisions and leave at dawn,' hailed Skyrah with raised spirits.

The following morning Clebe and Ronu were briefed on their duties, and should Namir return to the camp, what ever time of the day or night, she was to be informed straight away. It was practically a month to the day that most of the camp members had journeyed through the tunnel to attend Lyall's nuptials with Arneb, and now, here were the three of them, following the torches that paved their way for another reconciliation.

'Skyrah!' Lyall wrapped his arms around her. 'It's so good to see you. Look at you, you are blooming.' He stepped back to admire her bump and Arneb came over to embrace her friend.

'My dearest, it's only been a month and I have

missed you so much.' She kissed both cheeks with affection.

Lyall had acknowledged Meric and Chay and could be seen waiting for Namir to appear. He peered round the corner and his brow furrowed. 'No Namir today?'

'Namir isn't here Lyall,' Skyrah's voice quivered under the strain.

'What? Is he all right? Is he ill?'

She couldn't control the tears now, and all the anguish and held back emotion came flooding out in uncontrollable waves. Chay got a chair for her. Meric put her small bindle on the floor. Lyall and Arneb stood facing her anxiously.

'What is it dear sister? tell us,' urged Arneb.

'Namir has been taken!' She couldn't say anymore and motioned for Meric to tell them.

'I will take her upstairs to her bedroom, this is far too much to bear.' Arneb helped Skyrah to her feet. 'Come, you must rest now. Lyall will sort this out for you. I promise.'

The women took Skyrah upstairs to her room and Meric informed Lyall of the recent events.

'He's been gone for over two weeks now Lyall,' said Meric shaking his head gravely. 'We hadn't really been too concerned until now, we thought that maybe he had formed good relations with the new Emperor and was working towards an amicable alliance.'

Lyall threw a concerned look from his memories of old.

'I remember Cornelius being such a sweet boy,' continued Meric. 'He was a gentle natured lad with a passion for music, I never had any reason to think that Namir would be in any danger.'

'What did they want with him?' asked Lyall, remembering that anyone with that kind of power posed a potential risk.

'The Emperor had offered a peace treaty. Skyrah didn't want him to go, she was quite adamant you know.'

Lyall breathed a half smile, he recalled her forthright ways from long ago.

'But Namir was keen to install peaceful relations and so he went with them willingly,' said Meric shaking his head. 'I wish I had tried to stop him.'

But they both knew that if Skyrah hadn't managed to make him see sense, then no one else could have.

'He went alone?' asked Lyall raising his brows and his tone.

'No, Alun went with him,' Meric looked to the ground and took some deep breaths.

'What's wrong?'

'We found Alun yesterday morning in the river, his head was completely smashed in, he had been strangled as well.' Meric held a fist up to his mouth and stifled his emotions.

Lyall bit down on his lower lip and breathed heavily through flared nostrils. 'And Namir?'

Meric shook his head solemnly. 'I don't know

Lyall, I just don't know.'

'We have no time to waste,' Lyall shot himself into gear. 'I will assemble a search party straight away and I will leave right now.'

'Meric put his hand on Lyall's shoulder. 'Thank you dear boy, thank you.'

In the hours before Lyall's search party left for Ataxata, the castle was a hive of activity. The people assisting him on this mission had been summoned, the weapons were cleaned and the provisions collected. The blacksmith made sure the horses were shod while the armourer made sure the group were properly protected. The carpenter carved six foot long bows from a strong flexible yew and fitted them with strings of gut and waxed hemp. The fletcher made arrows from ash, birch and mahogany and attached fine feathers to the ends of the shafts. Their swords were lathed and polished before being concealed in fine scabbards and horses wore defensive headgear and protective socks round their forelegs.

By midday Lyall sat with his elite archers; Hali, Silva and Hass. He had donned his boots of supple black leather, soft lambswool breeches of light brown, a dark brown doublet and brown cloak with the Durundal coat of arms embroidered on the breast. He wore a waist belt of black leather from where his scabbard with Wolfsbane was secured, and slid a concealed dirk into the calf of his boot. The magnificent Tore was still able to wield a four foot long sword which hung at his side and Lace had accompanied him with her favourite bow which was secured across her back. Siri from the Giant's Claw and Dainn from the Hill Fort Tribe had also arrived to offer their support.

By the time the group were ready to leave, they only had half a day of sunlight left, but with a strong wind behind them and the chance of a good journey without setbacks, they would be part way across the plains of Ataxata by nightfall.

Lyall leaned down to kiss Arneb goodbye. 'Look after Skyrah for me.' He smiled a thin smile.

'I will,' assured Arneb. 'She is in good hands here.'

He squeezed her hand and nodded.

Meric and Chay stood by the entrance of the gates to wave them off. Lyall looked up to Skyrah's room and saw her standing against the window. She raised her hand in a trembling wave. He nodded back in recognition. The castle inhabitants had joined the throngs to bid farewell, and within minutes the party had galloped out of sight.

The October afternoon brought a hazy sun and a low chill; this time of year was full of swollen grey clouds and threads of silver mist. Thin trees stripped bare after the summer stood like rickety old men; gnarled, twisted and spindly. Meadows were even more sparse. The eagles swiped and the buzzards soared, stocking up for the winter days ahead.

They descended the ridge quietly, the horses hooves scattering out debris every so often.

'So tell us what you know about this new Emperor?' said Lace pensively. 'You haven't had much time to brief us.'

'Well I haven't got a lot to go on actually as the rat sent a couple of his guards to do his dirty work.'

'But he has come out of exile now?'

'Yes it would seem so. He must have got wind of his father's death and has come back to claim his inheritance; but why he needs Namir to sign a peace treaty is beyond me.'

'Don't you believe it then?' she continued.

'Only because Namir isn't back now suggests that the Emperor has an ulterior motive.'

'And there is the suspicious death of Alun, gods rest his soul; that had to be at the hands of the soldiers.'

'I agree,' said Dainn between thin lips. 'That was calculated circumstances to be sure and can only mean one thing.'

'You are right,' agreed Lyall. 'I am convinced this sculduggery was planned months ago, so my sincerest gratitude extends to all of you; I know that revisiting this place doesn't bode well.'

The group were somber until a voice piped up.

'We owe it to Skyrah and to Namir. We have to protect them as they have protected us,' championed Silva in their honour.

Everyone agreed.

They kept close to the path that they had taken coming back from Ataxata only a year ago; through passes, on the mountains, under grottos, over dales. Lyall saw a stag on the high ground, his head was up, surveying his domain, his huge rack of antlers almost held the entire mountain in its structure. It reminded him of their stag hunt and how empowering it made him feel. How alert and alive he had been that day, full of hope and optimism for the future; but that very same evening the General had descended on them and stripped them bare of all their childhood innocence and freedom. Yet here was the stag again, the Emperor of the forest, the image of power and freedom, of nobility and pride. And here he was, treading the path to meet its human antithesis.

They reached the eaves of the forest and rode into it without the slightest pause, even the breathless atmosphere didn't deter them, they had all faced greater monsters in the past. The echoes and disturbance of the forest tried to hamper their spirits. But these were warriors of the highest calibre, a strangled wind and choking tree branch was of little consequence to these brave souls.

They made camp in a shallow bowl tucked well inside the overhanging bank of a rooted oak. Dainn nudged the life out of a smoky fire of damp wood. Tore took food out of his pack and handed out strips of smoked beef jerky. Lace shared her provisions of cured ham and cooked duck eggs. Hali offered a flagon of ale.

'I was sorry to hear of Laith's passing,' said Siri. 'He was a great man and deeply respected.

Lyall nodded and touched his arm in gratitude. 'And I heard about your loss as well - the Giant's Claw has also lost a great leader.'

Siri nodded, 'He never recovered from the battle...a sad day for all concerned.'

'I am sorry to hear that,' said Dainn, 'I never knew Thorne - but I heard what a great man he was.'

'He truly was Dainn, one of the greatest.'

'Makes it all the more paramount that we install peace across the subject kingdoms. We must learn from these great men and follow in their stead.'

'Hear hear,' came the collective response.

'It started in Ataxata and it finishes in Ataxata.' 'Well said Dainn,' said Tore. 'And now my thoughts are with Namir. Poor man, just married, his wife is with child and we cannot be certain of his whereabouts.'

'We will find him,' said Lyall with conviction. 'We have to.'

They didn't pass Namir, even though they looked out for him at every turn. Skyrah had told them how ill he was and didn't know what state he would be in by now. Had the Emperor been kind and compassionate, or had he been neglected and treated like an animal? No one knew for sure.

They had made good time on this second leg of the journey, they all knew the urgency of their operation. They all kept each other going reliving stories of the famous battle and when Dainn stole Tore's crown in the boxing ring. The day that Hali came third

245

after another clan woman had pushed Lace into second place in the archery. Lace evoked feelings of awe as she detailed how she had first used a bow and arrow defending her younger sister from a charging wild boar. 'I just loaded, aimed and fired; straight in its eye it went. But the beast didn't go down until I sent another one down its gullet.'

Lyall remembered a similar outcome when he and Namir were still novices hunting a boar, but they did it together. Lace did it on her own.

'That's when I knew I had to marry her,' said Tore triumphantly.

The two of them shared an affectionate glance.

'Every step nearer to Ataxata makes me anxious about what we are going to find.' Lyall's sigh was heavy.

'I know exactly what you mean,' echoed Silva.

\

They were now on the high road to Ataxata, passing field after field of hoed soil, and tufted meadows with herds of Aurochs grazing. A pony and trap jaunted by, the rider tipped his cap to the group. They all looked at each other and then back at the pony and trap.

'Should we stop him and look in his cart?' asked Dainn suspiciously.

'I think we should,' agreed Tore.

\   But they found nothing and so they carried on.

Lyall led his party on through the previously bustling market streets and down the once colourful avenue of pink and gold houses with an assortment of different shaped roofs. But there was no life here anymore; the city of Ataxata was a wasteland. The rubble of broken buildings and fragmented statues lay scattered all around them. Sand and dust had blown down empty streets, through the pillared walls and porticos, covering everything in a thick layer of dull grey powder.

The party was silent as they continued through the broken city, their horses' hooves eerily loud in the wake; not even the corvids flew over here. Turning into the palace grounds three guards came running up, hands ready to unleash unforgiving swords, words ready to deliver.

'In the name of Emperor Cornelius of Ataxata, state your name and your business.'

'My name is Lyall, I come in peace with my seven comrades. I seek an audience with your Emperor to discuss the whereabouts of my brother Namir.'

'Is the Emperor expecting you?' continued the guard, flanked by the other two with swords drawn.

'Maybe he is, my brother has been detained by him for nearly three weeks now. He was due to return after a couple of days. His wife and myself fear for his safety and we need the assistance of the Emperor in finding him.'

'Dismount here, remove your cloaks and surrender your weapons. I will inform the Emperor of your arrival.'

A youth ran out and took the reins. Another relieved them of their swords and bows, another carried the cloaks and doublets. The dirks remained in their boots.

'I will feed and water your animals,' said Macus obligingly and led them into the stable block.

'Your possessions will be returned when you leave,' said the other youth, and with the coat bearer behind him, followed on the heels of Macus.'

The eight of them waited, facing the dormitory. Six of them felt sick to the stomach, the other two could only imagine what they were going through. Up in the tower Namir had heard the thunder of hoofbeats and had his head pressed against the wafer thin opening. He recognised them at once and started shouting. He was banging on the wall, looking for things to throw out, but there was nothing; the Emperor had made sure of that. He saw the stool, but he didn't have the energy to break it up; besides, the legs wouldn't fit through the holes. Namir could see them looking in his direction. He was screaming at them in desperation. His knuckles were ripped raw and bled with the pummelling. He was pleading with his brother to look up. But Lyall and his troop looked everywhere except upwards.

The Emperor soon appeared and invited them in; a tall regal man, not much older than themselves, but looked senior by definition. Namir slid down the wall of his prison and collapsed in a tearful heap.

'Welcome to my home,' said Cornelius in a grand tone. 'I understand you want news of your brother.' He directed the second part to Lyall and then addressed the ensemble. 'Please follow me.'

They passed through a world of opulence and grandeur and for the first time they saw through the eyes of Skyrah when she was taken into the palace. Every wall was adorned with precious polychrome marbles; frescoed ceilings were enriched with gold, glass paste and lapis lazuli. There were water features that gleamed bright orange with well fed carp. There were fountains, whirlpools and wells made entirely from mother of pearl mosaics. Every wall and ceiling and pillar was inlaid with gold, ivory and tourmaline. There were sunken gardens inside vast rooms complete with exotic ornaments adorned with playful golden cherubs. Two more rooms full of art depicted magnificent epic scenes and the most celebrated artists of the day were commissioned to display their fine works for the Emperor. They saw the enormous dining room that had a revolving domed ceiling that constantly moved day and night like the heavens, and trooped past the grand carved staircase that disappeared from its curve into the first floor apartments.

Following their guide he led them into a room of mirrors with a magnificent crystal chandelier as its focus point. Two guards stood to attention as the Emperor went in.

Leaving the eight guests to stand, Cornelius sat on the raised dais and his jewel encrusted golden shoes glistened under the lights. Flaxen hair covered his ears and a rich golden jacket sat atop a pure white silk shirt with a ridiculously large medallion of office on show. Wearing black breeches and black slippers, well groomed hands were clasped on his lap and deep blue eyes shone out of a handsome face.

'Now please, how can I help you?' he addressed them with a smile and a helpful tone.

'Well,' began Lyall, undeterred by the spectacle. 'I understand that you summoned my brother to take part in a peace treaty?'

'Yes that is correct.'

'And you assured his wife that you would only detain him for a couple of days.'

'Yes that is correct also.'

'But I have to inform you that he has not yet returned home; and myself, his friends here and most importantly his pregnant wife, are deeply concerned about his safety.'

'Hmmm,' Cornelius tried to show concern.

'I also have to inform you that Namir is not well,' Lyall continued. 'He is still recovering from an injury sustained in the battle,' he paused to compose himself from the raw emotion. 'And he needs regular doses of a particular herb, so I hope you can appreciate why we are so anxious.'

'I see,' Cornelius stroked his chin with a manicured hand and then summoned a guard over. A lot of nodding and looking over to the guests went on, followed by some raised eyebrows, a range of facial expressions and tilted heads. Then the guard went out of the door and the Emperor spoke again. 'I am sorry but it seems that you have had a wasted journey.'

'Really?' Lyall frowned.

'Yes, I did indeed have an audience with your brother and when we had duly signed the treaty the next day, he was free to go.'

'So how long ago did he leave?' asked Lyall with a tone of malaise.

'I am not sure; let me think,' Cornelius paused as he looked to the ceiling for some random figures. When he was satisfied with his story he rolled off the deception on the tip of his tongue. 'It was only a few days to be honest with you; he rested overnight in one of my stately rooms after he had dined with me. Then the following morning we signed the treaty and by the afternoon he was on his way again.'

'Are you quite sure about that?' Lyall's voice was hollow.

'Oh yes quite sure, I distinctly remember thinking what a nice man he was and what a shame we couldn't spend more time together. I could honestly see us as friends.'

Lyall disregarded the sickly smile instantly. 'I am sorry but the journey would only take him a couple of days at the most.'

'He did say that he wasn't very well,' lied the Emperor. 'So maybe he had to stop off somewhere.'

'But where?' Lyall was agitated. 'He only knows one route and we have followed that path; so even if he had succumbed to illness we would have seen him. I am sorry but there is something not quite right here.'

251

Cornelius glowered. 'I do not like your tone and I do not like your accusations Master Lyall. I have invited you into my home to help you as much as I can, and all you do is stand there and dismiss every answer that I give you.'

'I apologise my lord if I have come across ungrateful,' said Lyall between clenched teeth. 'But with respect, I hope you can understand my concern.'

The Emperor offered another solution when the guard returned, but only after a subtle nod had passed between them.

'You can search the place if you like; my guards will take you round; maybe he has fallen foul of his injuries in the grounds. I will be horrified and saddened if the poor man has been laid out somewhere needing assistance all this time. So, as it's imperative that we delay no further, you are welcome to see inside the dungeons, inside the dormitories, the stables, the outhouses, everywhere in fact. Be my guests.'

Lyall looked at him suspiciously but erred on the side of caution. Oh yes he looked dashing with lashings of charm and charisma and every inch a regal lord. But underneath those fancy clothes and that sickly fake smile, lurked a sinister character that was possibly even worse than the previous dictator. Cornelius broke the icy stare and gesticulated an outstretched hand.

'Please - follow my guards.'

Lyall went to go, but there was something else that hadn't been discussed, he paused and turned around. 'There is one more thing though.'

'Yes,' Cornelius looked bored now.

'Namir had a travelling companion.'

'Yes.'

'He was found downstream, washed up on a bank on the clan's territory; a few weeks after your soldiers had escorted Namir and Alun out of the camp. His head was smashed in and he had strangulation marks around his neck.'

Cornelius grimaced. 'I don't know anything about that.'

'So you didn't know that your soldiers had agreed to let a companion travel with Namir?'

'Yes of course I knew about that, I am told everything. But I don't know how your man died. According to my soldiers he was fearful of the fog and turned back. He must have fallen off his horse, stumbled and drowned.'

'Yes, of course, because a horse would naturally ride close to water in a fog wouldn't it?' Lyall posed the ridiculous allegory. 'And that doesn't explain the severe traumas to his body.'

The two of them held an unsavoury stare. Lyall could see right through him. Cornelius broke the stand off. 'I am tired now,' he said with jittered nerves. 'I have helped you all I can and offered you a favourable solution; there is no more I have to say and so I bid good day to you.'

'Pity Namir wasn't allowed the same courtesy,' Lyall seethed with quiet anger.

'Excuse me, I could not hear you,' said the

Emperor craning his misinformed ear.

'I said of course, we have taken up too much of you valuable time. Your Excellency has been most helpful.' Lyall bowed from the waist without taking his eyes off the man and took his leave with his entourage.

The guards dutifully took them down into the dungeons of the palace to where Laith had been imprisoned. They were taken to the dormitories where they themselves had been imprisoned. The stables were full of horses, the store rooms were full of furniture. The outbuildings where full of dust and decay. Namir was nowhere. Lyall stood in the courtyard and looked around. 'Where are you brother? Where are you?' He spotted the ancient tower in the distance. 'What's that over there?'

A guard stepped forward. 'It hasn't been used for years, it is unstable and on the verge of collapse, even the rats won't go in there.'

Lyall looked for a long time and dismissed the guard's rantings, warbling at his side. But he remembered the tower by his castle; how derelict and unsafe it was. The sound of hooves made him turn away.

'Your horses and apparel sir,' said Macus diligently.

Lyall recognised him at once and held a gaze trying to will the information out of his eyes, but Macus was clearly afraid and dropped his focus to the floor. Lyall looked around once more as he donned his doublet and cloak; he put one foot in the stirrup and looked up at the tower again. It was lifeless, devoid, empty. Surely Namir would have made some kind of communication by now if he was trapped in there. But maybe he couldn't, maybe he was shackled and chained; sick or even dying. Lyall took his foot out of the stirrup and gave the reins back to Macus. His friends went to dismount as well but he held up his hand to stop them.

'It's all right, I won't be long.'

The guard's face was ashen. 'I've told you it is not safe in there, the steps are worn and the doors are dangerous.'

'I will be the judge of that, either you take me there or I shall go by myself.'

He started the long walk over to the tower, followed in hot pursuit by the jittery guard who was looking anxiously over at the others on horseback poised with their weapons drawn.

'Open this door,' he demanded.

The guard threw it open for him and he was faced with the same stone steps that Namir had to climb. He wrinkled his nose at the rank, dusky smell that came from within.

'You see it is very unsafe,' whined the guard. 'No one has been in here for years.'

Lyall looked at him in disgust and began the ascent to the top of the stairs where he came across another bolted door. 'Open it!'

The guard turned the lock, pulled the bolts free and as the hinges creaked open the full horror of the room was exposed. Lyall retched. A smell of dampness, sweat and urine made him gag and he had to take in tiny sips of air through a gloved mouth. It did little to stifle the putrid air and he suddenly felt nauseous and had to swallow the rise of vomit that came to his throat.

The room was small and squalid; it would have been dark too, save for the bars that speared a small window and allowed a few beams of light to pierce through the gaps and stab the wide uneven flagstones.

He walked in while the guard remained at the precipice, ready to run if needed. Lyall felt the palette, it was still dented from the weight of a body. He looked out of the window and could see his friends. He called out to them but they could not hear him. He wiped his fingers on the bars. There was no dust. He saw the stool and wiped that as well; still no dust. He thought that strange. He looked around again for more clues. But there were none. 'What is this place used for?' he wanted to know.

'I don't know,' cowered the guard. 'I thought it had always been condemned, I honestly didn't know any of this was here.'

Lyall glared at the cowardly creature. He looked him up and down. No one told the truth in this gods forsaken place and he pushed past the frozen excuse of a man. 'There's nothing in there,' he called out to his comrades. 'Sheathe your swords, we are leaving.' He pulled himself up into the saddle. Bade his farewells to Macus and spurred his horse into a gallop out of the courtyard.

Out yonder in a paddock, out of sight and far away from prying eyes, Namir was bound and gagged in an excruciating fashion, while his horse was tethered next to him.

Inside the hall of mirrors the Emperor was seething. He bit hard into his knuckles until they bled. His eyes were fixed on the ground seeing only lies and deception in its path. His rage was fuelling with hatred and venom, and he breathed deeply in and out of flared nostrils. 'How dare he lie to me. How dare he. Sending out messages to his brother to come and save him, does he think I am that much of an ignoramus that I won't know what has been going on?'

He stood up and prowled the length of the hall of mirrors, shaking his head and grinding his teeth. 'Does he think I am an imbecile, does he really think that he can get one over on me and that I won't see it?' His golden coat flapped around him as he paced and turned, his face con-caved as he became more angry.

'That brother of his, accusing me and challenging me. How dare he!' And with that he flew out of the door towards the tower and waited there for Namir to be brought back.

Round the corner on the open road Lyall was venting his concerns. 'Namir is not dead, he is alive, I know it, he has to be somewhere close by.'

'But we looked everywhere. We checked everything,' said Dainn.

'That Emperor, he is not to be trusted, I saw it in

his eyes.'

'I agree with you Lyall,' said Lace. 'That man is a loathsome creature.'

'We will check out every hovel and outhouse to see if we missed him,' said Lyall gravely. 'We will look in every cave and hollow on our journey back. We have to search everywhere and make it known to all the clans for miles around to look out for him. It might take us several weeks, but right now I fear for his safety where ever he is. I pray that his spirit guides look after him. I pray that he is elsewhere and not in that place, for if he is still in the palace; his life is in even more danger than before we went there.'

Lyall was even more concerned than ever. 'I never imagined I would meet anyone more vile and wicked than the General, but after meeting that young Emperor, I fear he is the most extreme type of sadist.'

He remembered Laith saying to him: '..... *just when you think you have met the most depraved human being, there will always be one more who is even worse.'*

'What can we do?' asked Tore.

'We check first if he has made it to a clan village that he knows of. After searching the clans I am going to the Clan of the Mountain Lion and moving everyone to the castle.'

'I noticed how you didn't tell him everything, particularly who you are and where you come from.'

'No, I didn't dare, but I will take the clan back with me to safety. We should be safe for now because the winter is upon us. But Namir is not safe at all. Unless he is with clan people, then he will die.'

He kicked his horse into a gallop and with the others in pursuit, made haste to the ridge of the mountain.

Namir was now back in the tower and the Emperor was throwing what little possessions he had out of the room. He stripped the cloak off his shoulders and threw it out of the door, he ripped the shirt of his back and launched that down the stairs. His boots followed one after the other. Namir was pressed against the wall shivering in fear.

'You lied to me!' he bellowed.

'I haven't lied to you,' Namir retreated further.

The Emperor whacked him round the head and nearly knocked him out. 'You didn't tell me about a brother and an army.' He kicked him in the ribs with a wicked force.

'You didn't ask about a brother, he doesn't have an army.'

'Don't you be insolent with me!' and a cruel fist punched him in the face.

Blood trickled down his jaw, the swelling started immediately.

The Emperor bent down and tilted his face menacingly close to the red mess that Namir was in.

'As a punishment you will stay in here for the rest of your life. You will be fed on rice and water so that you live long enough to think about the errors of your ways. You will not see your brother again, you will never see your wife and child. And that is the price you will pay for lying to an Emperor.'

Then he saw something shining round Namir's neck, he reached for it between his fingers. 'And what is this?'

'It's mine, it's a picture of my mother,' Namir's voice trembled.

Cornelius howled with laughter. 'Really? Your mother? Well you won't be needing that anymore will you?' and he ripped it from his neck.

Namir roared and lunged at him but he was too weak, stumbling back again he tried to make sense of the Emperor's behaviour. 'Why do you hate me so much, what have I ever done to you?'

'It's what you could do to me that concerns me. That's why I have to stop you now, while I can, before you kill me and take what is rightfully mine.' He put the locket in his top pocket.

'I don't want what you have,' whimpered Namir frantically. 'I only want my simple life. I don't want any more than what I already have.'

The Emperor kicked him again in response. 'Stop lying to me you dreadful creature; I should kill you here right now.' He paused and lowered his tone. 'But where would be the decency in that?'

He straightened his apparel, wiped the blood off his fist with a silk handkerchief and strode towards the door. He turned as he reached it.

'This is the last time you will see me. If you choose to tell me about your brother and his army then I will set you free. If not, then you will die in here and rot.' He looked about the small squalid room; it didn't take him long. He opened the door, stopped and reached into his pocket. 'Someone once told me this was an almanac.' He looked at the contents dismissively, then at Namir. 'I   think you might be needing this.' And he threw Namir a pack of cards.

The door was closed and bolted. Footsteps retreated down the steps. And then there was nothing. Namir was now frozen, injured and dreadfully weak. He rolled up into a tight ball and wept. And all he could think about was what his father had told him all those years ago:

'You must remember that not everyone is good and honourable, happy with the simple things in life and just content with what they have been given. There are so many that will go to sadistic and brutal lengths for even more recognition and power.'

28

They had been travelling for most of the day. The autumn air was cool and tiny fireflies drifted and shimmered in the diminishing sunlight so it seemed they were journeying through a strange kind of vortex.

The party had covered some considerable distance and the dark grey clouds of Ataxata seemed a million miles away now. Leading the troop across barren land and over glacial mountains was hard going and it was late afternoon when they reached the walls of a fort. A crescent of dark stone that formed a huge impregnable wall. It soared from the land around it like a miniature mountain, with turrets and towers standing proud against a blood red sky. The stone gatehouse was in the centre with two lookout towers either side. A new citadel formed the centrepiece and with its walls a paler shade of grey; it hadn't yet shown the ravages of time and was completely free of bearded moss and patches of lichen. Beyond the curtain wall there appeared to be more than one hundred hectares of animal grazing land complete with its own slaughterhouse, storerooms and outbuildings while within the wall was a town for about five thousand inhabitants or more.

'Who goes there?' came a booming voice from one of the towers. A hiss of raised bows with deadly poised arrows were aimed directly at them.

'We come in peace,' said Lyall honourably. 'I am King Lyall of Durundal, these are my comrades and I am searching for my brother Namir, I wondered if he had been taken in here.'

'Why would your brother be here?' came the hollow reply.

'Because he had been held by the Emperor of Ataxata against his will. He is sick and I believe he is lost somewhere. I am hoping he is with you.'

'Wait here.' The Captain of the Guard whispered something to a sentry who sped of in the direction of the central buildings. The arrows were still aimed at them. The horses moved about noisily, swaying their heads and grinding their snaffle bits against their teeth. The party were getting jittery now as the minutes ticked silently by.

'What's keeping them?' said an anxious Hali.

'They have to get permission I guess,' answered Lyall as reassuringly as he could.

Lace began to feel the weight of her bow strapped to her back. Tore had his hand on the hilt of his sword. The others sat quietly waiting for news.

Eventually the gates to the fortress were slowly opened and Lyall's procession filed in. The guard in the tower pointed towards the main building and the soldiers lowered their weapons.

'That is the Grand Committee Room, that is where our leaders will help you.'

A stable boy ran up and waited for them to dismount so he could take the horses.

'You won't be needing those weapons here either,' said the Captain with a glare and signalled to the returning guard to relieve them of their armaments.

Toro and Lace hesitated.

'We are peaceful people,' the Captain assured them. 'We are sentries to keep out those who wish to harm us and nothing more.'

'How do you know we are peaceful?' queried Dainn.

'Because your enemy is the same as ours. Now please, our leaders are waiting for you in the Grand Committee Room.'

The Captain turned and went back to his lookout post, the horses were led away and the weapons were taken to the guardroom and would be stored till they went back out through the gates.

Lyall's group looked about them with eyes as equally wide as their mouths.

'I should take note of this place,' said Lyall with a heart full of admiration.' It is the most incredible fortress that I have ever seen.'

Even though the sun was going down they could still see that the buildings were light and spacious and comfortably arranged. The white plastered walls made them look new and clean and the few people who were still working, running errands and going about their

264

business, mingled about them wearing long grey robes and wide smiles.

One of the buildings looked like a school; though empty at this late hour, it was complete with climbing frames, a maze and a small allotment for the children. Another was a place of worship, and a group sat reading from a book in front of an administrator. The many shops were closing down and the outside stalls selling fresh fruit and vegetables were now giving away their left over produce. The last of the day was fading but they could just about see that the fields out yonder were full of sheep, cattle, pigs and geese, while more acres were yielding wheat, corn and barley. Grapevines hung in huge glasshouses and orchards of apples, pears, and plums were scattered beyond that. Candles and torches were beginning to be lit now, and their ambience changed the atmosphere of the town entirely. Following the procession of light the party made their way to the grand portal of the committee rooms.

The huge double doors stood open and the light from a hundred candles poured out onto the stone steps before them. For a few moments they stood and waited but then Lyall led them up the flight of polished ramps to the yawn of its mouth. Stopping at the entrance, he waited for his comrades. 'Everybody all right?' he asked, searching for reassurance himself as well as for every one else.'

'Yes,' came the collective response.

After another pause they stepped through into an enormously high and wide hall. The polished wooden floor stretched away for a seemingly impossible distance, and the high domed ceiling, which had them tilting spellbound heads as far back as they could reach, was decorated with the most exquisite frescos, studded with gilt stars and celestial moons.

Making their way through the vast room they noticed that the illuminating light source came from the monstrous black standing candelabras that lined their path and the only recognisable sound was of their boots against the vacuous empty space.

At the end of the hall ran a long oak table and seated there were seven females. They all bore the same lines of maturing years and all wore the same long white robes with golden sashes. One sat in the middle and had a noticeable air of superiority by definition. Wearing long braids of greying hair around a smiling face, she stood up and addressed the visitors.

'Good evening travellers and welcome to our community. My name is Myra, and I am the Matriarch of this fortress; these ladies here are my deputies and they help keep the fort a working progress.'

'Good evening to you ma'am, and thank you for inviting us in to your home. My name is Lyall, I am the King of Durundal and these are my comrades from different clans across the subject kingdoms.'

'Clans?' spoke up one of the deputies, wanting to know more.

'Yes, we are all clan members. We collectively

form some of the biggest clans around: the Clan of the Mountain Lion, the Giant's Claw and the Hill Fort Tribe.'

Nodding heads and impressed smiles acknowledged the introductions.

'So why do you call yourself a king?' another deputy asked.

'Because I was brought up in Castle Dru by the King and Queen of Durundal; until General Domitrius Corbulo massacred them in an unprovoked assault. My parents and the rest of my people were slaughtered, the castle was razed to the ground. The queen was my mother. The Clan of the Mountain Lion took me in after I managed to escape. Namir saved my life... I later discovered that the leader was my real father and Namir was my brother.' He quavered as he recalled the many times they had stood by each other in the wake of fear. How they had protected each other and risked their own lives to spare the sibling. But this time his brother was on his own...in the pit of hell...with no one to help him...no one at all...

A voice startle him back to the present.

'And you have returned to the castle to take up your birthright?'

'Yes, that is correct. And to restore it.' Yet at that moment he had a fleeting regret. Because just maybe, Namir would be safe right now if he hadn't have gone.

He could see Myra nodding her head with her deputies to acknowledge his response. 'I am very pleased to have made your acquaintance and I hope that our two communities will remain as peaceful allies.'

He bowed and permitted an honorary smile. 'That is my wish also.'

'Now tell me King Lyall what brings you here?'

'My visit is due to some very grave occurrences. I am searching for my brother Namir and my search has led me to you.'

'Yes, my guards told me this,' Myra looked at him earnestly. 'But why would your brother be here?'

'Ma'am if I might be given a few minutes to explain.' Lyall waited for the nod of her head to continue. 'My brother was taken by soldiers who work for the Emperor in Ataxata some three weeks ago now. His riding companion was found dead with serious head injuries in the river a few days since. His wife came to me to seek his whereabouts, as she, and now we as his family, are very concerned about him. We have just come from the palace, Namir's last known whereabouts, and the Emperor Cornelius told us that Namir was released a few days after he was taken. If this is true, then he has not returned and he could be anywhere now. He is very sick and he will need help. He might be disorientated and will probably descend on the first place that will give him sanctuary.'

'I see, though could you tell me why was he taken in the first place?' her voice was solemn.

'The Emperor offered a peace treaty,' Lyall started. 'But I believe it was a ruse to get him away from his clan. I don't believe that any peace treaty existed.'

'Why would the Emperor want your brother?' asked another deputy.

'I think he fears him. Last year we were prisoners there, but we escaped. It was Namir's intended, now his wife, who poisoned the guards and the Emperor Gnaeus. The General launched an attack on us, but we, collectively as clans, defeated him.'

'You killed the General?' exclaimed the Matriarch.

'Yes we did.'

The seven women began talking fervently amongst themselves.

A pause followed and the Matriarch spoke again. 'Who is this new Emperor ?'

'He is the the exiled son of Emperor Gnaeus. He is called Cornelius. With his father dead he has returned to Ataxata, but we believe him to be just as evil if not worse than his father.'

The group of women nodded their heads with even sterner expressions.

'Thank you for warning us Lyall,' said Myra sharply. They shared a grave expression and she spoke with her contemporaries, before divulging their own origin.

'We are Smilodon people,' she began. 'We are like you. We are clan. More than ten years ago our small community was ravaged and depleted by the same General that you have mentioned. He was looking for the Seal of Kings.' She stood up and made her way towards him. 'The same search that took him to your

269

castle in Durundal it would seem.'

Lyall looked sickened, but was equally mesmerised by the Matriarch before him. Her long white robe hung elegantly off her statuesque frame and he could see her face bore the lines of age but was still incredibly beautiful. He was transfixed as she spoke again.

'Only a few of us survived, and after we buried our dead we set to work to build a fortress that would withstand any attack from any type of threat and our people could live in safety again.'

'It is truly spectacular,' praised Lyall looking around. 'I applaud your determination and steadfastness.'

'Thank you Lyall,' she looked at all of the clan members now as they too, hung on her every word, totally captivated by the graceful smile that she wore. She held out her hands to them. 'We meet today as friends and family; all of you, you killed the same people that slaughtered our mothers and our fathers and our children. We are indebted to all of you.'

Lyall swallowed hard, his friends stood proud.

She continued. 'We have the same blood, we have the same dreams and share the same ambitions. We want only to live in peace and harmony with our fellow human beings.'

'I agree,' said Lyall, with a following echo from his group.

She addressed only him now. 'Your brother has not been here, and unfortunately I agree with you, the new Emperor is not to be trusted. But if your brother should end up here then he will be welcomed and looked after until we get word to you at Castle Dru in Durundal. I can promise you that Lyall.'

'Thank you,' he quivered with an emotional stance.

'But for now, you are my honoured guests for the evening. Rooms will be made up for all of you, where you can bathe and get changed and then I invite you to join us for a celebratory supper. I want you to meet with the people who run our community. There are many of us that keep this fortress safe and answer all needs. It is a working progress that I want to share with you all. We will work together to fuel the rewards of peace and celebrate the honour of friendship.'

'Hear hear!' came the collective response.

The elder stateswomen stood up on the raised dais. They saluted with fists on their hearts and spoke passionately with their souls. 'To peace, to prosperity, to pride.'

Lyall's accommodation was particularly splendid and the fragrance of aromatic petals and essential oils wafted round the room. A deep tub with ornate taps in the shape of a sabre toothed tiger, bubbled in the corner as it was being filled. He looked out of the window, and from his high elevation, stretching out before him lay the magnificent Smilodon fort.

The moonlit glow from a bright full moon had turned the white buildings a sheen of silver and the jewelled spire of the Grand Committee Room shone like a beacon reaching up to the sky. In the square below hunched figures rushed about their business; lovers found a quiet corner to embrace and the porter was sweeping up the dusty walkways. He watched for a while before moving into the comfortable warmth of his spacious room. It was sparse in the way of furniture, but the wood panelled walls intrigued him with more golden inlays of the Smilodon amid a range of stucco carvings of wild beasts and mythical figures. He went to a table and found a simple goblet next to a decanter of wine; he poured himself a glass, sat back in the deep winged chair and savoured the taste of the smoothest, sweetest claret he had ever tasted.

'Your bath is ready King Lyall,' came a trill sound from the other side of the room.

'Thank you,' he called out to the chambermaid.

Finishing off his wine he placed the goblet back on the small round side table and made his way to the bath tub. He pulled the decorative screen between him and the rest of the apartment, discarded his clothes and sank down into the well of the bath. He closed his eyes and leaned his head back against the roll of the lip. Mixed furious thoughts filled his worried mind.

He took in deep breaths and tried to relax, but the thought of his brother coiled up somewhere in excruciating pain furrowed his brow and he found himself grinding his teeth. He lowered himself right under the water and let the warmth spill over his face; he massaged his scalp and blended the oils through to the ends of his hair. 'This feels so good,' he thought to himself and then sat up again. 'I'm sorry Namir, I feel like I am betraying you somehow. You are living in hell and I am here in these palatial surroundings. But I know you are somewhere brother, I know you are alive, and I know this is not the end. I will have you safely back home soon.' He lowered himself under the water again and let the warmth spread over his entire body.

Fearing he would fall asleep in the undeniable comfort, he stepped out of the bath and into a robe that the maid had left him. He poured another goblet of wine and sipped it slowly as he looked beyond the window again.

'Would you like some help dressing my lord?' asked the maid.

'No, no, I will be fine,' he chuckled quietly before turning round to acknowledge her. The last person to dress him was his mother and he found it amusing, though his amusement was benevolent rather than mocking, and he didn't want to offend the girl.

The maid was small with short black bobbed hair, she only looked about fourteen years old; wearing a long pale blue dress with a white pinafore apron and moved about her errands on brown leather lace up boots. She busied herself arranging his evening attire.

'I have left a gown on your bed my lord. If it pleases you, I will take your clothes and have them cleaned by the morning.'

'Thank you, that would please me greatly,' he raised his glass as a sign of his appreciation.

Smiling courteously and dipping down into a curtsey, she then went to the bath and emptied out the water; he heard it disappear down a pipe and into a reservoir under the streets of the fort.

'Amazing,' he thought to himself, listening to the last drops draining away. 'Castle Dru shall have this when I return.' He went to his bed and put on the white silk tunic top over grey flannel trousers then slipped into the black velvet slippers that were left beside them. His hair, still wet from his bath, clung in dark strands to his scalp. He tousled it into place with his fingers and sat in the chair again; thinking, contemplating and sipping on wine.

A gong sounded an hour later which brought him abruptly out of his doze. He went outside to greet his friends, all wearing the same ensemble. He was quick to notice Lace in her long shirt and loose flannelette trousers. 'Wouldn't you have preferred a glamorous robe?' He asked with a wide grin.

'Not at all, these are more than adequate and extremely comfortable,' she stroked the soft material and performed a twirl with ease.

'The maid offered her a robe,' said Tore. 'But my good lady wife said she would be fine with what she had been given.'

'I suspect the maids weren't expecting a woman in our party,' suggested Lace.

'Very true,' said Lyall. 'But with their Matriarch and her Deputies preceding over events, I am glad we have you here to represent the women of our clans.' Lyall took her hand graciously to seal an honoured kiss.

'Well thank you kind sir,' she smiled and curtseyed before him.

'I think we all look fine specimens and each one of us has been groomed and pampered in admirable surroundings,' said Dainn glowing from head to toe.

'I agree,' said Silva. 'I have never felt so clean.'

'Or smelt so good,' said Hali.

'The girl trimmed my beard,' said Siri, smoothing a finely razored stubble.'

'And mine,' said Hass, sharing the same experience.

'There is lot we can take away from this experience,' proclaimed Lyall enthusiastically. 'I shall endeavour to incorporate as much as I can into our own Castle Dru. But now my friends, let us go and meet our hosts and enjoy the rest of our stay.'

They collectively took their seats in the Great Hall amongst others wearing the same silk tunics with grey flannel trousers, and those who wore white robes with gold sashes; and spoke with honoured guests and acquaintances who had a story to tell.

The chatter died down as the huge doors opened and dozens of young people entered carrying platters and other containers of every imaginable sort of food; and at the head of the procession walked the Matriarch looking even more beautiful and radiant than when they had seen her earlier. Her braided silver hair was piled up high on her head and she wore the purest, whitest silk dress that moved elegantly with her and hung on her tall slender frame like a second skin. She took her place at the head of the table flanked by her deputies and she remained standing to address the assembly.

When every one was quiet she made her announcement. 'Honoured guests, ladies and gentleman, it is my very great pleasure to introduce the young people that sit amongst us.' She gestured towards Lyall and his party. 'These are my friends and they are your friends also. I invited them here today after I heard their story. These are brave people from the same blood as us and I have welcomed them into our home.'

Fearing they had suffered the same fate as themselves, a sympathetic wave rumbled round the assembly room.

The Matriarch held up her hand for order.

'But these young people have done more for us than you perhaps are aware of.' She looked around the room at the rows of elders; all of them concealing the trauma of watching their own people being burnt to death or hacked to pieces by the General and his legions. Each one of them now hanging on her every word and eager to know what these courageous people had accomplished. And she delivered what they wanted to hear; in a strong passionate voice she raised the roof. 'For they have defeated The General Domitrius Cobulo, they have killed The Emperor Gnaeus of Ataxata and they have put to death the countless soldiers that assisted them both in burning down our land and massacring our people a decade ago.'

A wave of shocked surprise rumbled through the tables, gasps of delight echoed round the room. Faces worn with a lifetime of unending horrific visions were now replaced with the guise of retribution. A roar of appreciation went through the rafters, they stamped their feet, they clapped their hands, they rattled their goblets, tears flowed in as much abundance as the wine and she had to wait a while for calm to be restored again.

'Please, raise your glasses to Lyall, Hass, Hali, Silva, Siri. Dainn, Tore and the undeniably exquisite Lace. Because now, with the undisputed heroism of these young people; at last, vengeance is ours!'

The whole assembly rose together and lifted their tankards, goblets, glasses and vials; anything to raise a toast in. They stamped their feet again, cutlery was rattled, the table was pummelled and the rafters nearly came off the joists as they proclaimed:

'Vengeance is ours.'

'And one last request my lords and ladies and honoured guests,' her voice rose loud over the celebrations. 'To Namir, who is lost at the moment. But I, and all my people, will pray for his safe return.'

29

Two weeks had gone by and it was now well into November. They had been to the clans of The Giant's Claw and to the Hill Fort Tribe; but to no avail, Namir was not there. No one had seen him.

Siri and Dainn stayed with their respective clans and assured everyone they would keep a vigilant look out. The only clan the party hadn't been to was the Marshland Tribe, but as that was so much further north and Namir would have needed to pass at least four clans, including his own to get there, it wasn't on Lyall's list of high importance. But Tore and Lace knew what to do, so they bid their farewells and made their way back home, ahead of the bad weather in front of them.

But now Lyall had more pressing matters to deal with and he needed to move the Clan of the Mountain Lion, for fear of reprisal by the malevolent Emperor Cornelius.

Skyrah was with her mother and Meric at the castle. All Lyall had to do was to get everyone else to move out - and that was going to be the hardest part. The remaining followers sat on the edge of the forest and discussed their options.

'I have to build a fortress like Smilodon to take everyone.' Lyall was thinking out loud.

'Everyone?' asked Silva, quite overwhelmed at the mammoth revelation.

'It can be done,' Lyall said with the courage of his convictions. 'You saw Smilodon. You saw how it accommodated all those citizens. I am tired of our people living on dreams and schemes, running away, always fearful, never safe.'

'What do you propose to do?' asked Hali.

'I am going to build another Smilodon Fort with a school and a place of worship. I am going to spread the fields to have more livestock and yield more grain. There will be additional outbuildings for animals, extra barns and storerooms for produce. If they can do it. We can do it. We must do it.'

'But what about the clan members who don't want that, the ones who chose to stay here because they don't like change,' Silva put the realistic perspective on Lyall's vision.

'Did you see the Smilodon people? Was there anyone there who looked unhappy? No, because they felt safe. Namir can't guarantee safety here. It's too open, it's too vulnerable. We live in changing times where people kill and steal or any other number of dastardly means to take what is not theirs,' Lyall shook his head. 'We have to be more protected. No one can guarantee absolute safety, but Smilodon has done a darn good job and I want to do the same.'

'I still say that people won't like it,' said Silva

accepting Lyall's reasons but stating the awful truth.

'You are right,' said Lyall. 'People don't like change and given a choice they will always stay with what they know and what they are familiar with. But our people don't have a choice now, and I am not going to let anyone die.'

'We could take a chance and leave them,' suggested Hass. 'You will have to knock parents out to get them through the tunnel, and there ain't no way they goin' over any mountain.'

'I am not prepared to take that chance Hass,' raged Lyall stoically. 'Castle Dru and all its land is equal to Smilodon. We can do it. Those people did it. Come on, think of your children's future. Think of your future.'

'You are right,' said Silva. He had been listening to all the points raised and was considering all of them carefully before he came to his conclusion. 'If we want peace and prosperity, then everyone has to be moved. Whether the Emperor lives or dies, there will always be someone out there depraved enough to take what is not theirs. I say we do it Lyall. The Clan of the Mountain Lion has been attacked too many times now and with two leaders up at the castle, only the foolish would try to challenge you.'

'Thank you Silva, and I appreciate you coming forward with your support.'

'We need to do this as quickly as possible then, the weather will be turning soon,' said Hali firmly. 'I think we should make haste.'

'Agreed,' Lyall was relieved. 'So my strategy is this. I will talk to the clan and convince them that this is in their best interests. Then, Silva, I would like you to stay here with me and help me get the clan packed up, make sure they don't take too much in the way of provisions, it will make for easier transporting that way. Hali and Hass, could you go through the tunnel and explain to everyone up there what is happening, make sure you inform Skyrah first; she will be out of her mind by now. Silva, I want you to start leading the animals over the mountain pass, you know where to put them when you reach the paddocks and fields, you have turned and fenced them after all,' he smiled with a grace to his expression.

'What will you do with the camp when everyone has gone?' said Hass diligently.

'I will burn it to the ground. The winter is upon us and that will bring snow, whatever is left in the form of embers will soon be covered over and all evidence of that civilisation will be gone.'

'What about the tunnel,' said Hali.

'I have thought about that as well.'

'And...' they collectively said together.

'Once Namir is back safely with us, I'm going to have to blow it up.'

'What?'

'I know, it pains me to do it, but I have no choice. Namir will agree with me, I know he will. After what has happened here recently I can't leave it open.'

Worn faces looked at each other with raised

eyebrows but who were they to argue with his reasoning? Instead, they kicked their horses into movement and the party trooped into the Clan of the Mountain Lion amid a rapturous welcome.

All were jubilant to see the warriors return safely, but spirits quickly waned when they saw that Namir was not with them.

'I can see you are troubled Lyall, do you have news of Namir?' voiced Ronu beneath a furrowed brow.

'I'm sorry to say that I do not, I am deeply worried and need to speak to the clan as quickly as possible, can you get everyone together for me?'

'Of course I will, I shall do it at once but is there anything I should know?'

'You will find out soon enough dear friend, but please, make haste and get everyone together, for this is a very important decision I have had to make.'

Ronu looked at him for answers but Lyall jutted out his chin in an attempt to speed things up.

The clan were summoned amid whispers of concern. Bustling bodies weaved their way to the meeting house trying to make sense of it all. To be honest, most of the clan had gone anyway. It was only a handful of elderly people left there now. These were the members that were happy with what they were born into; who believed that their totems and spirit guides could protect them against anything, that the menhirs were their walls of strength. But now a far more ruthless predator was out there, a predator that needed a stronger defence.

'Friends, colleagues, families, I come to you with urgent news.' He looked at all of them in turn, looking every inch the regal lord and his dress evoked an air of righteousness. 'I have been to the Palace of Ataxata in search of Namir,' he paused briefly. 'I could not find him.'

A gasp went up and worried faces hung in front of him.

'I have travelled to the Giant's Claw and the Hill Fort. I have been to a huge new fortress built by the Smilodon people. I have searched in caves, grottos, fields and barns. But still I cannot find him.'

'What are we going to do?' came an urgent request from the back.

Lyall held up his hand in an attempt to continue. 'I believe Namir is in danger. I believe he is being held somewhere against his will at the palace. I believe the Emperor was lying when he said he wanted a peace treaty signed.'

'Why would he lie?' called out another voice.

'Because he is just as evil as his father, and probably the father before that... and while people such as this exist in the Kingdom of Durundal, then you are all in danger as well.'

'What's the answer then Lyall?' asked a worried mother. 'Everyone is up the castle now, we have little to defend ourselves.'

'That is my concern,' he said sternly.

'Lyall, what are you proposing?' asked Ronu, almost knowing what the answer would be.

Lyall looked at the worried faces, the people who had lived a lifetime here, the ones who rejected his offer once before. But would they now change their minds?

'I want to take you all back to the castle with me. After what has happened, Namir will support this decision. It is the only answer for the safety of our people. Those of you who came to the wedding will know how strong the castle is now. It is on a vast scale already. But I am going to make it even more substantial to accommodate a growing community.'

Everyone was looking open mouthed at his revelation.

'You will have your dwellings around the outside of the castle but within a protective wall. You can live as you are now, but you will be living under the protection of a citadel and a force that will safeguard you and your families.'

He paused waiting for a heckler - there were none.

'You can grow your own crops, rear your own animals. Nothing much will change apart from your surroundings. But I cannot leave anyone here to perish at the hands of a madman again.'

'We have lost good men,' called out Clebe from the back. 'Too many have died now, Alun was the most recent and we all praying for Namir's safe return. We are living in dangerous times, and sometimes we have to go out of our comfort zone for the sake of safety and progress.' He looked at his wife, who had wanted to go with Arneb and the others in the first place. Ellise was pleading with her eyes. He gave her the answer that she wanted. 'I say we go.'

She looked up at him in astonishment and threw her arms around him.

'Can I go and pack?' she asked him excitedly.

He nodded in agreement.

Enelle looked at Ronu, she was also desperate to leave.

'I say that Lyall is right,' he said in full support. 'We are not safe here anymore. I shall go and prepare the horses.'

'And I shall also go and pack,' she trilled.

'Is everyone with me?' Lyall called out with strength in his heart.

A cheer went up and he knew he had the clan on his side. Looking back to the party who had stood by him these past few weeks he nodded and smiled.

'Please, just take what you need, provisions will be there for you. You will only need a few things I promise.'

The clan was a hive of activity. The shepherd gathered his small flock and the goat herder collected his animals. Chickens were put in baskets. Children took hold of their dogs.

Lyall went to stand by the stones. Tall, impressive, magnanimous in their very presence. The home of the gods, the sepulchre of the spirits. He felt a breeze lift him and he felt surrounded by love and hope. He closed his eyes. 'Help me make the right decisions.'

Ronu and Clebe joined him to pay their last respects to the place that was once their home.

'Things are changing too quickly Lyall,' Ronu said gravely.

'I know, and I am truly sorry to have to do this, I really am.'

'While there is life there is hope - maybe we can return one day.'

Lyall looked at him, then to Ronu, 'What do you think Ronu?'

'I agree, a home is always a home, people come and go and the land is forever changing; but it is still home. Maybe it will be again one day.'

The breeze quickened, it curled round his ear as if pleading for a reprieve, one last chance before being set alight and its very existence forgotten and damned to the pits of the earth for eternity.

Ronu continued. 'But I think we should secure the cave entrance, we can camouflage it to make it invisible to the outside world. It would only be us that knows about it.'

Lyall looked to Clebe who was nodding his head in agreement. 'All right, we seal the cave.'

Skyrah came out when she heard the rumble of the horses and the last of the clan had come through the tunnel. Arneb was settling them in to their temporary accommodation. A stable boy came out to take the destriers from him.

'You have heard then?' Lyall threw Skyrah a

stricken glance as she approached him.

'I have; Hali and Hass told me,' she shook her head with worry.' What are we to do Lyall, I know he is still out there somewhere?'

'I agree, I know he is still alive. The Emperor said that Namir has been released,' his face looked stern.

'What is it Lyall?'

'I don't trust that Emperor, there was something in his eyes. That's why I have moved everyone here in case he descends on the clans like his father before him.'

'Do you think Namir is still there then?' she asked with uncertainty.

'My gut says he is, but I do not know for sure. I looked everywhere I could; but that Emperor is devious and cunning with a wicked streak and an unpredictable nature.' He paused to reflect what that would mean for Namir and then thought out loud. 'With the bad weather just around the corner, there is nothing more I can do right now - except pray for a miracle.'

30

The inclement weather had brought change and the grand summer foliage had broken down to mere embers of bony limbs, strewn like corpses on the pathways while dispatched leaves spread out like fallen heroes on the sodden ground. Now, all that was left of those long, hot, sunny days was a fragile glimpse which paled easily into a distant memory.

Namir had always held on to his pride and dignity, especially in front of those who tried to strip him of both, but mostly for himself. If the guards opened the door when he was sobbing, he would wipe away his tears and look them straight in the eye. When they slopped his food onto the floor and told him to eat it like an animal, he would scrape it back into the bowl and eat it properly. He had told himself that if he could just hold on to those two things then he would be all right, he could cope. But asleep, when he dreamed of things beyond the walls and woke with the memory of Skyrah and his clan, that's when he came close to the brink, and every day without them sent him further into despair.

Lyall had been and gone so any hope of rescue had diminished with him. And now the Emperor thought he had been lying about everything so that line of release was now an empty dream as well. Each day he received a bowl of rice and a mug of water, and received the usual request for truthful answers. But like his father before him, he couldn't divulge his knowledge about his brother and his army. He just could not implicate Lyall; and the Emperor would kill them both anyway, then he would massacre his clan.

'Oh no, the clan, they were in danger, so much danger now. Skyrah and their unborn child.'

The thought terrified him. Hopefully Lyall read the Emperor's face, hopefully he saw the malevolence when he looked in those demon eyes. Lyall would move them all; he knew that. Lyall was still half clan.

But he knew his fate was going to be worse than his father's. He was actually going to die in solitary confinement while the mother of his child gave birth alone. At least Lyall and Arneb would look after them he had thought. His child would never want for anything. But while he knew his family would be safe, the thought tore him apart.

'It's history repeating itself isn't it. She's going to end up at the castle for the rest of her life and my child will never know me.' He shouted through the slits, he bellowed and screamed. But no one heard his cries.

Most nights he had the same recurring nightmare where a raven tried to carry him away. The talons ripped through his face and gripped on to his cheek bones. Even in his dream he could feel the excruciating pain and the tears felt as warm as blood.

He tried to remove its claws with his hands, but the bird lifted him even higher and as the drops of blood oozed down his face he woke himself up in a hot sweat. 'I'm going to die in here, I'm really going to die in here. The raven is a sign.' He was beside himself with confusion and he tried to calm himself with deep breathing. But he was too scared to sleep now. Each time his eyes closed with exhaustion, he forced himself awake again. He was too afraid of what he might see in his dreams.

For six weeks she had been confined to her room, but gradually, Gya had started to find her feet again. First, she took brief walks around her room; then as she had got stronger she had ventured out into the palace corridors and weaved her way around the sparkling indoor maze. She had sat on the veranda for a few minutes every day and then disappeared into the warmth again. But this day at the end of November was the first time she really felt back to her usual self. She felt good, she felt alive, she was much stronger. She had got dressed and decided to go for a stroll outside. This afternoon the hallway was warm and bright with candlelight, even the floor seemed tepid beneath her feet. She was thankful of her woollen garments though and braced herself for the chill outside. The doors to the pavilion were guarded by a pair of hunched soldiers leaning lazily on their swords. One was tall and skinny, the other short and plump, but dressed exactly the same they looked quite comical. As she crept through the doors and tiptoed past them, they immediately

290

straightened up and held their swords up high, hilts against their breastplates.

'Good to see you looking so well Mistress Gya,' said the short one, nodding to her graciously.

'Thank you, it feels good to feel more human again.'

'Mind how you go Mistress Gya, don't spend too long out there, the weather is about to turn at any moment,' the tall one sniffed at the air as he announced his prediction.

'I won't,' and she pulled her cloak tighter round her shoulders.

'Would you like us to escort you mistress, before we take our tea break?' the tall one continued.

'No, I will be fine, you go and warm yourselves up,' she smiled to herself contentedly. She had heard Cornelius complaining about the slovenly guards and their constant tea breaks. 'I won't be long out here anyway.'

'Thank you mistress.'

The guards sheathed their swords, opened the doors and headed for the kitchens at the other end of the building.

In the distance was the tower, hidden from view, and to all but a few, completely desolate and empty. Inside though, a man was on the verge of giving up hope. After three weeks his face was healing. The bruises on his ribs were now a mottled shade of green and yellow. But his body was pale and thin, he was as weak as a day old lamb. Every night he had engraved a mark on the wall as he looked up to the moon. Fifty two nights he had missed sleeping with Skyrah, fifty two days he hadn't told her that he loved her, he had now broken the promise that he had made on their wedding day.

The morning had brought daylight and he was relieved that the dark had been swallowed up at last. Sounds of creaking hinges and grinding metal was another welcome relief, for it proved that he was still alive and gave him a small olive branch of hope with a voice attached to it. He called the guard over.

'Please, you have to help me, I am very sick. I need the yarrow flower. Please can you bring it to me.'

The guard laughed smugly. 'This is all you've got today my lad, no yarrow flower here.'

A bowl of rice and mug of water was put on the floor and then the guard lowered his face closer to Namir's. 'Have you got any more to tell the Emperor?'

'I don't know any more.'

'Well that's just too bad - maybe you will remember something by tomorrow.'

The guard looked at the frail figure before him and for a split second Namir thought he saw a glint of pity. But the guard quickly turned and with a clatter of bolts against grating metal he was gone. Namir was on his own again. He could still hear the guard laughing all the way down the steps to the lower floors. He looked at the deck of cards that Cornelius had given him. He shuffled them and laid them out, one by one he looked at each card in detail. The faces of kings and queens looked up at him, the pictures of hearts pulled at his own, the black images scared him. The numbers made no sense at all. He tried to work out what they meant, but by the afternoon he had tired of them. He had no use for anything the Emperor gave him, so instead he went to the empty window to view the outside that was so torturously out of reach.

But this time, an inquisitive raven was perched on the sill looking in at his prison. Her head was jerking and twitching as she faced the man, and her feathers ruffled as she tried to keep warm. Namir smiled at the bird.

'What brings you here today little friend?'

The raven cocked her head and blinked.

'I have nothing for you,' said Namir dismally. 'You can see for yourself, it is far colder and more miserable in here than it is out there.' He showed her his meagre surroundings. 'You have far more than me.'

The raven looked at the cards in his hand.

'Oh these, you think this is food do you? I'm sorry, it's not, I don't have any food either.' His face was solemn. 'These are all I have. But look, you can have them, and then you can see for yourself.' He looked at the interested bird, and between the cold weathered rods of iron, he slowly pushed the cards out. One by one, she took them in her beak and sent them spiralling to the ground. They both watched every one fall, and when there were no more, she cocked her head, ruffled her feathers again and as her seraph wings took shape, she flew off into the distance.

Namir found himself quite emotional and sad to see her go. 'Goodbye little bird, stay safe and warm, I wish I could go with you.'

He watched her until she was just a speck on the horizon, and that's when he finally understood what it all meant; for each one of the fifty two cards represented each day he had been imprisoned in the tower. The dream about the raven carrying him away was a sign. It all made sense now. He knew that he would die that day. There were no more cards, there was no food or medicine. There were no more days to be spent in the tower, and no more terrifying dark nights alone. He went back to his bed to die and had no idea that a saviour was so very close.

Down below Gya was taking her walk. She had seen the falling cards and made her way over to their resting place. With ardent eyes and dextrous fingers, she carefully picked them out from the talons of bracken that clung on to them, and then looking upwards for a sign, all she saw was the crown of the building disappear into the low hanging clouds. 'What is going on?' she asked herself and walked round to find the entrance of the tower. She looked around, not a soul was there. It was deathly quiet, but the door was ajar and she slowly pushed it open.

The steps were uneven and Gya brushed her fingertips along the wall to keep her balance. A faint draught that smelt of urine made her retch, mildew and decay was rank in the already stagnant air; the walls were soft and powdery and in the dim interior her hands recoiled from something slimy. As she climbed further, a rod of light gleamed on to a patch of crumbling wall, revealing the creeping black stonewort and clinging damp moss. At the top, and from whence the beam of light had come, she saw a door reinforced with iron strips and barred with iron bolts. She held her ear close to it to seek out clues - but there were none. She carefully slid open the bolts and gradually opened the door.

Her eyes fell on him and she instantly knew who it was. She fell at his side when she saw him. His dark hair was grey with dirt and lack of sunlight and fell in twisted hanks around his jaw; he had grown a beard which was equally tangled and filthy. His trousers were rotting in the damp and his exposed chest was hollow, the bones protruding through pallid skin. His knuckles and fingernails were red raw and bleeding by pummelling the walls. His lips were split and he bore evidence of a beating on his face and body.

'No, no, what have they done to you?'

Namir opened his eyes wearily. 'Am I dead?'

'No you are not dead. I am here to help you,' she kissed his cold hands.

'How did you find me?' his voice was weaker than hers had been two months ago.

Gya showed him the cards.

He smiled weakly and remembered the raven.

'What happened to you?' She was desperate to know.

'I have been here for fifty two days - I feared I was going to die in here.'

'Why are you here though?' her expression was one of astonishment and pity.

'The Emperor - he sent soldiers - to sign a peace treaty - but he wanted to ask me questions - I told him everything I knew - he thought I was hiding something - he has beaten me - starved me - and left me.'

She stood up. 'I will go and get help.'

But Namir's response was panic driven. 'No! No! You can't! Don't tell him - please - he will kill us both - he's insane - please - just take me now.'

'Namir, I have medicine back in my room. I must get it for you. I have only just recovered from a sickness myself otherwise this would never have happened to you.'

He reached for her arm to stop her. Gya threw back her cape and showed him her Smilodon tattoo. 'We are the same brother and I know what you and your people did for the safety of our clans.'

But Namir had sunk back on the bed before she could finish. Gya took off her cape and put it round him. She then flew out of the door, charged down the steps, through the palace grounds and stormed into the Emperor's private rooms. The Emperor was sitting at his desk, dressed in his regal attire, signing official documents. He looked up at the intrusion.

'What have you done?'

He put his pen down and sat back in his chair. 'Excuse me, you can't just come bursting in here and start shouting at me like that.'

'What have you done?' Gya repeated herself with both hands firmly on his desk.

Cornelius sat forward. 'I ask you again. What do you mean. What have I done?'

'There is a young man bedridden up in the tower. Why is he there?' Gya was furious.

'Oh him,' Cornelius stood up. 'He is helping me with my enquiries.'

Turning his back on Gya he walked towards the window with a thoroughly malevolent air about him.

'What enquiries pray may I ask?' Gya demanded from behind him. But her mind was now on a pendant that lay on his desk. She had never seen this before and barely noticed his answer as she opened it.

'I needed to know who attacked the palace, I needed to make sure that they wouldn't do it again.' The Emperor was looking out of the window with his hands clasped behind his back.

'What are you talking about?' Gya was still looking at the locket and noticed an inscription on the back. '*Namir.*' 'You bastard,' she thought. 'You absolute bastard.'

Cornelius was still droning on. 'We talked about it back in May, don't you remember? We said that we would find out who attacked the castle and that I would put an end to it, by death if need be.'

Cornelius could still not face her. So she put the pendant in her pocket and tore into him.

'But we spoke to Macus and he told us that it

was the clan boys and a young girl. He told us that, and I said not to do anything until I was better, because I wasn't strong enough to discuss the matter in greater detail with you.'

Cornelius turned round now to face her and spat out an answer for his errant behaviour. 'I don't need you to make my decisions for me. I don't need to run everything past you. And I certainly don't need a woman's approval. I am the Emperor here not you, and it is my duty to take what steps I need to take to be sure.'

'To be sure of what precisely?' Gya moved closer, her expression filled with rage.

Cornelius backed away. 'I needed to be sure that they wouldn't descend on the palace again, that I would be safe. I needed to be sure that Macus had told me the truth.'

Gya erupted and stood right next to him. 'Of course Macus had told you the truth why would he lie about something like that? But now I'm going to tell you something young man.' She pulled up the sleeve of her shirt and showed him the tattoo of the Smilodon on her arm. 'You see that?'

Cornelius nodded his head as an answer.

'That is my animal tattoo, it is a Smilodon, it protects me, it watches out for me. That man you have imprisoned in that small tower, the one who is probably dying up there because of you; he is not a warrior, he is not your enemy, he does not kill for pleasure. Yes he is strong, cunning and clever, but he does not take what is not naturally his. He is the same as me, he has my blood, my lineage, my ancestry. That is Namir. He wears the totem of a predator, just like mine, it is his animal tattoo. Because people like us have to protect ourselves from people like you.'

'You are wrong Gya... because he does have an incredible force, he does have horses, he does have weapons.' Cornelius seethed in his attack and magnified his response. 'One hundred men on horseback bearing weapons of steel came asking about him.'

'What?' Gya was taken aback.

'After three weeks, an army of men came looking for him. A man calling himself his brother enquired about his whereabouts.'

'So what did you tell him?'

'I told him that he wasn't here, that I had let him go.'

'So you lied to him?'

'They told me that he was very ill and needed special medicine. I thought they would attack me there and then. There were so many of them and I had no back up.'

'So rather than hand him over so they could take him back to safety, you lied to them and kept him up there! What were you thinking?'

'The prisoner had lied to me. He said he didn't have an army. He told me nothing about a brother with an entire regiment. He had to be punished.'

Gya was beside herself now. 'But they would have left you alone if you hadn't taken Namir in the first place. Just like the Emperor and the General wouldn't have been poisoned and attacked if they hadn't interfered with other people's lives. Who do you people think you are that you can just march onto another person's territory and do what you like just for your own self importance and self gratification?' She tried to compose herself as Cornelius turned away. 'I am clan Cornelius, I am a clan girl born to the Smilodon people. Remember my story about how I was a coward and watched my people being burned and ripped apart in front of my eyes?'

Cornelius looked towards the horizon outside.

'I can tell you know that the men who massacred my family came from here.' Cornelius turned. 'Yes Cornelius; General Domitrius Corbulo massacred my people on the orders of your father, the Emperor Gnaeus of Ataxata.' She hissed the words out, her mouth square with venom.

'Why have you never told me that before?' Cornelius faced her, hands clenched behind his back.

'Because I wanted to spare you the awful truth; that you are descended from a monster who had so much desire for power that he would stop at nothing to get it. But now we know what really happened don't we? We now know how he took those boys and made them fight to the death in horrifying conditions, and how he plundered and pillaged every clan and every castle for miles around in search of the Seal of Kings. That's why he attacked my clan, to find the Seal. And I have to tell you now, how I followed the blood of my people and how it brought me to Ataxata, and how it took me to the palace and I swore on that very day that I would kill the General and your father.'

'So why didn't you?' Cornelius' voice was thick and insulting.

'Because I loved you too much, I couldn't put you through any more suffering. You had lost your mother and your sister. I just couldn't do it; even though I hated them much more than I loved you and wanted them both dead, something stopped me.'

'You should have done it. I hated them as well.' Cornelius turned away again and looked out of the window.

Gya hovered by the Emperor's shoulder and continued airing her truths. 'But what happened was, that man up there killed them for me. Namir and his people with the girl they call Skyrah; they did it. I owe that man everything, and you have nearly killed him.' She started to pace about the room, thinking, contemplating, planning her next move. She was crimson with rage, her hands clasped behind her back.

Cornelius continued with his line of defence.

'He lied to me about his army. You can never trust these kind of people. If I let him go he will get his army to defeat me.'

'But if he dies then his brother will come back with an army anyway.'

'Well then I will imprison him also.'

'You sicken me to the very core Cornelius, just like you were with the turtle on the paradise island, you

301

couldn't leave it alone could you, couldn't just listen to the people who knew best and wanted the turtle left alone on its own ground where it had come to spawn in peace year after year. No, not you; just like your father before you, you can't see the severity of your actions and the ultimate disasters that will inevitably follow, even when it's staring you right in the face.' Gya turned on her heels, she was much too angry now and couldn't bear to be in the same room as this possessed soul.

But Cornelius' temperament suddenly changed like the tempestuous sea wind and he leapt out in front of her. 'How dare you come into my room and speak to me like this, accusing me of all sorts and telling me what to do. Who do you think you are?'

Gya was forced to stop in her tracks and faced him again. 'Your father said something similar to me when I was trying to save you.'

Cornelius was now a finger's breadth away from her face. 'Well I must be more like him than I thought.'

Gya reached in even further. 'Right now that is my greatest fear.'

Cornelius snapped back. 'Here you go again Gya and I am tiring of you and your ramblings. You forget your place in this palace. I should have you locked up in the deepest dungeon and throw away the key for speaking to me the way you do.'

Gya stepped forward and lowered her tone. 'He said that to me as well - now please step aside; I am not going to let that man die.'

She ran to her room, scattering everything from

her table except the things that mattered; bottles, tablets, potions, liniment, a flagon of water. She hurriedly put them in a leather pouch and then spun on her heels to get back to the tower. Down the marble steps she flew, along the vast hallways and adjacent corridors, past the magnificent state rooms. The guards were still on their tea break as she swept through the huge doors to the gardens. Scurrying along the path to the outside tower she moved quickly. There was no time to lose. The stairs were tiring her now, she pushed herself to her limits to reach Namir. Throwing the door wide she called him.

But it was empty. He had gone. She looked for him everywhere, even though it was an absurd thing to do. But she couldn't believe that he had moved, he was far too weak. But then her mind played even more absurd tricks; had the guards got to him first? Or worse, Cornelius?

'That man will surely perish if I don't get to him,' her voice was fraught.

She ran to the stables. The urgency in her voice was rife. The stable boy came out at once. 'Macus, have you seen anyone; the guards, Cornelius, or a young man, he is very thin and very pale, he would be wearing my cloak?'

'No Gya I haven't seen any of them, I am sorry. Who is the young man you speak of ?'

'Your saviour, and mine, and I hope it is his totem guiding him and not those who would wish to harm him.'

'It's Namir isn't it?" Macus looked anxious. 'I recognised him when he first came here.'

'Yes, it is him.'

'I did nothing to help him Gya.'

'You didn't know Macus. I didn't know till now.'

'But I did know, I knew exactly what they were doing to him.' His voice was solemn.

Gya put her hand on his shoulder. 'We all have moments when we are afraid Macus, but you learn from them and you step up the next time.'

He looked at her with searching eyes. 'What can I do to help now?'

'You can saddle me up a horse and be quick about it, I have to find him before he dies out there.'

'Do you want me to come with you?'

'No it's all right, I should be able to track him easily enough.'

Macus quickly got the fastest horse ready and brought him out to the pacing Gya. 'Here, you will need my coat as well, the weather is going to change, I can feel it.'

Gya looked up into the swollen grey sky. 'Yes you are right, thank you Macus. Are you sure you are not clan?'

He smiled and helped her into the warm apparel. 'No, just a farmer's son, so we have been brought up with looking out for change.'

'Farmer's son, clan girl, we are the same Macus, we can both sense change.'

She had one foot in the stirrup when a loud

booming voice came up behind her.

'You are not going anywhere Gya, or is Gye or Marquis de Beauchamp? Whatever your name is, you are an imposter and I did not give you permission to leave.'

Gya looked at Macus with a withering look; she took her foot out of the stirrup and faced her accuser. 'You are going to have to fight me to stop me Cornelius, you do know that don't you?'

From behind his back Cornelius produced two swords. 'I thought you might say that.' And threw one to Gya. 'Take the horse inside Macus, I will be needing that in a few minutes.'

The words came pale and thin from the Emperor's mouth. Macus did as he was told and taking back his coat, gave one last look at Gya.

31

Dragging himself along, Namir picked out the vast plains that were heavy with the bulbous clouds of frozen snow. He was heading towards the forest now, he remembered that direction from another time. After what seemed like hours, he could barely see the grey outline of the mountains on the horizon; his boots were sodden and his feet were freezing as he made his way over the barren fields. Straining, Namir took another step, it was fragile and heavy at the same time. He was very weak now. 'I can't go on,' he cried. 'I just can't, I've got nothing left.'

His body wasn't his anymore; the weather was turning now, his body just wasn't strong enough. 'I have to find a flowering yarrow, that's what I need. There should be some still here in the undergrowth.'

But his disorientated mind led him to the wrong plants and his search was futile. He rested a while beside a trunk and woke up feeling even more cold. How long had he been there he wondered, he had no concept of time anymore. The first flurries of snow had started and already he had a thin layer over him and he wore it like another coat; he brushed it off and stood up heavily but he knew that within the hour he would be covered again. His steps were now dragging. He had to find shelter, or should he keep going, he didn't know which to do. He thought that if he stopped moving he would surely die, but he was getting very weak now. 'Perhaps I am going to die anyway,' he thought to himself. He pulled his cloak tighter round him.

He had found a lambswool tunic, boots and a pair of breeches to wear in the stables. He didn't have time to get a horse. He had heard someone coming. Fearful it was the Emperor he had disappeared quickly. But he was thankful for the time to get these clothes, even though the weight slowed him down.

He felt rocks beneath the crisp white blanket and looked out for a cave, but the powdered crystals were falling so heavily now he couldn't see very far at all. Overhanging trees held out their branches for him to grip onto and each time they released a fresh falling onto him. He would stop soon he thought to himself, only a few more steps, he could build a fire, he would soon be warm. His body ached now. His old wound felt as if it had opened up again and a thousand daggers were twisting inside him.

He gripped his stomach and groaned. 'Help me please.'

He heard a noise and turned on his heel, his ankle twisted and he dropped to the ground as the pain shot up his leg. 'Lyall, I need you, where are you in my darkest hour.'

Whatever he heard had moved away, maybe it was a snow leopard he thought, but that would leave him alone wouldn't it? The snow leopard was his animal totem, no, that wouldn't harm him.

He stood up and limped along, grabbing branches, then he heard it again, the same noise. There was someone there.

'Lyall, is that you?' his loud whisper was fuelled with panic. 'Lyall, I'm here, I'm very cold.'

There was definitely something out there.

'I can't walk anymore. Help me. Please.'

He lay down on a snowbank, sprawled out with his face upwards and looked towards a swollen grey sky. He didn't know whether it was night or day, they had morphed into one now. The drift had made him blind and the grey tinged boundary made everything seem dark. He didn't know how long he had been walking or what had happened to him. How on earth had he ended up here? Was it a bad dream?

'No,' he said out loud. 'Dreams are never this real.' He remembered a woman though, a beautiful young woman. He tried to reach out for her but she kept melting away. The woman made him feel happy and warm, he remembered her smell, he tried to picture her face. But it evaporated into the cold air.

Then he saw it. A huge head standing over him. Condensation billowed from huge nostrils and tendrils of frozen ice hung from its mouth. It snorted once and sent particles of frozen spray raining down on him. Namir smiled, that's all he could do now. 'Have you come here to take me. Is this what happens when you die?'

The beast snorted again and pawed at the ground with its hoof. A jewel encrusted foot was inches from his head. He lifted himself up. Something else moved. Something came round towards him. It made a sound but he couldn't understand what it said.

'Who are you? What do you want?' His voice was fragile and thin, he could barely speak but the survivor in him wasn't about to give up just yet. He sat up on one elbow to get a better look. Snow was still falling and blocked his vision, he wiped at his lashes, they had frozen together.

The apparition was next to him now. 'Are you my saviour or my destroyer?' And then he collapsed.

32

Gya had grabbed the sword. She was not at her best, she knew that. After two months in confinement her muscles had stiffened, her fighting edge had gone. But it was nothing compared to the change in Cornelius; he was so consumed with hatred and loathing he would not be able to focus, and that was the secret of the sword; for accuracy is more vital than power.

He came at her like a man possessed, going straight for her heart, but she was light on her feet and leapt away. That gave her respite enough to calm herself and engage with her enemy. He came at her again, jousting, stabbing and dancing around her and howled with such words she really believed him to be a devil now. He aimed for her throat and her heart, the two places that would inflict certain death. She was blocking all the time while he used up most of his energy. She spun round on her heel and slashed him across the brow, his response caught her below the breast. They retreated, never taking their eyes of each other and fought in silence; something she had always taught him to do.

'Accuracy is more vital than power', she said to herself again.

Suddenly he leapt behind her and yanked her head back, but she slammed her hard boot down onto his soft slipper and he cried out in pain. Calling her every name under the sun he retreated again and composed his stance.

Inside the stables the horses were frightened, she could hear them shrieking and kicking the doors trying to get out amid the sound of Macus trying to comfort them. She had taken her focus off her adversary and he caught her under the chin, she wiped at the cut and saw the blood on her sleeve. Undeterred, she relaxed and studied his form, particularly the distance between him and the point of her sword. She waited patiently as he danced around her and then launched in catching his shoulder with a deep cut as he moved sidewards.

Her arm was aching and a nick to her lip caused her mouth to fill with blood. She spat it out and refocused. His obscene words were being thrown thick and fast, even quicker than his blade. She recoiled at both. She wanted to shout back at him but her throat was dry so she just grunted with every swipe. She was backing away from his fearsome advances, throwing herself to the left, then back again to the right, she ran up the stable wall and tumbled in the air till she was behind him. She took a section of his right ear off and as he spun round completely enraged she took the other ear off. His hand flew to the missing appendage so she slashed him hard across the thigh, his leg went out from under him and he stumbled.

He saw a disused steel bucket and threw it at her, it caught her temple and she staggered back. He picked up a rock that caught her in the chest and took the wind out of her, she held her left hand up to her throat, she couldn't breathe now. Short bursts of frantic panting got in the way of her precision. She ran into him screaming and bellowing, but he threw down his weapon, swept the sword out of her grasp with his left hand, and punched her in the stomach wth his right. She was now doubled over. He booted the sword away and then kicked her onto her back.

'You thought you could over throw me?' he bellowed, striking her in the ribs.

Pushing with her feet she tried to back away from him, but he pulled her back and stamped on her shin. She swallowed the scream. 'I taught you well Cornelius, I taught you well.' Her voice was weak and thin now.

'You were never a match for me.' And his spittle ran down her cheek.

He sat astride her and with both hands round her throat started to throttle her. The life was going out of her now, she couldn't breathe and had no energy left to throw him off. Her arms were useless, she had no power, no muscle, no energy to fight this brute. She wouldn't be able to save Namir. They were both doomed. This wasn't supposed to happen. On a better day she would have won, but coming out of confinement; he was right, she was no match for him.

But then she saw Macus out of the corner of her

eye and he leapt on the back of Cornelius pulling at his head to release the grip.

'Get off me you filthy rodent,' barked Cornelius. 'You are a servant and you are forgetting your place.'

Macus would not let go. 'I can't let you do this, there has been too much bloodshed here already and there will be no more.'

The Emperor roared in fury, he swung his arm behind him and grabbed hold of Macus by his shirt. 'By who's orders?' And he pulled him off his back and threw him against the stable wall. Macus slid down and a trickle of blood oozed from his head. Cornelius followed in with a rain of hammering blows. Macus' defending arms did little to stave off the ferocious attack.

'Cornelius no!' shouted out Gya, her voice strained. 'Leave him.'

Cornelius turned to her, his eyes were narrow and a wicked smile exposed hungry incisors.

'Eliminating three savages in one day! I think the General is guiding me.'

'You are possessed by something Cornelius, be it power, envy, or cowardice, I know not what, but you are a changed man.'

A brutal fist smashed down on her face. 'Coward! are you calling me a coward? How dare you!' He wrapped his hands round her throat again.

But Macus opened one eye, the other was bruised and swollen. His lip was split, his face was cut. He managed to withdraw something from his boot and slid it towards the helpless girl along the gravel. She inched at it with outstretched fingers, just a bit more, just a little further. She grabbed the handle and spun it in her hand. With one last ounce of effort she plunged it into the Emperor's side. 'Accuracy is more vital than power.'

His weight collapsed on top of her. She pushed him off and rolled away so she was laying on her back again.

'Are you all right?' groaned the boy in a shallow whisper.

She couldn't talk, her hands flew up to her throat and she calmed her breathing. 'Thank you,' she strained. 'You saved my life.'

'I didn't want to kill him Gya, but he left me no choice.' Macus was still recovering from the beating; legs outstretched with his back supported by the stable wall.

'I know you didn't Macus, neither did I.' Gya sat up awkwardly. 'I think you took the worst of it though.' Her face didn't agree as the palm of her hand nursed an injured jaw.

'There would have been more bloodshed if he had lived, and Ataxata needs to thrive again.' Macus exonerated his actions.

'I know Macus, neither of us had a choice,' she looked over at the corpse. 'But we need to get rid of the body before the guards come out.' The enormity of the situation became perilous. 'Are you able to ride?' She asked anxiously.

'Yes I think so.' He pulled himself up and winced as the blood rushed to his head.

'That eye will need looking at first.' She got to her feet and moved towards him but he pulled his head away.

'We haven't got time Gya, we have to get rid of this body. The weather won't wait for us and the guards will be doing their rounds soon, we have to go now.'

'Yes you are right. You take the body and dump it up at Break Pass Ridge. The gorge opens up into the bowels of the earth under a naturally formed bridge. I will find Namir and meet you there as soon as I can. Then we will travel to the Smilodon Fort. It's the closest settlement to Ataxata.'

'Your old settlement?'

'Yes, it's our only hope.'

Macus disappeared into the stables and brought out an old horse blanket. 'Here wrap the body in this and help me lift it onto the Emperor's horse. And get that bucket of sand to soak up the blood.'

The two of them pulled Cornelius face down onto his destrier, tied the stirrup leathers over the body and then began to cover up their tracks.

'Namir's horse is still here, I saddled her up. Hopefully the guards will think he has taken Namir back to his clan.'

'And when he doesn't return and we have gone as well?' She put the question to him gravely.

'We will need a saviour ourselves.'

33

She saw the frozen figure moulded into a snowbank; Gya had thought he was a corpse already, his body so skeletal and his skin so pale, even against the freshly fallen snow he looked even whiter. It was only after she had dismounted and bent over him she heard him whisper.

'Are you my saviour or my destroyer?'

'I am your saviour Namir, you will come with me now, I will take you to safety.' She bent down to him. 'Here, take this, it was given to me to replace lost minerals and vitamins. You need it now.' She gently poured the liquid into a thimble sized vessel and he took the healing nectar.

'Skyrah gives me the yarrow flower,' he whispered. 'But this tastes just as good.'

'Maybe it is the yarrow flower ground down into a liquid. It certainly helped me.'

He pulled the cloak tighter round him.

'You need fluid as well,' she offered a flagon of water. 'Just little sips, you are severely malnourished and your body will reject it if you take too much.'

'It's all right, I have little strength to take too much anyway,' his voice was patchy.

'But now we have to get you back up on your horse. She is here waiting for you.'

He got to his feet like a fragile old man, brushed the snow off his shoulders and leaned in towards his destrier. 'I've missed you my beauty.' She nuzzled in to him and he felt the warmth from her withers.

'Are you ready Namir? I think we should ride together so I can hold on to you. I don't want you falling off.'

Gya helped him up into the saddle and she sat behind him. That way he was sandwiched between two pillars of body heat. The second horse followed by way of a lead rein. As the hills grew steeper, it got more perilous for the horses. Drifts of snow cracked under their hooves and where the ground had solidified they began to slip. Namir was packed in so tightly that he had fallen asleep with the gentle rocking motion of his steed.

It was still light when she spotted Macus. He was waiting for them, standing in the middle of a natural bridge above a cavernous gorge. Far below raged the mountain floods.

'Have you disposed of the body?' she asked, dismounting gently so as not to wake Namir.

He looked down into the endless ravine. 'He won't ever be found again.'

She followed his gaze into the pits of hell and felt a sudden ache of remorse. 'Foolish man, it didn't have to end this way.'

'I think it did Gya. Too much power breeds

uncontrollable hatred and greed. I've seen it so many times and I saw it in Master Cornelius' eyes as soon as I told him about Namir's army defeating the General. I knew he wouldn't rest until he had absolute power. If we hadn't have killed him back there, then there would have been more blood on his hands.' He looked down into the ravine. 'I have stood by for too long and watched young boys be taken as prisoners and made to fight to the death. I have seen whole families ripped apart by despicable acts of cruelty.' He was struck with uncontrollable sadness. 'I could have saved Namir weeks ago, instead of which I stood back like a coward because I was too scared to do anything.'

'You are not a coward Macus. You must never think that. You said it yourself; you witnessed torture, you watched the General burn a family to death because their daughter escaped. Of course that was at the back of your mind. You were protecting your own family.'

'I still should have helped him,' he was frantically searching for answers in the gorge. 'It will haunt me forever.'

'Macus look at me.'

Eyes full of sorrow faced her.

'A long time ago, I watched the General slaughter my people. I hid under a wagon while I heard my father begging for his life and my mother screaming for the life of her children. I can still hear the cries of my younger siblings as they died. The General killed all of my people and I did nothing. I was too scared and mute so I hid myself away and tried to block it out.'

They held the empowering silence while coming to terms with their lack of courage in desperate times.

'So where did you get your strength from?' he asked in awe.

'A wise old man showed me the way, he taught me how to overcome my fears, he showed me the way of the sword and how to find my courage. When I did that, I swore that I would get vengeance for the death of my people.'

'So you killed the Marquis and took his identity?'

'It wasn't as simple as that Macus. The Marquis took something of mine and didn't honour an agreement.' She looked down into the gorge. 'He paid the ultimate price in the end though.'

'And then you came for revenge, to kill the General and the Emperor?'

'I did; but Master Cornelius was a vulnerable young man then. I didn't want to corrupt him and change him into a monster by killing his father.'

Their thoughts emptied into the ravine. The irony was left there to fester.

'It seems that corruption and evil was always in his blood,' said Macus pitifully recognising the truth.

'I think it was... and he followed that spiral downwards... unfortunate man.' She looked up from the cavern and faced him. 'But destiny has shown you your own strength and courage Macus. You are a hero now, you saved my life and you saved Namir.'

Macus thought about it for a while. 'Well, when you put it like that.' He tilted his head with a shrug.

'Our destiny is always out there, it just takes a while to find it.'

'Thank you.'

Namir stirred and brought her back to the moment. 'This man here is another hero, and we have to get him to my village. Plus your face needs attention.'

'I had forgotten about that.' He winced when he touched his swollen eye and cut lip. 'But I thought you said the Smilodon Fort had been burnt to the ground with no survivors.'

34

Break Pass Ridge was a series of passes and steep twisting ridges that curved back down through glades and grottos that were dappled with the rays of a struggling sun. Back in the summer it would have been a truly wondrous sight. Meadows full of summer blooms would have heralded their arrival and supreme raptors nesting in the heights would have come down to hunt in those very fields, their lazy circles suspended on magnificent bronze wings that flashed gold from the sun. Alpine hares and mountain goats would have jumped from glen to glade and rodents would have burrowed deep in the marshes.

But on a day like today, the scene was of a glistening white blanket, tinged with silver from the refections, while the sky was a mottled shade of grey as the sun struggled to break through. Today, the sky was as solemn as the town of Ataxata behind them, and the snow fell softly and steadily, muffling the sound of their horses' hooves and sticking to their frozen faces.

They rode north, away from Break Pass Ridge, following the mountain tracks, over the weathered field and into the dense forest. Gya took the lead, keeping her mount to a steady pace and guiding with the reins whilst holding on to Namir at the same time. Macus followed her with the two other horses as best he could. Every so often they both glanced behind them to see if they were being followed, but the snow was their ally today and was covering their tracks within seconds. The guards would surely know that something was wrong soon, with Namir and the Emperor gone, plus herself and Macus, and four horses. What would they do to them? She dared not dwell on it. But her mind was working overtime now. Of course the guards wouldn't think that. They would think that Cornelius had taken Namir home, just like they had discussed. And they would not associate any link between Macus and herself - she hoped. Nevertheless, the whole reason for going this way was because of the tricky mountain path, and because not many people knew this way.

When they crossed another bridge Gya turned her horse to the right and followed the twisting course of the river for half a mile before scrambling up a stony bank and back amongst the trees again. Even though she was sure no one knew this way, she couldn't leave anything to chance. They could not stay on the road. Macus did not question her choice, he had every faith in her; she was a clan girl. And after the feat that Skyrah pulled off the previous year; who was he to question anything a girl did.

The snow seemed to be less furious now and the group were able to keep to a steady pace. The soft broken ground was still treacherous with half buried roots and hidden stones. She heard Macus' horse stumble and she quickly turned to check he was all right. They crossed another road, its edges lined with the mush of decaying leaves and topped with the recent fall of snow and rain. Up and down hills they went, through brambles and briars and tangles of underbrush and along gullies where they had to duck and dive below the weighted branches.

'Not long now Macus,' she called back.

Namir stirred in front of her. 'Are you all right?' she whispered, aware that he was awake now.

His groan was weary in response, and she couldn't make out what he was saying.

'We need to stop a while Macus, I need to give Namir some more medication.'

'I think the horses need a rest as well Gya, we have covered a good amount of ground so far and they are tiring.'

The wooded glade gave them protection as Macus helped to lift Namir gently down. He took a rug from the side of his horse and laid it out for the frail man.

'Thank you,' said Namir weakly.

'Here take this, and Gya poured another spoonful of medicine into his open mouth. 'It will help your recovery. And take these pills, they will give you added minerals.'

'Where are we going?' Namir asked through thin lips, licking every last ounce of the healing nectar and swallowing the tablets whole.

'I am taking you to the Smilodon Fort, it's my tribal home. The last time I saw it, the General was burning it down, but I am sure there must be somewhere untouched where we can rest in safety.'

'What about my home, the Clan of the Mountain Lion, can't we go there?' his voice was tiny.

'It is too far, you are not strong enough. Smilodon is the closest settlement I can assure you. I promise I will get you strong again, then I...,' she looked over to Macus, '...we, can return you to your people.'

Namir smiled a weak smile.

'Here, I have something that belongs to you.' She took the pendant out of her pocket and secured it gently round his neck. 'It's the picture of your mother.'

He clasped it and started to weep. 'How can I ever repay you?'

'You already have.'

A fragile hand touched her own as a sign of gratitude and he closed his eyes again as the medication began to work.

Macus was with the horses, feeding them from a bag of oats he had brought with him. He patted each of them and stroked their soft muzzles.

'You're a kind man Macus,' said Gya, noticing the rapport he had with the destriers.

'I love these horses, they are such majestic animals that only want to serve their riders.'

'Perhaps they have lessons to teach us,' Gya surmised.

'I think they do,' he agreed.

'Come and sit with me a while dear friend,' she said, patting the rug. 'You know all about me, so tell me more about you.'

'What's there to tell?' he said quietly, almost embarrassed to divulge the entire contents of his dull life to someone who had lived so much.

'I'm truly interested. How old are you? Do you have siblings? What does your future look like?'

'That's a huge task to answer in one go,' he stammered with a smile.

She grinned back and her expression encouraged him to continue.

'Well, I'm nearly twenty four years old now and been working in the stables for about ten years,' he laughed at the memory. 'Where does the time go? Now that I say it out loud, ten years is quite a long time.'

'Yes, it is,' she said thoughtfully, her own memories taking her back that same length of time to when her people were slaughtered.

'A fourteen year old whipper snapper, knee high to a grasshopper,' he laughed.

She tittered at the allegory.

'I had worked with my father on the farm since I was about four years old, helping drive big old Betsy on a mouldboard plough,' he drew a thin smile and breathed out a sigh of reminiscence.

'You've always liked horses then?' she asked, pulling her legs into her chest and wrapping her arms around them.

'I have indeed, Betsy was such a good old Shire; such a strong girl.'

She smiled at the affection.

'I loved working on the farmstead, I helped with the geese and the chickens, looked after the pigs. I played with the dogs which infuriated my father: 'They're working dogs, not pets!' he would bellow.' Macus relived the memory. 'I saluted the buzzard when I heard her mew, I aspire to the call. But I couldn't kill any animals; not even a rabbit,' he bit his bottom lip gently.

She looked at him sympathetically as he continued.

'The day came when I had to kill the sow. I had tended her since she was a new born. I had held her in my arms, petted her, stroked her and now I was expected to kill her for my supper. My father gave me a knife and said: 'Ignore the squealing, for she will scream and shriek from the pit of her stomach. But ignore it son, just ignore it.'

Gya winced, Macus recoiled at the memory, his head hung low.

'So what did you do?'

'I did what any normal fourteen year old boy would do in the same circumstances.'

Gya raised her eyebrows.

'I let her go. I told her to run and she did...we never saw her again!'

'Wow, and your father, what did he do?'

'Gave me a beating and a few strokes of the

cane for good measure, and then sent me up to the palace to earn a wage, saying I would be no good as a farmer and no good to him.'

'That must have been hard for you.'

'It was. I was leaving behind my mother who sobbed into her apron for days before I went. But it would have been harder to kill an animal which I would have had to do if I had stayed on the farm.'

'What about your father? Didn't he need help on the land?'

'I have two younger brothers, so they stayed and did all the hunting and killing; they're made of tougher stuff than me, I'm just a big old wuss.'

'You're not a wuss, you are a very caring man with a gentle nature. I can see now why you kept your head low at the palace.'

'I would have been sent back to the farm if I had been caught interfering; but my family or someone else's family would have been burned to death in one of those cages first. Skyrah managed to kill most of the palace so that wasn't an option when she did it. I still got a good beating from the General when it happened but it was Meric, the physician, who stopped the wrath of the madman that time and then Namir's army who stopped him altogether.' He looked over at the sleeping hero and then over at the horses. 'Look at them; so loyal, so calm and peaceful.' His mind was a conundrum of thoughts as he admired both. 'I should have been born a horse.'

Gya laughed. 'But then I wouldn't have met you

and had this lovely chat with you.'

'Well you wouldn't have missed much would you?'

She looked at him with a coy gaze, he dropped his eyes instantly. A girl had never looked at him like that before.

'It's so nice to meet someone like you,' she said. 'For too long I have faced death and destruction, greed and corruption. It's so refreshing to talk to a gentle, kind person with no hatred running through their veins. There's not many like you about you know.' She looked over at Namir sleeping and remembered the old man who had taught her. 'Well maybe just one or two.'

'I find it fascinating talking to you,' he replied gallantly. 'All your experiences, how you have overcome your fears. Your fights,' he smiled. 'You are really quite remarkable.'

She concealed a blush between her knees before looking at him again. 'You are remarkable Macus; for someone who hates conflict and battles, you have acted with such courage and valour today. You saved my life, Namir's life and now your own life has taken a completely different direction.'

He blushed at the accolade. 'I know. But I do hope that's the first and last time I have to assist in killing a living creature. I did it because I...,' he stopped himself saying the words and changed it quickly before he messed up. '...because I had to.'

'Well, I am forever in your debt and I sincerely hope that wherever we end up, it will be more peaceful, and maybe we can look after chickens, pigs, dogs and horses,' she smiled through her vision of the future. 'I really need a peaceful life now.'

He took her hand and kissed it. 'That's all I want from life too, a peaceful existence.'

She leaned in to kiss him on the lips, and he followed her lead. Against the cold of the late morning air, a warmth was suddenly catapulted around their veins. Their hearts beat like never before and the emotions of the last ten years evaporated in an instant. Something had happened to everyone that day. This would be the start of things to come.

'Come Macus, the daylight will not last, let's get Namir back on the horse and be on our way.'

He leaned in to kiss her once more. Namir was awake now. He had been dreaming about Skyrah.

35

A short time later Gya and Macus sensed they were nearing the end of their journey, as a vast canyon appeared before them and their pace began to slow. The mountains that bordered each side of the valley virtually disappeared as the route exposed a wide expanse of land where huge embankments and broad trenches acted as protective rings round the newly constructed city. Scattered boulders and piles of stones that once represented a bygone civilisation were the only evidence of a much simpler community and Gya couldn't believe her eyes.

'Is this the right place?' asked Macus in awe, for he had never seen anything quite like it in his life either.

Gya was speechless and Namir sat in front of her in his weakened state unable to take in the spectacle.

The entire settlement was divided into three areas and set into a massive hilltop plateau. The walls that encircled it went further than the eye could see and were set with a range of strategically placed lookout towers. Within the complex was the statuesque citadel; a massive defensive core that rose high out of the ground, protecting the entire settlement with precision and power; the last line of defence should any enemy breach the other components of this impressive fortified system. Another domed building with a spire that disappeared into the clouds preceded that, and around the inside lay more assembly halls and meeting houses set closely together in a uniform style. The city within this girdle of stone was equally impressive with tiled courtyards, bustling markets, a school of learning, a place of worship, and beyond that in the lower town, the dwellings where people lived were more scattered and varied. It was unlike any other place they had ever seen.

'Who goes there?' Came the booming order from the sentry guard.

The platoon around him raised their bows and with squinting eyes aimed their arrows.

'It is I, Gya. I am from the Smilodon Clan that was attacked in this very place ten years ago. I have Namir, leader of the clans with me; he is very sick and we seek assistance.'

The platoon instantly lowered their weapons and looked at each other in amazement, then they looked at their Captain for instructions. The Captain was issuing an order to a guard below him who could be heard scurrying off at once. The huge gates were opened and the troops stood to attention as they entered.

The soldier saluted her. 'Welcome home Gya, and we have been given orders to send Namir to the infirmary straight away.'

Namir was still sitting in front of her barely hanging on. As soon as he felt he was safe, his eyes glazed over and he collapsed.

'Guards! Guards!' came the frantic orders from the Captain.

Four soldiers threw down their weapons and leapt to catch Namir as Gya released her grip on him.

'Get him to the infirmary at once!' came the order. 'Do not stop for anyone, or anything!'

The guards disappeared with Namir into the warren amid the mollified gaze of his rescuers.

The stable boys were at their side now and took the reins as they encouraged them to dismount. Gya and Macus jumped off, albeit a little worn and weary and let the lads take their horses to the stables. They were now facing the Captain looking totally dumfounded.

'How did you know about Namir?' she asked.

'Namir's brother, King Lyall of Durundal came looking for him about a month ago, he was with seven comrades.'

'Eight of them?'

'Yes, only eight ma'am.'

'Gya rolled her eyes. 'Cornelius told me it was an entire army.'

'No ma'am, only eight warriors I can assure you. I let them in myself. The whole fort knows about the battle of Ataxata and how the murdering scum of a General has been slain and the Emperor Gnaeus poisoned. We are indebted to them. King Lyall and his party stayed overnight but they were on their way by dusk the next day as they had to check other clans. We have been under orders to be vigilant ever since.'

'Namir will be pleased to know that, but they had a wasted journey going to other clans I am afraid,' said Gya solemnly.

'How so?' asked the Captain.

'Because Namir has been imprisoned this whole time at the palace. We had to kill the Emperor Cornelius, Gnaeus' son, to get Namir out.'

The soldier went down on one knee to express his gratitude. 'My bended knee is not enough dear lady.'

'It was both of us; Namir and I would surely be dead if it wasn't for Macus.'

The sentry saluted Macus. 'Noble knight, it is my honour.' Out of the corner of his eye the sentry saw the Matriarch approaching. He stood to attention and waited in that position for her to reach them.

'Has Namir been taken to the infirmary?' she asked hurriedly.

'Yes ma'am, he has.'

'Good, excellent, now who pray are these dear people.'

'This is Gya ma'am, from our own Smilodon clan,' said the Captain with a proud stance.

Gya dipped in a curtsey in front of the Matriarch.

'And this is her noble knight, Macus.'

'Well I'm not really a knight,' Macus began, and bowed to the lady. 'But thank you sir for the accolade.'

'You killed the Emperor, you are a brave knight

from the highest order in my book.'

The soldier saluted them both, bowed to the Matriarch and went back to his post.

An extended hand began the introduction

'My name is Myra, and I am the Matriarch here. I run the Smilodon Fort with several other leaders, who you will all meet in due course. But for now we have to get you two treated as well.'

Gya hadn't realised how weak she had become, she had been so preoccupied with getting Namir to safety that she hadn't really thought about herself. She felt her head going dizzy and she reached out for Macus. He was there instantly to grab her as she collapsed in his arms.

'She has fought bravely for the past two days,' he said to the Matriarch as he followed her through the streets. 'She fought with Cornelius, and she saved Namir. She is a remarkable woman.' He kissed her forehead as he carried her in his arms.

'You all look like you have had to fight to survive,' noticed Myra.

'Sometimes we have to fight to get to where we want to be,' Macus answered.

The Matriarch knew exactly what he meant and carried on through the winding paths that would lead to the infirmary. 'I will talk to you in more detail later,' she said kindly. 'But I am aware you are dreadfully fatigued and need medical treatment without delay. We are nearly there.' She led him up some steps and in through the huge double doors that led to a massive room.

The infirmary was the third largest building in the fortress, after the imposing Citadel and Grand Committee Rooms. The floor was panelled with lengths of polished rose wood where rows of beds were sectioned off with moveable embroidered partitions. A ceiling of porcelain murals and gilt edged cherubs fed into tiled walls of diverse mosaics of the Smilodon symbol and raised stuccos of wood nymphs and beautiful goddesses. At the far end of the room, patio doors stretched from floor to ceiling, which, in the summer months and warmer days, opened up onto a manicured lawn that led further to a man made lake. Pillars, fountains, grottos and gazebos adorned the equilibrium of tranquility; and scattered in between were places to sit, lay, curl and repose.

Faint weaves of steam rose from the sunken pool which ran adjacent to the patio which was constantly renewed and warmed from the pipes below. The whole room smelled of ginger and lime while wafts of yarrow essence filled the air.

They could see Namir laying on a bed with four physicians around him.

'Will he be all right?' asked Macus with a concerned look.

'He will be now; I promise you,' Myra assured him patting his arm. 'Put Gya on this bed, I will send a couple of maids over.'

Macus put her down on the bed and started to take off her outer garments; he saw the Matriarch talking to some girls who hurriedly collected various bowls, vials and cleaning potions. Myra then went over to Namir and the girls came over to help him.

They were separated now by the partitions. Macus was stripped of his clothes and bathed with the warm water. His facial wounds were cleaned with a medicated gel and left to administer their healing properties. A soft white robe was draped over his body and a vial of soothing liquid was given to him. As he slipped under the cool silk sheets on the sleigh of a bed, his head gradually gave way to the aromatic smells and he succumbed to sleep.

Namir lay there a couple of beds down while nutrients and minerals were being administered into his skeletal frame, like the flow of oxygen and other essentials through the life giving umbilical cord. Slowly his body began the process of repair and as the hours and days passed, the rate increased. And as the new cells were forged, so he began to get stronger.

36

Namir came to his senses slowly, a hazy light obscured
the grey blur of sleep; he opened his eyes believing that
he was in the castle, but the sounds of running water
weren't familiar, neither were the surroundings.
Someone was humming, the air was scented. It took a
moment for him to place the sweet smell; a special
essence used for the sick. He breathed in the incense
and placed it as a waft of yarrow flower igniting his
body. He smiled at the recollection and knew he was
safe. He didn't know where, but he felt warm and at
ease now. He pulled himself up onto his elbow, though
every fibre in his body felt heavy as he moved and
became aware that he was on a proper bed now, not just
a palette or a pile of animal skins. This bed was
massive. It was as wide as three of those put together
with raised sides of rich mahogany, a soft plump pillow
supported his head and a smooth yellow silk sheet
covered his body. He looked beneath the covers, his
clothes had been discarded and in place was a soft
white tunic. He had been bathed and his skin looked
clean and of a better colour now. A young girl came
over to him and the humming stopped.

'Master Namir, are you all right?'

'Where am I?' his voice was soft and curious.

'In the infirmary of the Smilodon Fort.'

'How long have I been here?'

'Several weeks now, Master Namir. You were in a very bad way; very dehydrated and suffering from malnutrition. If our Gya hadn't got to you when she did, you would certainly have died.'

'She gave me pills and potions... I remember now.'

'The contents of those pills and potions have been tested and analysed; she saved your life Master Namir.'

'I need some water,' his voice was becoming fragile again.

She took a small drinking bowl and poured from a water jug.

'Here, you must drink slowly though, just small sips, the physicians are tending to you and say you must not rush things.'

'Yes I remember,' and slowly the events of the past year began to piece together again. 'Where is Gya now?' I need to see her.'

'She comes down every evening with Macus to see you and say goodnight, they will be both be here later; but now you must rest. The physicians will be here soon.'

After dozing off again he was roused by voices and opened his eyes to see another figure coming into the room. Dressed in a long violet gown with a gold embroidered rope round his middle, he wore a maroon physicians cap over his sparse white hair and came over to him carrying a tray of various goblets, potions and vials.

'Good afternoon Namir,' said the man with a small bow and a smiling face.

'Good afternoon,' replied Namir sitting up and leaned against the enormous pillow.

'I am pleased to see that you are recovering well. Me and my contemporaries have had to administer your nutrients via hourly drops; so it's very reassuring to see you up and able to take your medicine on your own now.'

'I have been asleep a long time,' said Namir still feeling fatigued.

'I know, we had to induce sleep, it makes for quicker healing,' said the physician, concentrating on his task of pouring precise measurements of potions from one vial to the other and then mixing from one goblet to another. When he was finished, the cordial was offered to Namir. 'This is your special tonic now.'

Namir took the goblet and peered inside. The liquid looked like green algae. He looked at the goblet then at the physician. An air of caution spread across his face.

'Your body needs this Namir, you must be careful what you eat right now, we do not want to overload your stomach. In a few days I will speak with our chefs and have them prepare some light dishes that will be suitable for you.'

Namir knocked back the infusion in one go, he

licked his lips and raised his eyebrows with a satisfied manner. 'That's actually very good, thank you.'

The physician smiled a contented grin. 'We aim to please here.'

The young girl came over. 'Would it be all right for Master Namir to take a dip in the sunken pool today?'

'I think that's an excellent idea,' said the physician looking at Namir. 'Just for a short time though, and maybe a couple of strolls round the room; nothing too much mind you, just a little to get his muscles working again.'

'Of course sir.'

She helped Namir over to the sunken pool. Carefully as he went, he slowly dipped a toe to feel the ambient temperature, when he was satisfied that it wasn't too hot, he sat on one of the seats that had been grooved into the sides. Covering his legs and lower torso, he had never felt anything so divine in all his life, aside from the touch of his wife that was. He leaned back in the crevasse and let himself be subdued in the jets of steam that coiled around his withered limbs. Looking out into the garden he thought that even its presence brought about a feeling of well being and was acutely aware of the healing process this place offered. Glowing lanterns lit up the sanctuary at this time of year and were hung in the most aesthetically pleasing places. He could see a curved bench by the side of a lake which even at this hour hailed an illuminated fountain of golds, silvers and greens. Nearing the end of December, the trees and bushes were covered with dense layers of snow, and looked almost magical in the glimmering moonlight. The maid brought over his cup of water and placed it next to him.

'Is there anything else I can get you Master Namir?'

'No, thank you. I am perfectly content.'

'You will hear a gong in a few minutes,' she said softly. 'Please do not be alarmed, it's only the dinner bell summoning the elders and guests to the Great Hall for supper.'

'That's where Gya and Macus will be heading I am guessing.'

'Indeed they will, and then they will come and see you,' she smiled.

He was in no rush to leave the refuge of the infirmary, and so it didn't bother him at all that his two saviours would be feasting on gourmet food and being entertained with delightful conversation while he supped alone on his water bowl.

At eight o clock precisely, Gya and Macus duly arrived to visit him and were thrilled when they saw that he was sitting up and looking more like his usual self. His hair was back to its glossy black layers now, his colour had returned and he sported his usual clean shaven look. The locket had been polished and could be seen glinting beneath the white tunic that he wore. He was back in his bed now and sipping from another vial of nutritionally dense cordial that the physician had

341

prepared.

'Namir I am so pleased to see you looking so well,' enthused Gya. 'You had me so worried a few times back there.'

He smiled at her. 'I need to thank you Gya for saving my life and bringing me back to this incredible fort.'

'You are most welcome. Though I have to be honest, I never dreamed that my people could rebuild a place on a scale of magnitude such as this.'

'It is truly remarkable isn't it,' he answered. 'I am astounded at their feats.'

Gya almost blushed with pride before relaying more revealing news. 'I believe that Lyall is drawing up plans as we speak to replicate it.'

'He's been here?'

'He came here looking for you,' said Macus. 'He told the elders everything about the battle between the clans and the palace and how he thought you had been imprisoned by the new Emperor. He said he had searched everywhere but couldn't find you.'

'The guards moved me from the tower while Lyall was talking to the Emperor,' said Namir witheringly. 'They knew that Lyall would look for me there, so I was bound and gagged and put in a meadow with my horse until he had gone.' He winced at the recollection.

'Lyall thought as much, but couldn't be certain. Cornelius told him that you had left the palace after the treaty was signed, so he scouted the clans searching for you - just in case Cornelius was telling the truth and you had fallen ill somewhere.' Gya shook her head in shame. 'The Smilodon people were aware and looking out for you.'

Namir shook his head as he took in all the information and reflected. From the lie to get him away from the camp, to his friend's sudden disappearance.

'Does anyone know what happened to Alun, he was supposed to be my guide but he went missing on the first night?'

Gya shook her head again. 'Sorry Namir, he was found downstream by members of your clan.'

'What had happened to him?'

Gya looked to Macus to deliver the horrendous news.

'He suffered a massive injury to the head Namir. He had been murdered.'

Namir bit down on his fist. 'I knew it. I knew he wouldn't have left me. He was an honourable man and would not have run away from his duty.'

'If it makes it any easier for you,' said Gya humbly, 'we have been told that he was given a pyre burial and that his soul is now in the afterlife.'

'Yes, that does make it easier to bear,' agreed Namir after contemplating the alternative. 'At least his totem brought him back, so our people could pray for him and give him an honourable ceremony.'

'It was after that sighting that Skyrah went through the tunnel to get Lyall's help,' said Gya choosing her words carefully. 'Some wondered if his totem chose him to alert the clan of the danger you were in.'

Namir pondered, not sure how to answer that supposition, instead he conveyed his thoughts of the living. 'You know, I have witnessed some dreadful things in the last few years,' he shook his head in dismay. 'But that new Emperor has so much hate and bitterness, he is a dangerous man.'

Gya and Macus looked at each other in disbelief. He didn't know.

'The Emperor is dead Namir, he won't be bothering you or anyone else again,' Macus almost whispered it.

Namir nearly choked on his potion. 'How?' he stammered, knocking back the heavenly liquid.

'Gya killed him,' Macus declared.

'Well it was both of us really,' Gya reacted humbly, raising an eyebrow to Macus.

'I merely threw a knife to her, Gya was the one who killed him. I cannot take any of the glory.'

'I know of another woman who did that,' said Namir proudly. 'Happily I am married to her. And I am truly honoured to be in the presence of such courageous human beings.'

'Your wife has been informed of your whereabouts,' said Macus kindly, wanting to share the news that Namir most sought. 'She is at Castle Dru with your brother and his wife and is in fine health.'

'How does she know I am here?' Namir looked shocked.

'A guard was deployed to the castle as soon as you arrived,' Macus clarified for him. 'Lyall was promised that he would be informed straightaway should you arrive here; and they kept to their word. The guard dutifully returned with news from the castle.'

Namir put down the vial and sobbed into his hands.

Gya sat down beside him and put an arm around him. 'Your whole clan is safe Namir, Lyall moved them all to the Castle.'

'Everyone?' He looked up from a teary face.

'Yes, everyone. I don't know how he did it, but everyone is there praying for you.'

'I can't wait to see them,' he sniffed back a runny nose.

'In a few more weeks Namir. The weather is treacherous out there, we wouldn't even attempt moving you now. You have to get strong and the weather has to improve greatly,' she urged.

'Let your people at the castle look after Skyrah, and let the physicians here look after you,' said Macus, raising Namir's spirits.

Gya threw Macus a loving smile and touched his hand affectionately.

The three of them discussed at length their tales of the past few months. Gya relayed her story from when she was a frightened little clan girl to the present day and Macus relayed the accounts from the palace over the past few years. Both of them talked about what they had learned from Myra, the Matriarch.

After two hours of chatter the maid came to break up the ensemble and switch off the lights. 'You can see him tomorrow, he will still be here,' she assured them, filling up Namir's water bowl and patting his pillow for him.

Gya kissed his cheek, Macus rubbed his shoulder. 'See you tomorrow,' they said together. 'May your dreams be sweet and filled with joy.'

Namir lay back and closed his eyes and filled his head with the sweetest dreams of his beautiful wife and unborn son living safely under the protection of Lyall and Arneb at Castle Dru, while he gathered his strength and fortitude under the watchful gaze of those at the Smilodon Fort.

37

After exactly one month of treatment, Namir was well enough to be moved to the main building where he was given a very comfortable apartment next to Gya and Macus. She had taken to reading to him from the books in the library during his time in the infirmary, so now that he was out of there, she was going to teach him to read and write as well. Macus' literacy skills were a little thin, so she had taken it upon herself to be their tutor; and so during these long winter months, it proved to be a highly valuable few hours in the day.

As well as having his own personal tutor, Namir had his own maid who would run his baths, bring his clean clothes and change his sheets every day. His room was spacious with a huge bed fit for a king; a deep sunken bath complete with jet steams of yarrow essence, a window that looked over the gardens and a mirror that ran the length of one wall.

The maid had closed the window for fear of him getting a chill, but he opened it wide and breathed in the fresh December air. He felt the air igniting his soul once again and let out a sigh of relief for his much welcomed freedom and good fortune.

This would be the first time that he would dine

in the Great Hall with the Matriarch, his friends and the appointed guests and dignitaries, all in the same room, together.

That evening he donned a long sleeved gown and slipped into a pair of grey flannel trousers and black slippers. He followed his friends to the Great Hall where a banquet was awaiting him. The Matriarch was standing alongside her deputies and began the applause as he strode in nodding to the dignitaries.

Taking his seat, the congregation were still on their feet and he kept rising to accept the fanfare. Gya and Macus sat either side of him and the Matriarch had to chime her glass with a silver spoon several times to get order.

'Thank you everyone, thank you,' she said over the gentle rumbles.

As it quietened sufficiently, she addressed the man himself. 'Namir, I think you can see by this reaction, that we all hold you in high esteem.'

He smiled and bit his bottom lip with an air of embarrassment. Gya touched his knee with pride and Macus patted him on the back.

'But to everyone concerned, I do not need to introduce this fine young man, you all know who he is. This is the man, whom, with his brother and their legions, defeated the General and the Emperor of Ataxata; and it is for this reason, that our own Gya from the original Smilodon Fort, who witnessed those very same monsters brutally killing her own people, has taken such heroic steps to save him.'

Namir kissed her cheek and the roars went up for Gya once more.

Myra continued, 'I am so proud of all those in the infirmary who have worked day and night to bring this man back from the brink of death.'

Namir, Gya and Macus joined in the applause and nodded their heads in agreement.

'I know that you will wish to return to your family at Castle Dru soon Namir, and we will be sorry to see you go, but please come back and see us whenever you can and be sure that you will always be given a warm welcome.'

Myra was holding back tears as the crowd responded with a request for a speech from the great man himself. She sat down and dabbed her eyes with a handkerchief from one of her deputies.

Namir was on his feet now to a rapturous applause and had to wait a while for calm once more. When all was settled he found a composed voice and addressed the room.

'Thank you everyone for this amazing welcome, and thank you for bringing me into your home,' he looked around in awe. 'Words cannot express how I feel right now.'

The assembly were mute, you could hear a pin drop.

'But just as you have created a magnificent spectacle here, you all know that it has been a team effort that has accomplished this extraordinary feat. You know that the Matriarch and her deputies oversee it all and make sure that everything runs smoothly.' He smiled in her direction. 'And the battle against the forces in Ataxata was much the same.

My brother and I were part of an incredible team. A mass of likeminded people who were brave, determined and steadfast in their duty to protect their kingdom came together that day. So many were involved in that victory, just like your achievements here at the Smilodon Fort. For it is not the accomplishment of just one person, or from the hands of the man who holds the sword; success comes from the joint efforts of many people, with a lot of skills and an abundance of pride and determination who all strive for the same thing.

Yes, I am the leader of the Clan of the Mountain Lion, but I can't take all the credit. It was all of my people who saved us from the grip of a devil, and it was my duty, along with my brother Lyall, to lead them. So I will take your kind words back with me, and tell everyone at the castle that you are indebted to them all. Thank you.'

The Matriarch stood up and bowed to Namir. 'You are a remarkable man with a remarkable brother in King Lyall of Durundal. I acknowledge your humble words of reverence and honour for your fellow men and women. But you are a strong and exemplary leader, who speaks with fairness and selflessness, duty and pride; and you will remain in our hearts as Namir, King of the Clans.'

He smiled at the accolade and nodded his head in her direction. Raising his glass he proclaimed his allegiance.

'To the clans and their leaders and all those who serve with them, may we live together in harmony and prosper together in peace.'

The whole room was on its feet and gave this humble man the thundering rapturous applause he deserved before sitting down to celebrate in the knowledge that good does conquer evil, and that a humble and gracious leader exudes far more power and respect than the tyrannical one.

38

Another month had passed and the worst of the bad weather had also been and gone. Namir and his party had expressed their gratitude and bade their goodbyes to the leaders of the Smilodon Fort and were now heading through the market square and past the many houses where the people had come to their doorways to bid them farewell. A flock of white doves had been let out to symbolise peace and prosperity and they spiralled up into a soft grey sky towards the spire of the Grand Committee Rooms to where the Matriarch and her deputies stood watching.

The buildings that lined the streets glowed in the January afternoon and the Smilodon Fort bunting flapped frantically in the cool of the day. At the gates the guards stood to attention and a horn blower hailed a fanfare as Namir and his party waited for their horses to arrive. The Captain came over to salute him and offered Namir his own personal greeting.

'I trust you have enjoyed your stay with us Master Namir, and please, if I may be so bold; if any of your people want to come and stay with us at any time you know they will be warmly received.'

'Thank you Captain for your kind parting words.

Myra and her deputies have already invited us back again in July for the Summer Ball, so I will probably see you then.'

'Most definitely Master Namir, most definitely, and I look forward to seeing you and your family then.' The Captain looked round when he heard the sound of horses approaching and took the reins from the stable boy. The young lad stood cap in hand as he watched the brave warriors mount their destriers. Namir looked straight at him. 'Thank you for tending to my horses while I have been detained; they look extremely well cared for.' Namir patted his horse and the lad looked starstruck. 'Goodbye for now. Be sure, I shall return in the summer.'

The trumpets blazed, the people clapped, the children ran from the school building, and with banners waving and hands held aloft, Namir led Gya and Macus out of the fortress gates.

The party stayed close together as they shared their experiences at the Smilodon Fort; what they had taken most from it and what they would remember the most.

'For me it has to be how very one is treated as an equal,' said Macus. 'Every person has a role to play in the network and is regarded with respect and admiration; even the Captain of the guards spoke to us as though it was his fort, but that's because it's what he is accustomed to. I thought it was incredibly humbling, and coming from where I have, that was most noticeable to me.'

Gya nodded her head in agreement. 'I agree with you Macus; but for me, it was seeing the Matriarch and her lady deputies in charge, it really resonated with me. For ten years I had to live as a man so I would get the recognition that I deserved. For as a woman, I would have been overlooked and cast aside. Even Cornelius changed towards me when he found out I was a woman, and it's something I will never get used to. I hope that what they achieved at Smilodon is the way forward, because for me, peace only prevails with uniformity, mutual respect and listening to each other.'

Namir had been listening to their reasons and had formed his own. 'I agree with both of you. I personally can't see a successful future where one person thinks they are better than another person. We all have skills and services to share, qualities and gifts to teach, and each service is an important function in a thriving community. I agree with the female Matriarch; I only have to think of my Skyrah and how she has reacted in the face of adversity, plus I have to tell you that it was she who begged me not to go to the palace, she was the one who saw through the lie of the offered peace treaty and the pretence of the officers. Is that a quality that all women have? I don't know,' he raised his brow and drew a thin smile in acceptance. 'But equally, the characteristic that stood out most was the organisation and distribution within the walls of the fortress itself. The whole community was catered for and cared for, even the children, certainly the infirm, and the people with years of experience were considered the hierarchy. I applaud their tenacity and steadfastness and I will endeavour to work with my brother alongside Skyrah and Arneb to produce something that comes even half way close.'

'Hear hear to all of those comments,' echoed Gya and Macus together.

The party edged ever closer to the castle and with the clip clop of hooves on the ground and the billowing of horses nostrils, they reflected even more on what had just been discussed.

Eventually they rode onto a path that ran west, and each of them turned to whatever thoughts were uppermost in their minds. Macus was deciding whether he was strong enough to ask Gya to marry him. They were so akin now and having shared an apartment for the past few months, it seemed the most honourable thing to do. But what if she said 'No,' what if she declined him? She was such an independent woman after all, was marriage what she really wanted? The conundrum held his voice silent for some time while he assessed the situation.

Gya was contemplating whether she should make the first move on the same subject; after all, she had spent the past ten years as a man; she felt she knew them as well as she knew herself, and that meant she could be waiting years for Macus to summon up the strength. And as he had just recently found the hero within himself to fight back at a corrupt organisation and those power hungry individuals in authority; was it too much to expect him to find the courage with this conundrum. Her face expressed the air of confusion while she firmly held her tongue.

Namir was trying to piece together a vision of what the castle would look like now. He had last seen it some four months ago and wondered if Lyall had made any changes to it in light of what he had seen at Smilodon. Certainly more living space was needed with the arrival of the clan. He tried to piece together his own interpretation and felt certain that Lyall would be busy at work creating a place that was exactly the same as in his own mind's eye. But before he could start making any visions in his head, the fortress was in view and the three of them spurred their destriers into a gallop and descended on the castle at full speed.

It was Skyrah who spotted him first and waved frantically from her window, she knew he couldn't see her, but called at the top of her voice to Lyall and Arneb. They thought she was going into labour and so crashed through the door practically tripping over Chay and Meric who had also darted into her room.

'Lay down Skyrah, just take deep breaths,' Arneb was guiding her back to the bed.

'No, Arneb, I'm fine really I am.'

'So what's wrong?'

'Look, look out of the window,' Skyrah was ecstatic and Arneb followed her gaze.

By now, five faces were pressed against the leaded window pane and Lyall grabbed Arneb.

'He's back, look he's back.'

This was the best news anyone could ask for.

They all rushed downstairs and out into the courtyard, the gates had been opened and Namir sat there with Gya and Macus in total awe at what Lyall had achieved in such a comparatively short time. He leapt off his horse and ran to his brother. Tears flowed and they embraced for what seemed like an eternity. Neither of them could control their emotions. Lyall stood back to look at him. 'Thank the gods Namir, thank the gods.'

'It feels so good to be back brother; I have missed you,' and Namir flung his arms around his brother again.

Lyall could see his saviours over Namir's shoulders. 'Who are these good people?'

Namir turned to introduce his guardians. 'This is Gya and this is Macus, and I owe my life to these two, because without them, I would have died and been left to rot in the tower forever.'

'I looked in there,' Lyall was distraught and angered at the same time.

'They moved me. I saw you Lyall, I called out to you but you couldn't hear me. But the Emperor knew you would look there so he moved me to a meadow close by.'

'Lyall was grinding his teeth now, 'I knew he had done something like that, I just knew it.'

'But these two people saved me and have been at my side ever since.'

Lyall went over to them. 'I will never be able to thank you enough, you have given me back my brother and I am indebted to you. My home is your home now, we are family.'

Gya was touched by the welcome. 'Thank you Lyall, you are most kind. But when you hear my story about what the General and the Emperor did to us, then you will realise it is I who am indebted to you.'

'Whatever it is Gya, we are indebted to each other.'

He embraced Gya warmly and shook Macus by the hand. 'I knew I recognised you Macus.'

'I'm sorry I didn't say anything at the time,' Macus couldn't shake off the feeling of remorse.

'Macus don't apologise, Namir is safe now because of you and we shall talk about your heroics later. But please, leave the horses here for now; you must come in and I will show you to your rooms.'

They turned to face the door that led into the castle and a lone figure had just arrived there. Heavy with child and not long to go, Skyrah was almost silhouetted in the doorway. The party stood still and looked at her. Even Namir took a startled breath as his eyes rested on the vision before him. This guiding light who had shone the torch for him when he was at his lowest point, now stood there like the brightest star in the sky. Without taking his eyes off her, he patted his brother on the shoulder and walked slowly over to where she was standing. By now there was a silent congregation around them as news of his return had spread round the castle. Friends old and new watched as the two of them were finally reunited. The lovers brought together as young children had never been apart. Even when first imprisoned at the Palace in Ataxata, she was sure she could see his shadow in the dormitory. But this time, the longest time, it was only his unborn child and his brother that kept her going.

Under a rising full moon he flung his arms around her and kissed her tear stained cheeks. She was sobbing as she stroked his hair and touched his face, she squeezed his arms and put her hand on his heart. 'I never gave up hope Namir, I never gave up.'

'My love, my love...,' he broke down. 'I dreamed of you every night, and every waking hour I pictured this moment. You kept me going Skyrah; in my darkest hours, in my lowest times, it was the thought of you and our baby that gave me the strength to survive. And if ever I thought I loved you more than life itself, nothing can compare to what I feel right now.' He kissed her hands.

'I knew you were alive. Just as I could feel our baby alive in my womb, I could sense that you were alive in my heart.' She hung on to him tightly, she was never going to let him go again.

He put his hand on her swollen belly and smiled up at her. She felt a kick and moved his hand to where she felt the movement. 'Your son is welcoming you home I believe.'

Namir was relieved to feel the baby come to life under the warmth of his hand. 'This is truly a miracle Skyrah,' and he felt the infant kick again.

The amount of activity inside her womb surprised her as well, there was never usually this much flurry - but then a pain shot through her abdomen and she groaned.

He moved his hand away instantly, fearful that he was pressing too hard. 'Have I hurt you?' his voice was anxious.

She grabbed hold of him. 'No you haven't hurt me Namir, I think this baby wants to meet his father. Now you are here, he can't wait to see you,' she breathed deeply and doubled over with another stab of pain.

'Somebody help her!' he called out frantically.

Meric rushed forward. 'She is in labour Namir, help me get her up the stairs.'

'What! Already?'

'Namir, it is time.'

Skyrah's revelation that the baby was full term caused a brief calculation of dates before Meric spoke again.

'Come, we must get her back to her room.'

Arneb rushed ahead to prepare her bed. Chay went to get water and towels.

'What can I do?' asked Gya

'Come with me,' said Namir.

Macus was left holding the horses and took them round to the stable.

It was a long night for everyone that last day of January. Arneb and Chay never left her side. Lyall and Namir had waited outside on the floor for hours. Gya sat with Macus at the top of the stairs and watched intently as Meric went in the room and came out again many times that night.

'Any news Meric?' Namir would say urgently.

The healer could only shake his head.

'Well at least you are back in time to witness the birth brother,' said Lyall trying to lift Namir's spirits.

'But I'm not allowed in there, shouldn't I be with her?'

'I think it's in case there are any complications,' said Gya trying to reassure him. 'When they know everything is all right you will be called in.'

Namir looked at Lyall for answers, but there were none.

All of a sudden they heard Skyrah screaming his name. Namir shot up from his seated position and raced to the door. 'I have to go in there, I have to, she needs me.'

Meric came out and ushered Namir in. He fell at Skyrah's side and wiped her feverish brow.

Too exhausted to speak, she squeezed his hand and started to push. Sweat was pouring down her face and onto her chest. Her legs were pulled up and she had them spread wide. Her long gown was covering the baby's entrance, but it didn't hide the blood.

Namir was more than anxious now when he saw the crimson sheets. He looked silently at Meric for answers.

Meric's tone was hushed. 'She is giving birth Namir, sometimes there is a bit more blood and sometimes it takes a bit more time.'

After a few minutes she screamed again and he

felt her squeezing his hand and with gritted teeth she bore down to push with all her might.

He wiped her face and kissed her hand. 'I love you Skyrah, I love you.'

She looked at him but still couldn't speak, instead another wave came across her and he could feel all her strength going into the push.

'I can see the crown,' called Meric excitedly. 'Your baby is coming.'

'Skyrah! He's coming, come on push him out, let us meet our son.'

She bore down and with one last effort pushed down to force her baby out. She fell back exhausted and Meric handed her the infant to hold.

'Do you want to cut the cord Namir?'

'Yes... I will... thank you.'

Meric handed him a clean knife and held the grey and purple cord gently. Namir ceremoniously and proudly severed the life giving artery in two.

Meric waited to take delivery of the placenta - but then his face turned a whiter shade of pale and he looked totally ashen.

'What's wrong?' said Namir with his own fixed worried expression.

'There's another one, there's another baby coming out. You have to push again Skyrah.'

Meric delivered the second infant easily and gave the child to Namir.

'It's a girl,' cried out Namir in delight.

'And I have a girl here,' exclaimed Skyrah.

'We have twin girls,' shouted Namir from the top of his voice.

He went outside the room to show off his new offspring. 'I have daughters, I have twin daughters.'

Inside, Chay and Arneb were cleaning up Skyrah and putting a clean gown and fresh bed linen on for her. When she was ready, the people waiting outside were allowed in. She was sitting up with the first born in her arms. She looked up at Lyall, her pride swelling in quantities. 'Would you like to hold her?'

'Yes I would Skyrah. I would be honoured. But Namir, with all the excitement of your return and the unexpected birth, I have neglected to tell you that Arneb is expecting our own baby in June.'

Skyrah gave Arneb a knowing glance and Namir knew that Lyall had deliberately waited for a happy outcome before sharing his own joy.

'That's wonderful,' said Namir enthusiastically. 'I just couldn't be happier for you both and this has to be the greatest day of my life. To be reunited with my family and have two healthy daughters delivered to me; what more could a man want?' He kissed his new baby on the forehead and couldn't take his eyes off of her.

'Have you thought of any names?' Lyall asked, looking lovingly at his nieces.

'Well not until now, but if it's all right with Skyrah, I would like to name them after the two women who saved my life.'

'Of course my love. I think that's a wonderful idea. So what are their names going to be?'

'Well the first woman who saved me was Gya; so Lyall, you are holding little Gya.'

'And your one?' Lyall asked.

'This is Myra everyone, meet little Myra.'

39

Namir stretched his feet towards the fire and sighed contentedly. He was getting used to this ritual every evening, and for the last five months he had never felt so comfortable back in the loving arms of his family; and with the addition of a very affable wolfhound at his side, it somehow added to the familiar sense of security. He stroked the canine gently and patted her head while he rested.

Meanwhile out in the Great Hall, the sounds of the tables being dressed and servants scurrying about told him that supper would soon be served. This was a regular occurrence now as well, with his wife, his brother and sister in law, and of course his rescuers, Macus and Gya.

He found himself reminiscing about clan life and was glad that the camp hadn't been burned to the ground, especially with his main perpetrator dead, there really was no need for such drastic measures. One day he would take his daughters there, to see where he had been raised and to stand amongst the menhirs and summon the spirits and guides once again. The thought made him feel warm inside, but this was his life now, and everyone felt safe and content inside the castle walls where they sustained a rich life from the available resources. Gya was the school mistress and taught the children everything. Macus had decided he would rather stay working with the horses and was elevated to Chief Groom.

This month of June had been another grand month to remember, Arneb had given birth to twin boys; Canagan and Laith, very fitting he thought. Macus and Gya had got married, the young hero had finally found the strength to ask for the heroine's hand in matrimony. Skyrah and Arneb were busy organising costumes for the Summer Ball at the Smilodon Fort. Lyall was occupied preparing a Gathering to celebrate their birthdays, and introduce the clans to the new heirs, and of course, display his remarkable achievements to their new friends from the colony.

Namir sat back contently to sip on the finest red wine and pick at the ripened figs at his side.

Suddenly the wolfhound sat bolt upright, her ears pricked forwards to a knock at the door. She paced to the front and waited for it to be opened.

'What does the sentry want at this hour?' Namir said to himself. 'It had better be important.'

The familiar sound of his twin daughters began to echo faintly down the stairs. Their noise drowned out the activities where the wolfhound was keeping guard. He smiled to himself. The twins certainly took after Skyrah's side of the family he thought. He could never fathom where they got all their energy from, and neither could he understand why everything they did needed so much noise. A sudden movement caught his eye and he tried hard not to look surprised as Gya slipped into the room. 'Are you all right Gya?' he asked with a perplexed gaze. 'You look like you've seen a ghost.'

'I think I have Namir,' said Gya, totally ashen.

'Well?' he questioned her with his furrowed brow.

'It's the Empress; the young Empress Ajeya. The Empress Ajeya of Ataxata. She wishes to see you.'

40

A tense silence filled the air when Namir had finished his story.

'Cruel places breed cruel people,' she said and hung her head in shame.

'None of this is your fault Ajeya, you are here to pledge allegiance and that is the future,' he reminded her.

A tear ran down her cheek and it didn't go unnoticed. By now a few torches had been lit and the fire crackled in the great hearth but most of the Whispering Hall remained in darkness now.

A knock at the door had everyone on their feet when the visitor was announced.

'Dainn from the Hill Fort Tribe your majesties.'

The golden haired man rushed in and bowing before the two men, took Ajeya's hands in his own and kissed them fondly. He then held her within the tenderest of embraces and smoothed the hair from her face to see her radiant beauty. 'Are you all right my love?' he asked with concern.

'Yes I am,' she wiped away the tear.' It was good to talk with Lyall and Namir about everything, and I have no burning questions anymore.'

He kissed the top of her head and went over to embrace the brothers. 'Thank you for this Lyall and Namir, it means a lot to both of us.'

'Dainn, you are one of our most respected friends, a staunch ally whom we have depended on for so many years. It was a small gesture compared to your loyalty,' Lyall offered.

'We have been through such a lot together and it now looks like you are about to become an Emperor,' Namir put an arm around his friend's shoulder.

'Well I don't know about that,' Dainn laughed. 'I seem to recall the last time we spoke about the palace in Ataxata, we had visions of razing it to the ground.'

'Yes I remember saying that,' said Namir feeling a stab of pain from the past.

'It's up to my dear lady wife though,' Dainn said taking his place by her side again. 'It's her inheritance and her birthright, so she must do what she deems fit.'

She smiled affectionately in response and knitted her fingers in his.

'Please, you must join us for supper. We have plenty of room for you to stay with us, for as long as you like.' Lyall's request was passionate. 'I know that Arneb and Skyrah would want to meet you both - properly.'

'Thank you Lyall, it would give me great pleasure to shake the hand of the woman who saved my husband's life.'

'She saved all of us,' said Dainn humbly.

'Everyone would like to meet you,' said Namir.

'You are the original hare, the young girl who gave our father the inspiration, your name is legendary amongst our clan.'

'Thank you,' said Ajeya, taken aback by the accolade. 'It seems we are all indebted to each other in one way or another.'

'We certainly are,' said Namir.

'Gya and Macus will be there as well,' said Lyall. 'They are also a big part of our lives and will be able to fill in any gaps that we may have missed. So please follow me, the night is still young and there is much more to tell.'

Ajeya and Dainn followed Lyall and Namir into the Great Hall where they shared even more stories of heroism and fantastic feats and dreams for the future, all the while feasting on gourmet food and supping on the grandest wines with raucous laughter amid the occasional tear.

And yet some hundred or so miles away, in a deep ravine, somewhere between the mountains of Durundal and the city of Ataxata, in a dark, damp, hollowed out cave; a lone disfigured vagrant was hunched over a weak fire, with a tattered leather-bound book at his side, skinning a rabbit and planning his revenge.